P9-DWB-935

More praise for
CONJUGAL BLISS

"The ribaldry is on a par with Henry Miller at his best. . . . John Nichols has taken a lusty swing at the radical feminist pitch that men are predacious exploiters of women out for one thing only. The result is scenes from a marriage made in bohemia during a season in hell."

—*The Philadelphia Inquirer*

"Sexy and funny. And who couldn't relate to the difficulties of marriage between fortysomething professionals with baggage from previous relationships?"

—*Albuquerque Journal*

"Cleverly conceived and ever so lightheartedly offered."

—*The Anniston Star*

"Lively, personable narrative and a myriad of piercing insights on the politics of marriage spice this piquant, entertaining domestic comedy."

—*Publishers Weekly*

By John Nichols:

Fiction
THE STERILE CUCKOO
THE WIZARD OF LONELINESS
THE MILAGRO BEANFIELD WAR*
THE MAGIC JOURNEY*
THE NIRVANA BLUES*
A GHOST IN THE MUSIC
AMERICAN BLOOD*
AN ELEGY FOR SEPTEMBER*
CONJUGAL BLISS*

Nonfiction
IF MOUNTAINS DIE (with William Davis)
THE LAST BEAUTIFUL DAYS OF AUTUMN
ON THE MESA
A FRAGILE BEAUTY
THE SKY'S THE LIMIT
KEEP IT SIMPLE

Published by Ballantine Books

CONJUGAL BLISS

BLISS

A Comedy of Martial Arts

John Nichols

BALLANTINE BOOKS • NEW YORK

Sale of this book without a front cover may be unauthorized. If this book is coverless, it may have been reported to the publisher as "unsold or destroyed" and neither the author nor the publisher may have received payment for it.

Copyright © 1994 by John Treadwell Nichols

All rights reserved under International and Pan-American Copyright Conventions. Published in the United States of America by Ballantine Books, a division of Random House, Inc., New York, and distributed in Canada by Random House of Canada Limited, Toronto.

The lines from "The Equilibrists" are from *Selected Poems* by John Crowe Ransom, copyright 1927 by Alfred A. Knopf, Inc., and renewed 1955 by John Crowe Ransom; reprinted by permission of the publisher. The lines from "Circles on the Water" by Marge Piercy copyright © 1982 by Marge Piercy; reprinted by permission of Alfred A. Knopf, Inc.

Library of Congress Catalog Card Number: 93-1245

ISBN 0-345-38790-2

This edition published by arrangement with Henry Holt and Company, Inc.

Manufactured in the United States of America

First Ballantine Books Edition: February 1995

10 9 8 7 6 5 4 3 2 1

THIS SLEAZY PIECE OF FICTION IS
GINGERLY DEDICATED TO:

Juana and me, Bill and Audrey, Karen and Mike, Janice and Guillermo, Pop and Jackie, Virginia and Susan and Leo, Marian and Tony, Larry and Carol, Mother and Lou, Jo and Gene, and Ruby, and Ronnie and Carol, Rosa and Alan, Annie and Kenny, Roger and Kathleen, Phaedra and Jim, and all other friends and foes and lovers and strangers (and my children and their children and our step- and step-stepchildren), dear to my life and to my larcenous heart, who are now, or ever have been, involved in the magical and tragic aspects of the garbled and glorious martial—excuse me, *marital*—transduction of affect.

I love you.
I pray that we all survive.
I *worship* laughter!

"STOP! *Párale* right now! *¡Chingao!*
The way you two are fighting you're
gonna end up in bed together!"

—Ana Castillo
So Far from God

The fight started this way.

Moe Bubbles and Susan Dice, Ed Griffin and his wife, Emily, and Zelda's crazy pal Weezie Bednarik and another couple came over for dinner. It was our six-month wedding anniversary celebration. Half a year, by God! We drank champagne and red wine and ate smoked oysters and tiny little clams and had cheap caviar on crackers. The main course was a veggie lasagna. For dessert we gobbled Häagen Dazs ice cream on slices of homemade cherry pie. In due course somebody passed around a doobie, but I am not a smoker.

Then the whole thing crumbled when my chubby sidekick, Moe Bubbles, pulled out a vial of cocaine with a little silver spoon attached to it on a chain and offered freebees to whoever wanted. Zelda went into the bathroom to have a snort and I pushed open the door while she was in the middle of it. That pissed me off. All her sanctimonious twaddle against my kids' using drugs. I was enraged.

I asked everyone to leave. With her former second husband Zelda had been a real cokehead, but she had insisted it was all over now. She *hated* drugs. More than once she had implied that my son, Woody, was evil incarnate because there were whispers he worked for a guy who was growing pot.

And then this. What a fucking hypocrite.

I got very brusque with all our guests. I really hurried

them out. Weezie Bednarik started squawking at me with her new stupid hand puppet. Susan Dice, Moe's main squeeze, who had diabetes and smoked cigarettes like a fiend and loved anything contraband and chemical, raised a stink, but I was in no mood to trifle.

After they had all split, Zelda tried to make amends. We were both pretty drunk, I'll admit. I wanted her to leave me alone, however. I was pissed. "Don't bug me, Zelda." But she kept coming at me, playfully giving little punches, saying, "Aw, c'mon, don't be an old stick-in-the-mud. You know how much I love you. Let's get it on." I guess she was pretty high or stoned as well as drunk. She slurred a little. She had the sparkle in her eyes that is usually irresistible.

But I kept backing away, saying, "No, leave me alone, please." I was in a rotten mood.

So she slugged me. *Whack!* First time ever, by either sex, that I'd been clobbered. It stunned me. I never saw it coming. For a few seconds I didn't even know what had happened. Momentarily I completely lost my bearings and sort of ineffectively paddled at the air where her hands were pawing.

"Quit that," I snapped. "Get out of here. Leave me alone. I don't like you."

Zelda, challenged, gets a fierce eagle look in her eyes.

She was wearing a thick leather mastiff belt sprinkled all over with metal studs. She unbuckled it and wrapped the tongue end around her fist and took a swing with it at me. The thing had a mega buckle. I fended it off, but it really hurt, and, frankly, it scared me too. So I struck back, real quick, three punches—chop!chop!chop! I actually knocked her down on the kitchen floor. Then I stood over her, utterly appalled, shocked, and paralyzed. I mean, I'm so big and she's so *little*. I burst into tears and blubbered, "Oh Jesus Christ I'm sorry!"

I expected God to nail me with a thunderbolt right then and there. I had never before hit *anybody* in my life.

Zelda is small—five two—and you might even say petite, but she is not exactly a patsy, or an easily intimidated person. She bolted up off the floor and ran out of the kitchen, cursing me in no uncertain terms. She grabbed my latest Sidney Bard manuscript off a coffee table and threw it across the living room: *Splat! Flutter!*

Pages everywhere.

Next, she found a wineglass and fired it at my head. She was swearing and storming around, kicking things, fit to be tied. A tall blue flower vase bit the dust. Cats were leaping out of the way in every direction. Fuck the cats. I hated the cats.

The dog ran into our Beverly Jog and hid behind the water heater.

By the time Zelda locked herself in the bedroom, I was sitting on the kitchen floor, my back up against the stove, sobbing. There were pieces of shattered glass all over the place.

We had been married exactly six months, two days, eleven hours, five minutes, and—

Thirteen seconds.

After a while I crawled into the living room and gathered up pages, fitting the manuscript back together. When I pretty much had it in order, I picked up all the other refuse. I swept the kitchen and fed the dog and the cats and washed all the dishes. Then I opened the last bottle of champagne and sat at the kitchen table, drinking it and reading a Bernard Malamud novel called *God's Grace*. The novel is about a guy named Calvin Cohn who's shipwrecked on an island with a few chimps, a couple of baboons, and a gorilla after a second flood caused by a nuclear holocaust.

Things didn't turn out so hot on that island, either.

Soon I heard the bedroom door open and Zelda went into the bathroom. The tub started running. She began sloshing around in there. As always, that sloshing gave me a prickling sensation down in the old groin area.

Let me explain something before we go any further.

Zelda is petite, yes, but also voluptuous. She has beautiful ample little tits and an almost hourglass figure. I can squeeze both her buttocks in one hand. She has large velvet brown eyes and dark, *dark* hair that's always sort of professionally tousled. At cursory glance her features seem like the kind that are always defined as "delicately chiseled." But then those eyes light up and there's something joyously fierce and gleaming in her look, which is tremendously powerful. Sometimes I think of her as a sort of pint-sized legendarily gorgeous Israeli sabra dressed in desert cammy fatigues, toting an Uzi or an AK-47. And I think her name ought to be Rebecca or Ruth or maybe even Sarah—

But back to the bathroom.

When I opened the door, Zelda was lying in lots of steam, eyes closed, soaking up the atmosphere, calming down. Lots of bubble stuff (which I hate) frothed in the water. Truth is, I'm allergic. I can't stand most soaps and perfumes. Zelda loves perfumes and bath oils and the coconut mousse that tames her wild and crazy hair.

That had long been a bone of contention. On more than one occasion Zelda had said, "You don't ever use deodorants, so you always stink to high heaven."

I had explained a hundred times that I don't use deodorants because they are artificial poisons that kill the environment. Talk to a wall. It's a fact, though: I heartily enjoy a woman's natural smells. Sweat is sexy to me. Same with the *real* odor of Zelda's vagina. Unfortunately, she always uses douches and powders to keep the odors neutral or sweet scented down there. When I tried to explain, she didn't understand. She was embarrassed to be funky.

I told her she had beautiful facial skin, leave it alone, quit slobbering on the powder. Her reply? "I'm getting old, Roger, and as soon as I score the money, I'm gonna have a face-lift, and in the meantime I'll be goddamned if I'll give in and accept the aging process."

Her idol is Elizabeth Taylor.

Zelda did not open her eyes when I entered the bathroom and sat down on the toilet lid. I said, "I'm sorry." Her great stoneface didn't crack. I added, "I guess I overreacted, that was stupid. But you scared me with the belt."

Zelda pretended to be deaf and mute. Her lovely breasts were sort of half floating in the water. Naturally, the prominent nipples were stiff. So I undressed and lowered myself into the tub between her legs and began to kiss her. Pretty soon we were fucking. She kept her eyes closed the whole time and didn't say a word. When I bumped forward, water sloshed all around her throat and her wonderful breasts eddied and changed shape like a pair of incredible pink jellyfish. I turned her over and had at it from behind. She started making lots of noise, which really turns me on.

We came together in a truly joyful abandon . . . I think.

But in bed later it started all over again.

It always does.

Zelda has a mind like a steel trap, she never forgets anything. She never forgives anything, either. Maybe she pretends to, but you cross Zelda, buddy, and that's like money in the bank, drawing interest. And sooner or later, in one situation or another, that interest is certain to pay big dividends.

Like, negative dividends.

"I saw you making eyes at Susan" were the first words

she finally said about the k-fuffle. Susan is a Christian Scientist—the diabetic, remember? Zelda added, "I saw you touch her a couple of times, also. I saw you put your arm around her shoulders."

I said, "Oh for Christ's sake." I could never think of any intelligent retort when Zelda got on one of these jags.

My wife said, "I know you used to fuck her, even if you deny it. Weezie's former hand puppet told me."

"Weezie's full of shit. I hate this town."

Zelda said, "I hate it, too. It's full of creeps like you."

That pissed me off. I said, "You claimed you loved it before we got married. You said you wanted to move here and live in this house forever."

"So I was wrong. How was I to know?"

Actually, I love my scum-sucking little town. I've lived here twenty-two years. That's a lot of water over the dam. I muttered, "I never fucked her." And that was the truth.

Zelda said, "You told me you did."

That's another thing about Zelda's remarkable memory: She will twist facts at will in order to make a point.

I said, "I told you we *thought* about it once, but she has herpes and I was scared."

"You said you went to bed together and she sucked you off and you came in her face, and then you masturbated her with your fingers."

"That's not 'fucking.' "

I couldn't *believe* I had told Zelda all that. But see, things were different when we were just courting, before we made The Commitment. In those days we shared all our darkest secrets. We were still capable of being "best friends." We laughed at each other's bawdy adventures with different lovers. We were totally open and unashamed and candid with each other.

Little did I know the grave I was digging.

* * *

Yup, I lay there in bed beside a clammed-up Zelda, incredulous that I'd ever told her one fact about my former life. Especially my former sex life. But when we were courting, the relationship was friendly and funny and zany and happy and silly and slapstick and unthreatening. Or so I thought. We laughed all the time. We teased each other. She had boyfriends down in the capital, where she lived. I had girlfriends up here. Ours was a lighthearted commuter affair for almost a year. We met on weekends. We joked about our respective paramours. We never took ourselves too seriously. Eventually I concluded: This is the woman for me. Zelda. She's not jealous or defensive or insecure. She would ask me a million questions about my other lovers and my sex life and my erotic habits. I answered all queries truthfully. Yes, I am a candid man. What have I got to hide?

I asked her about her lovers, and she answered back, though later, when I thought about it, her replies were never all that detailed. They seemed frank, but in retrospect Zelda had kept the lid on most of the gory details. Zelda enjoys grilling, but she is less ebullient as a grillee.

No problem. I had always figured in time she would come around. They always do. If you're open with people, eventually they'll loosen up. It's simply a question of establishing trust. Which is a given, soon as they learn there's nothing to fear.

Zelda said, "You had no right to throw everybody out. It was humiliating to the max. We were having a good time."

"You told me you were through with cocaine. You hate drugs."

"Oh God, Roger, get off the soapbox. One hit of toot isn't gonna shatter the Empire State Building."

7

"I don't care. After all the times you have trashed Woody for getting in trouble, I feel—"

"Bag it, Roger. You're so uptight you make me puke."

I bagged it. And I lay there, staring at the ceiling. And I'll admit it, right then I hated her guts. I wanted to fetch the ax and smash her brains out with the flat side.

Nobody sleeps.

By and large, I haven't had a good night's sleep in six months.

Naturally, lying beside Zelda, pretty soon I'm horny again. Like, she is so *warm*. Not that I'm prejudiced or anything, but Zelda is a very ripe peach. And it happens that all my life I have really loved making love. I used to think I could fuck my way to immortality. Like, sooner or later, right at the moment of an intergalactic climax— *boom!*—I'm in a heaven populated by millions of Marilyn Monroe, Jane Mansfield, and Anita Ekberg lookalikes.

Yeah, I hit puberty in the fifties.

I took Zelda's hand and closed the fingers over my quivering dick. She jerked her hand away abruptly.

"You disgust me," she said. "You really do. I hate you."

Okay. I stared at the ceiling, thinking about Susan's mouth. Susan Dice, Moe's current squeeze. Though Susan is a Christian Scientist, she loves cocaine, she drinks like a fish. Yes, that is erotic to me, but also crazy. Scary crazy. When Susan becomes obsessed about doing things, she does them. I was once in a car while she drove it at a hundred and twenty miles an hour. I screamed at her to slow down, but she wouldn't listen.

Susan carries a loaded gun in her handbag. Once she shot a guy for breaking and entering. She chews bubble gum and lives on a macrobiotic diet and looks anorexic. Anorexic like an erotic snake. I never counted so many contradictions in a single person. Susan smokes dope and cigarettes. She's a dancer, ballet and modern. You watch her move on stage, it's like watching death all sinuous and you want to ball it. So what if HIV is abroad, leveling the planet? Susan kisses like an evil beast sucking you into something wonderful, corrupt, decaying. She has thin lips and slightly protruding teeth and a faint Texas drawl. Her mouth is shaped like that movie star's, Barbara Hershey. She is caustic and cynical.

Susan and I never went very far because I was afraid of her. I wish I hadn't been afraid, but that's life. Moe Bubbles, on the other hand, likes them perverse and crazy and dangerous. So they were perfect for each other, Susan and Moe.

I asked Zelda, "Are you awake?"

No answer.

Zelda can go to sleep after a fight, but not me. I'll never understand that. The emotional atomic bomb explodes over ground zero—our home—and an hour later she's cutting Z's. I lie awake in bed all night, arguing back, making my case, chewing her out, trying to explain, bitching about life, planning a divorce, contemplating suicide, worrying about the kids, listening to dogs bark, hating my life, wondering how I got into such a pickle, reminding myself to file quarterly taxes before next Thursday, wanting to fuck.

But she's sawing timber, happy as a little old clam.

So I roll over on top of my wife and start the parade without her. Zelda sort of halfway wakes up and mutters something and eventually gets into it, but moans softly, "You go ahead without me," so I go ahead without her.

Then I lie by her side once more, and process the whole damn argument again. While she, snoozing away, snuggled against me like a milk-fed kitten. I'm still so tense that it

9

feels as if my chest is paper thin and my heart is about to jump out and land in the wastebasket over there by her million-dollar chifforobe—

"Two points!"

Around dawn I get up, slouch into the bathroom, and pop two ten-milligram Prazepams. It feels almost as if I'm doing a Dutch act. I am terrified of artificial sopers. And get this: Only six months ago I was footloose and fancy free, I had a half-dozen girlfriends, I had money in the bank, and life was a bowl of cherries.

Hey Roger, what *happened*?

What happened—to be perfectly straightforward and concise—is that Zelda and I got married.

It was a great celebration.

Hang on to your hat, dear reader: we are now jumping back in time six months.

My friends Betty and Alex came from New York; Zelda's friends Carol and Seamus arrived from L.A. The idea was to have a regal week-long whoop-de-do *after* the wedding, the longest reception ever, also a barn raising to fix up the house, making it palatable to Zelda. It would cost me an arm and both legs, but I wasn't averse. I have an addictive personality. I like all the hoopla and passion around celebrations. If you got it, flaunt it, that's my motto. Easy come, easy go. As long as I can make it, I never feel a compulsion to hang on tight. Something else always comes along anyway, so you're gonna spend it no matter what.

Plus, hey, right about when I was rolling in clover. Last year's Sidney Bard novel, *A Sticky Wicket on Planet Zeus*, was going great. The second one in the series, *The Catacombs of Luray*, was on film option, and I stood to garner two and a half percent of the shooting budget up to one hundred K as soon as they commenced principal photography. Which would be the minute I finished the script (I hoped). Too, I figured I only had about four more months of writing left on the next intergalactic thriller, *Return of the Perseid Meteor Thugs*, and then I could turn it in for what would be a less-than-immodest advance.

And I was smoking on the Zane Adams script I'd accepted back in June, when the IRS began to complain about my 1988 and '89 tax returns.

But other than that, my mortgage payments were under five hundred a month, the truck was paid off, I had no other debts except a kid in college, so why *not* get married, ay?

An aside, here.

The guests who did *not* come to our wedding were anybody in her family, and nobody from mine.

The reasons for this were simple. Zelda and I both come from megadysfunctional bloodlines. Zelda's mom committed suicide when Zelda was thirteen. Her dad, Budge, an alcoholic, still works in a secret capacity for Dow Chemical, apparently inventing new kinds of tactical napalm. Her sister, Trish, is a thirty-two-year-old topless go-go dancer in San Diego, married to a right-wing bodybuilder, Winthrop Haley, who trains porpoises to jump through flaming hoops at Sea World. Her younger brother, Ken, a genuine Nazi, sells antiquarian condos in Petaluma.

My father, an accountant for GE, died from pneumonia when I was two. My mother next married a guy named Harold who serviced vending machines in a tri-state area until they chucked him in jail for racketeering. Then Ma got hitched to a very rich stockbroker who violated an obscure provision of the Securities Exchange Act and joined hubby number two in the slammer. Her fourth helpmeet, Gilbert Moffet, was a dentist in Oneonta until he retired three years ago. They bought a Winnebago and live in Montana in the summer, in Arizona when the snows fly.

I'm the only offspring of my real dad. I have two half-sisters from the racketeer—Beth, and Laray Savant. That's right, Susan legally changed her name to Laray Savant, hoping it would make her a better actress. Instead, she now works as a security guard on the Alaska pipeline. She packs a .357 magnum and also raises sled dogs in hopes of one day winning the Iditarod. Beth is a lawyer in Poughkeepsie, specializing in personal injury. Her husband, Don, an entrepreneur, became filthy rich during the energy boom, buying deep gas wells sight unseen and unloading them at a criminal profit before any drilling began.

They all think Zelda and I are bona fide weirdos.

At the time of our wedding, Zelda hadn't talked to her dad, or her sister and brother, in seven years.

I still get postcards from my mother and Gilbert about twice a year. Invariably they show jackrabbits with deer antlers, enormous grasshoppers tied over the saddle horn of a quarter horse, or a trout bigger than Moby Dick being hauled on a long flatbed trailer hitched to a Ford pickup truck.

And sometimes a tipsy mule is kicking over an outhouse.

The ceremony took place in my (correction, *our*) own back field on a September afternoon so beautiful it seemed as if cherubs stroking little harps and baby violins were about to descend from the radiant blue sky and play for us while we said our vows.

Attending the ceremony were only a handful of select friends. Betty and Alex, of course, and Zelda's buddies Carol and Seamus. Carol is a large, bosomy happy-go-lucky Valkyrie who runs a catering business to the stars. Seamus is a wifty pencil-thin gangster who sells illegal drugs. If I didn't mention it earlier, Betty is a foot taller than Alex, and she makes a good living "acting" in neo-Nazi sado-masochistic fly-by-night soft-porn films. I used to have a whole collection of her best work. I even tried some of it out on Zelda when we were courting, and it sure seemed to light a fire under her back then.

Alex teaches philosophy at NYU.

All the children came too, of course. Woody and Kim, my blood creations; and Gabrielle and Jennifer, hers.

Then there was Moe Bubbles, also Ed and Emily Griffin (Ed's my tennis partner), and Zelda's gonzo friend Weezie Bednarik, who can cathect only through a hand puppet.

The guy who made our marriage legit was my pal David Barbeau. David is an interesting specimen. He earns a living teaching people how to catch trout. He is also a stone alcoholic who always carries at least a dozen vodka shooters in the Velcroed pockets of his fishing vest. You want poetry with a fly rod, however, David is your man.

Back in the wild and wonderful seventies, David completed a mail-order course in ersatz theology and, for twenty-five bucks, became a minister in the Church of the Everlasting Gospel's Ethereal Light. It's a bogus organization that allows you to legally marry people at close to a couple hundred dollars a pop.

Which was David's reason for joining up in the first place.

Zelda and I choreographed a wonderful ceremony.

First of all, she had bought me a black silk shirt that would've made Elvis envious, so I was of a slightly more tony bent than is my wont.

Zelda herself wore a low-cut peach-colored jersey minitube that made her look about a hundred times more enticing than the next most erotic/beautiful woman in the world you can name.

She also sported a pair of silver hoop earrings and three-inch-high fuck-me pumps, and her thick Navajo cornlady bracelet.

David made it through the formal part of the ceremony without too much New Age tripe. But then he had to call down from heaven a Column of Light in the middle of which he ordered us to stand silently for three minutes. During that part I felt like a royal horse's ass. Zelda kept running her finger surreptitiously up and down the crevice between my buttocks.

Then Zelda and I recited together a poem by John Crowe Ransom called "The Equilibrists." Our favorite part was verse twelve:

> *Great lovers lie in Hell, the stubborn ones*
> *Infatuate of the flesh upon the bones;*
> *Stuprate, they rend each other when they kiss,*
> *The pieces kiss again, no end to this.*

We had drawn up our own marriage vows and recited them to each other. They were sincere and loose and high-spirited, not your normal bill of fare. We promised to treat each other with compassion, joy, understanding, humor, flamboyance, erotic derring-do. We promised to respect each other's freedom and independence.

We had a ball drawing up the rules and regulations. Zelda testified that if she ever became pregnant, she'd have an abortion. I declared that if I ever got filthy rich, I would buy her three thousand dollars' worth of racy silk undergarments from Victoria's Secret.

It was all clever and irreverent and modern. The onlookers uttered many hearty chuckles during our recitation.

We both felt very glamorous.

* * *

Came time for the witnesses to speak. Zelda's eldest daughter, Gabrielle (twenty-one), read one passage from Ecclesiastes, another from Baudelaire's *Fleurs du mal.*

My daughter Kim (fifteen) grew all teary eyed and maudlin as she professed great love for me and Zelda and she just knew that all of us in the extended family would love each other forever.

My son Woody (nineteen), so loaded on liquor and dope he could hardly stand, said, "For the good of all of us, I sure hope this works."

Alex was his usual acerbic self. He thought for a long time, puffing on his pipe, then said, "Roger, Zelda—l'chaim."

When Betty said, "I trust you assholes know what you're doing," Zelda and I squeezed each other and chortled, "We do, of *course* we do."

We said that with all the confidence of Hitler invading Poland.

Carol went into a long rap about her struggle to release her inner child, and seeing us together so happy made her believe it was possible, if you really worked at it, to find joy on Earth, not just in the hereafter as she had heretofore been inclined to believe.

Seamus, an oily little sleazebag from Hell, raised his glass of bubbly and said, "You got a helluva deal, Roger. I envy you. You better take good care of the little lady."

Implied, naturally, was "or else."

The twit added, "You both are great people and you deserve the best."

He didn't know either of us from Adam.

Weezie Bednarik ran a motorized messenger service that specialized in novelty items, such as birthday strip-o-grams for roué bachelors, and Mr. Bluster Clowns with honking noses who visited sick children in the hospital. Weezie's hand puppet at this time was a green parrot called Adrian. In real life, Weezie could not express her

True Feelings. She was pathologically shy. And terrified of confrontation. About three years ago a local therapist, Madelyn Grinnell, had hit upon the idea of Adrian. Ever since, Weezie could express herself very well, thank you. But only by waggling the hand-puppet parrot in your face and channeling all her words through it. Him. Whatever.

At our wedding, Weezie was sobbing so hard we could barely understand Adrian's piffle. Which ran along the line that two people, even ones as beautiful as us, rarely got a second chance in life. So Adrian thought our liaison was a miracle. And the hand puppet concluded, "I think you guys should be on the cover of *People* magazine."

Moe Bubbles struck a heroic pose, one hand on his chest, the other hand raised in oratorical splendor. He crowed, "Oh most merciful God, please forgive these blessed children, for they know not what they do."

We all laughed appreciatively.

Ed Griffin is your basic yuppie nudge. He said, "You two are the most exotic couple I've ever seen. I envy you. I bet your adventure together will be joyful to the max. Your happiness makes *me* so happy I could sing."

So he sang that schmaltzy song from *Man of La Mancha*, "The Impossible Dream."

Then Zelda's youngest kid, Jennifer (eighteen), said, "Dominus pax vobiscum." And after a major giggle fit, she added, "Shredded wheat."

Marijuana.

It'll make your children stupid.

For the ceremony's pièce de résistance, Zelda and I buried a Barbie and a Ken medicine bundle in the middle of the back field. I had purchased the Barbie and Ken at Wal-Mart. We wrote our names in Magic Marker on the appropriate body—Zelda on the Ken, me on the Barbie. Zelda likes Native-American mumbo jumbo, so she tied around Barbie's ankle a diminutive deerskin pouch full of bee pollen, heishi beads, orange coral, a piece of turquoise, a crystal, a Mimbres pot shard, a goshawk feather, and the tiny jawbone of a wee pocket mouse.

After the wedding was concluded, Alex asked me, "What was that medicine bundle all about?"

"It's just theater," I explained.

Zelda cackled, "It's a dance we do with the devil." She waved a bottle of champagne, already high on the stuff.

Then she grabbed me by the hand and tugged me into the house, into the Beverly Jog beside the kitchen, where she leaned over my (excuse me, *our*) medium-sized Sears freezer and ordered me to take her from behind.

With a hearty "Hi ho, Silver!" I complied.

So where (and how), you might wonder, given such an auspicious beginning, did it all go so wrong?

Patience, jackass.

Friday night, after the wedding and the blowout that followed, Zelda and I bid our guests and children adieu and drove out to the mesa. We parked my truck (correction, *our* truck) in the middle of a sagebrush ocean. The wind howled but the sky was clear. You could count a billion stars. We lay on a double mattress in the pickup bed under sleeping bags, a duvet, and two comforters and were warm as toast. We held hands and shouted "Look!" each time a shooting star zipped toward Earth. Coyotes yipped, barked, and cackled.

We took turns being on top so the other could watch the heavens as we screwed. The wind whipped Zelda's hair, which was haloed by stars. We stripped naked. Icy wind raised goosebumps all over us, but they felt wonderful.

Starshine and moonbeams on Zelda's lovely breasts made strikingly divine and voluptuous shadows.

We never quit. Our cadence matched that of the tempestuous air. I thought, *Oh God I am so happy I hope this lasts forever.*

One of my orgasms resembled an explosion of the scent of vanilla.

Another was like falling from a great height into an enormous bin full of peacock feathers.

Perhaps it was midnight when Zelda said, "I can't believe how happy you make me feel. My blood has turned into helium."

"Me?" I pretended astonishment. "It's *you* who make me ecstatic. My teeth are floating. My skin wants to leave my meat and go curl around the aerial and flap like a flag in this erotic hurricane."

"Jesus," she chortled, "I married a writer!"

"I love you, Zelda."

"How much between one and ten?"

"Twenty," I burbled, a lunatic in love.

"Only twenty?" Did I actually catch a hint of irritation in her tone?

"I mean forty," I corrected, just to be on the safe side.

Not safe enough, apparently. "That's all?" she teased.

"You said between one and *ten*," I kidded back. "I'm already three hundred percent beyond perfect."

"That's nothing," Zelda cooed into my frozen ear, letting her tongue tip lightly rape the lobe. "I love you at least a hundred."

Okay, answer me this please, those of you with degrees in the topic. How come I didn't just quicklike tell her back, "I love you a hundred too"? How come, suddenly, on this sublime occasion, I felt a prickle of irritation with the fact that she'd upped the numerical ante of our game? How come yours truly required almost a full fifteen seconds to finally admit, "I love you a hundred too"?

Zelda fell silent. The wind coursed over us like ocean breakers. We listened to the roaring night. Sometimes you could smell little spurts of dry sheep dung. We held hands, squeezing back and forth, rubbing thumbs, staring at the stars.

Suddenly Zelda asked, "Is it better with me than it was with Christie?"

Holy Toledo. *Christie?* One of my former girlfriends. But how did *she* crop up in the back of our pickup at a time like this?

"Baby," I groaned, hugging Zelda with all my might and main, "there isn't even a remote comparison."

Next day the kids departed, returned to college (Gabrielle, Jennifer, and Woody) and high school (Kim), scattered to the four winds.

Then Zelda donned her General Patton persona, and suddenly—*biff, bam, holy kazaam!*—we were ordered to attack the house with a vengeance.

Let me offer a word of explanation: I used to run my pad the way Mussolini ran his army—total anarchy. There wasn't anything of value in the dump anyway. I had mattresses on the floor, plywood tables, thousands of secondhand paperback books, and ratty ten-dollar couches. The kids and I had watergun fights and snowball fights *inside* the house. Nobody ever washed any dishes unless they were hungry. Dirty plates were always stacked in the sink. During their childhood summer vacations Woody and Kim would construct an elaborate "fort" out of the whole house. This mess lasted their entire visit. Upside-down chairs and couches piled over with blankets

19

and mattresses—hey, it never bothered me. It kept them occupied. I didn't even own a vacuum cleaner. And I swept the place out once a year whether it needed it or not.

Enter Zelda.

Within a week of the wedding, our ramshackle dwelling looked like something out of *House Beautiful*. An old Dutch bread cupboard over here, a lovely Mexican trastero over there, a china cupboard in the corner, a Navajo Two Grey Hills rug on the living-room floor, and candlesticks on the windowsills, and Mexican paper flowers, and pretty little tin mirrors, and Native-American art on the walls, and scented soap in all the soap dishes, and a clean bathtub and a clean toilet to boot.

Zelda actually got down on her knees and showed Alex how to scrub the toilet with a funny gray porous block, I think it's called a pumice stone.

She handed me a can of Comet for scouring the tub.

"Use the entire can if you have to, Roger."

We probably hadn't scrubbed that tub in a year!

Before I could stop them, Zelda and Betty and Carol had taken brooms and knocked down all the spiderwebs in the kitchen, including an enormous black creation that extended all the way from over the stove halfway across the kitchen to above the refrigerator. My children and I had been assiduously cultivating that web for almost six years. We called its spider Big Al.

"Hey," I yelled, genuinely distraught when I entered my old kitchen now steeped in the throws of transformation. "Who killed Big Al?"

"I did," Zelda challenged fiercely, sticking out her chest and brandishing a broom like Friar Tuck. "You wanna make something out of it?"

No, no, of course not. Nevertheless . . .

* * *

On the following morning, at breakfast, during our second major planning session, Zelda said that the false ceilings in all the rooms really sucked. "They're ugly," she said. "What's underneath?"

"Vigas," I explained. "But when Bonnie and I bought this place, each room had a false ceiling. Bonnie ripped 'em down. We painted and stained the ceiling beams. Looked great. But there's a dirt roof on the planks overhead, and dust kept dribbling in. It raised havoc with my allergies. So soon as we got divorced and I had paid her off, I nailed up new panels to stop dust from dribbling down. Within days I felt a hundred percent better."

"I love vigas," Zelda said. "I can't live in a place with such ugly ceilings."

"Ask Alex," I said. "He visited when the vigas were exposed."

Alex eyes me unhappily. "Yeah," he admitted. "I sneezed a lot."

Zelda chuckled, "Oh Roger, your allergy rap is just a power-tripping shtick. All your life it's been something you've used to either get attention or manipulate people."

"Hey Alex," I pleaded, "Go ahead and tell her. Am I lying?"

Alex glowered at me, then smiled at Zelda. "No, he's not lying."

Zelda folded her arms, grinned right back, and said, "Neither am I."

That afternoon we six tore down those false ceilings. Then we stained the beams again so that they looked bright and shiny.

By supper time my eyes itched, Alex had started sneezing, Carol's nose was running, and Betty had a mild rash on the insides of both forearms.

Of course, we all pretended nothing was amiss.

Then it happened.

All of a sudden, out of the blue, two days later Zelda came totally unglued.

Let me set the scene:

Alex and Betty and Carol and Seamus are still around, helping to paint and plaster and build sheds and refinish the floors, and the party shows no signs of abating. We're actually having fun.

But now it's evening, the day's work is done. All of us are gathered in the kitchen, drinking wine, baking cookies, eating tons of garbage, having a jolly old time. Outside it's raining cats and dogs. But inside it is cozy as all get-out. A half-empty bottle of Wild Turkey 101, Alex's favorite, is sitting in the middle of the table, smiling at one and all. There's plenty of kielbasy and mustard and mayonnaise. The cassette player is blaring Tanya Tucker.

Then the phone rings, and my life changes forever.

The telephone in the kitchen hangs on the wall by the door. So I pick up the receiver and go outside onto the portal to escape the racket. I sit down on the old blue bench and close the door behind me so I can hear myself think. The dog comes over and humps my leg.

It turns out my ex-wife, Bonnie, is in a bit of a twit because our son Woody just got busted for DWI up in Boulder, and they also found a little cocaine in a Baggie on the floor of the car he was driving.

Actually, Bonnie is hysterical.

I tell her to calm down, calm down, I'll call a lawyer, send money, pay off all the usual leeches, have him sprung, then talk to the people I need to mollify in order to keep him in school.

All that has hardly exited my mouth when Zelda slams out the door at a hundred miles an hour, hits the driveway mud and skids, goes flat on her butt with a scream, and slides five yards right into the left front wheel of her Subaru. She rebounds erect, cursing, jumps in, starts the car, backs around spinning every which way, takes off in the downpour (using our north-south runway!), and disappears into the Dickensian night.

Alex appears in the doorway, seemingly perplexed. Alex is five feet four inches tall and looks like he should wear a Borsalino hat and chew on a Cuban cigar while cradling a tommy gun in one arm. He dresses that way too: black fishnet muscle shirts, tight blue jeans with a twelve-inch peg at the cuff, ox-blood Wellingtons with three-inch Cuban heels.

But in reality he's a gentle person, also an intellectual. He likes William James, Kierkegaard, and Kant.

I ask, "What the hell was that all about?"

He doesn't know. Zelda just suddenly went ballistic.

I tell Bonnie, "Listen, I got a little problem here, don't worry, I'll call Boulder, I'll figure it out."

I'm good at figuring things out. For other people. I'm not sure if I ever solved anything for myself.

Bonnie sounds as if she ought to be wearing the Borsalino and toting the AK-47. "If you would pay a little more attention to our son," she says, "and a little less attention to your stupid wedding party, maybe Woody wouldn't get in this kind of trouble."

I couldn't figure that out. Boulder is four hundred miles away. What does my postnuptial fiesta have to do with his DWI?

I said, "Calm down, Bonnie. Relax."

She breaks into tears. She hates me. She hangs up.

Alex hands me the bottle of 101.

23

But I am a civilized human being. I rise, enter the house, locate my glass, drop in three new ice cubes, and baptize the cubes with bourbon. Maybe I'm a schnook, but at least I'm a cultured schnook. I *never* drink from the bottle.

I spend an hour in the truck driving all around town in Hurricane Brian searching for Zelda.

I check all the bars—? Nope. All the eateries—? Nope. The Safeway and Wal-Mart parking lots—? Nope.

Mostly, then, I drive around aimlessly, worried sick about my kid and about the woman who became my wife only five days ago. It's raining so hard I can't see squat, until I notice the blinking cherrytop lights in my rearview mirror. Three sets of blinking cherrytops, to be exact.

I sigh and steer onto the shoulder and haul out the wallet and roll down the window and hand over the license, then I pop the glove box and find the insurance card and give that to Mr. Macho also. He shines his flashlight on the license, on the insurance card, and then directly into my face. I almost speak impolitely, but instead I simply turn my face away.

"What's the matter, officer?" I ask, laying on the sugar. But I am beginning to be aware that this night will not go down in history as one of my finest hours.

"You were weaving, sir," says the big damp lummox. "Now, will you kindly step out of this vehicle?"

By the time Alex springs me from the calaboose, I'm fuming. He informs me that Zelda returned about five minutes after I left. "So what was the matter?" I ask. He shrugs. She didn't say. She just went to her room and slammed the door and, he presumes, went to bed. He tells me Bonnie rang twice more in hysterics. Woody got to a phone and called her from Boulder in tears. Get him out of there, *please.* He's *scared.* They roughed him up during the bust. His nose is bleeding. Bonnie wants to know did I find him a lawyer? I bellow, "It's fucking ten P.M., so how am I supposed to produce a lawyer?"

"Hey," Alex remonstrates, "don't take it out on me. I didn't do anything."

"Fuck you, Alex," I tell him, "you're guilty by association."

We both have a good laugh over that.

At home, things aren't so funny. I bang open the bedroom door and ask what the hell was that all about? Zelda is lying on the bed in the dark, fully clothed, arms folded, smoke spewing out of her ears. She says, "You know." I say, "No I don't know, I haven't got the foggiest." "Oh don't you pull that phony naive act on me," she says. "Don't you dare insult my intelligence."

I can't believe what I'm hearing. I can't believe her tone of voice. This is Jekyll-Hyde territory, and I am flabbergasted. This never happened when we were courting.

" 'Intelligence'?" I say, trying to keep it down to a dull roar. "Excuse me, but I don't see any intelligence in this room. I don't even see a sentient human being. All I see is a lunatic."

"Get out of here," she says. "Leave me alone. You are such a liar it isn't even funny."

"No, I'm serious," I say. "What in tarnation was that all about?"

"I heard you whispering with her behind my back," Zelda finally admits.

"What?" I mean, I really meant it. *"What?"*

"You heard me. You're not deaf, are you?"

"Whispering with *who*?" I asked, utterly paralyzed with bewilderment.

"You and Bonnie," she says. "Sneaking out of the kitchen like that."

I say, "What?"

She says, "You heard me."

I say, "I heard a lunatic. What are you talking about?"

She says, "In case you don't know, *I* happen to be your wife now, and damned if I will have you and your old wife telling tales out of school behind my back. That is betrayal and I will not tolerate it. I will not tolerate secrets. I am your focus in life now, not her. I am nobody's second fiddle."

Ah so.

I open my mouth, but nothing comes out.

I make odd spastic gestures that are totally aimless and uncoordinated.

She could have told me almost any old story and I would not have been as astounded as I was by what she actually said.

Talk about left field.

In desperate search for a relevant gesture, I yank off my glasses and throw them through the nearest window. Though made of a lightweight unbreakable plastic, they punch right through the glass with a little crash and a follow-up tinkle.

When my kids were little, they always used to say it like this: "Uh-oh, SpaghettiOs!"

But let me back up a minute, here.

You need to know that I once lived with a woman named Gretal who had cancer. We cohabited for three years in the early 1980s. Gretal was a tough cookie. I once sat in a hospital room and heard a doctor tell her she had only three months to live. Gretal told that sawbones "Fuck you," then we went out to price wigs.

She bought a blond curly Dolly Parton number and a long straight black Cher/Elvira ensemble. I didn't like the latter all that much, but Gretal had a flair for both the theatrical and the macabre. She played jazz saxophone and she was good. Of course, in our little town you make about as much money hawking old Billie Holiday tunes as a migrant worker in the Mesilla Valley makes picking chiles. But Gretal was a girl who would survive, and she always paid her share, and she never took me for a nickel out of line.

I used to frequent Tony's Arrivederci and listen to her quartet. Peter on the keyboards, Jaimie on the bass, and Gretal on the horn. The guitarist–singer was Dodie Fenichell. She had great tonsils. She'd mellow you out with "Stormy Weather" and "Stardust," then whack you over the head with "Strange Fruit."

Sometimes they all shut up and Gretal did an a cappella solo of "Amazing Grace." She could project a husky alto voice that really made me shiver.

Unfortunately, Gretal did not have a pragmatic approach to her illness. She went on macrobiotic diets, changed gurus every two months, ate apricot pits and sunflower seeds. Name a cancer fad, Gretal tried it. I had to practically mug her and tie her up and drag her to radiation and chemotherapy. But between the two of us we sort of licked the platter clean. The three months that quack gave her, when initially the disaster was diagnosed, stretched out to eleven years and counting.

We quit living together for a variety of reasons I am not too proud of. Gretal was eight years older than me, and she'd had one of those lives you only read about in books like *I, Jan Cremer* or *The Biography of George Sand*. But life takes a toll on everybody, even international jazz courtesans, and Gretal was ready to settle down. Me, however,

I'd just broken up with Bonnie, my third Sidney Bard novel was getting some attention, and I had a letch for the kind of high life Gretal had lived.

In fact, what attracted me to Gretal in the first place was the adventure I craved. We argued about that a lot. Gretal claimed the greatest adventure was in the mind. She said that the high life wasn't all it was cracked up to be. Despite all her glamorous affairs, she insisted that now she was a one-man woman. She lobbied for marriage. I resisted. We had a tempestuous affair.

In the end, when Christie showed up at our front door in a skin-tight pink jumpsuit selling Amway products, I was ready to make tracks. I couldn't reach for my checkbook fast enough.

Gretal cornered is a saber-toothed tiger, and she fought a rousing battle. But eventually she had to give up, let go, and I traveled on.

We remained friends, however, and indulged ourselves with an occasional root for old times' sake.

Now: during the prolonged fiesta and domestic renovation after Zelda and I took the plunge, Gretal was not having one of her better weeks. In fact, the day after Alex and Moe Bubbles and Seamus and I repaired all the gutters on the roof, the shit hit Gretal's fan.

I learned about her problem when I stopped by her house to deliver some mail she was still getting in my post-office box (six years after our breakup!). I found Gretal in bed, in pain, in tears.

"How long has this been going on?" I asked.

"About ten days," she admitted.

"You asshole," I said.

"Shuttup." She pouted. "I'm sick of your remonstrations."

"Well, you're an idiot." I was worried sick. "You're supposed to go in at the first sign of a relapse."

"I hate it anymore," she said. "I'm tired of hospitals and doctors and oncovin and radiation therapy. I don't want to lose my hair again. Enough already."

So I bundled her up, packed a little suitcase, and lugged her over to the Sisters of the Virgin Mary. I checked her in and called the local quack—Zebulon Morrison—who specialized in leukemia and lymphomas. I made a second run to the hospital, with toothpaste and a toothbrush. Then I had to make another trip for Gretal's dental floss and a pink silk camisole.

In Gretal's immortal words, "I don't want to lie here looking like some kind of zonkered bag lady from New York."

I mention Gretal because of course she immediately became a bone of contention.

Not the Gretal situation exactly, not at first—Zelda wasn't that big a fool. But when, on the following afternoon, Christie called in tears to announce that her daughter Cazzie had just tried to commit suicide in a motel room with her lesbian social worker (who was thirty years older), and I pledged five hundred dollars to get Cazzie into a juvenile detox program, Zelda hit the ceiling. Ceiling, nothing, actually she went through the roof.

Yes, I'd always known that Zelda was proud of being volatile. You bet she liked high drama, it was part of the act. And I had always enjoyed her raucous flair. Above all else, during our courting days, the lady had kept me in stitches. What I hadn't foreseen, during that halcyon time, was the degree to which her act could change once the situation itself was different.

"What kind of a stupid situation *is* this?" she wailed.

"Six hundred to bail out Woody. Now five hundred for Cazzie. Why don't you just invite them all to come and *live* with us? I'll go back to nursing school and get my stupid R.N. and chip in my salary. Gretal can sleep in the guest room, Christie can have the living-room couch, and we'll put Bonnie in one of the sheds with Woody for her roommate as soon as they throw him out of school!"

Then she turned to my best friend from New York, who, along with the others, was shelling peas into a salad bowl, and said, "What do you think about that, Alex? Do you think we should invite Megan and María Teresa to come and live here, too? We could stick an Arab minaret on the roof with a gold pennant on it announcing 'Roger's Harem.'"

Alex looked at Betty, who looked at Carol, who looked at Seamus, who said, "Don't look at me."

"You can't help what happens in life," I said. I was still trying to be lighthearted. "You cannot simply order up perfect timing. When you're forty-five like us, you're toting extra baggage. And anyway, when it rains it pours."

"I am not forty-five," Zelda (literally) spat. "I am a helluva lot younger than that."

Instantly I apologized. The one irrevocable taboo with Zelda is age. If I were to reveal her true years, even now in this book being written so long after the fact, she'd hire an expert killer to whack me, preferably very slowly and very painfully.

Then Zelda said, "I am not going to be married to a man who is still carrying on affairs with every goddamn sleazy street slut west of the Mississippi."

"Hey, jeepers creepers," I protested. "I am not carrying on affairs. When we decided to marry, you know I quit messing around. But these folks are important in my life. They're my friends. I still care about them."

"Fuck your friends!" she explained.

In unison, Alex, Betty, Seamus, and Carol said, "Hey, Zelda, thanks a lot."

Obviously, I did not like Zelda dumping on my friends. Obviously, I was also in shock. Me *and* Alex and Betty and Carol and Seamus. Those latter four had quit shelling peas and were spectating the holocaust like monkeys watching the atomic bombing of their own private banana plantation.

I couldn't remember ever having a serious argument with Zelda when we were courting. Sure, we had teased each other about her boyfriends, my girlfriends, but it had all been in a spirit of good-natured fun. Zelda had never cast an aspersion on Bonnie or Christie or Gretal.

Well, I told myself, this transition time can't be easy for Zelda. She's moving to a strange town. She's occupying an unfamiliar house that I've owned for sixteen years. Many girlfriends and a wife and numerous children have been through these hallowed portals. Only a very balanced person would not have trouble with such ghosts. I don't blame her for feeling defensive. I would feel the same way in her shoes.

Alex finally said, "Relax, Zelda. You're not trying out for *The Gong Show*."

Zelda smiled, lighting up like fuel rods in a nuclear reactor just before meltdown. "I *am* relaxed," she insisted. "This is fun."

That night I said, "Honey, do you think it's wise to bring all that garbage up in front of our friends?"

"I don't know if it's wise or not, Roger, but if I don't say what I think when I feel it, it'll never get said. I've been in two marriages where I was bullied, intimidated, and cheated on, and I kept silent. You told me yourself you and Bonnie could never talk. Well, this time around we both need to express ourselves."

I said, "I think our fights are embarrassing them."

"We're not 'fighting,' " Zelda corrected. "It's a natural and important process. We're learning how to communicate. I think it's exhilarating."

"It feels like fighting to me," I ventured.

Zelda scooched over and lovingly cupped my testicles.

"Darling," she said, "if it ever escalates into real fighting, believe me, you'll understand the difference."

Then she mounted me as if I were a Clydesdale, but no blissful Christmas Budweiser commercial could have held even half a candle to what next transpired.

Years earlier, my dear friend Alex had suddenly up and married. When he called me and told me he was going to do it, and described the volatile wop who was the lucky lady, I said, "Alex, you're crazy, don't do it." He laughed and did it anyway.

There followed three years of total chaos. In the end she threw a meat loaf at his head, so he broke her jaw, she called the cops, he wound up in jail, and she ran home to the parental fig tree and tomato plant in Brooklyn and sued him for a hundred thousand bucks. The day the divorce papers arrived, Alex had a heart attack and wound up in intensive care for twenty-three days, where he read Thomas Mann's book *Joseph and His Brothers*.

On Wednesday afternoon of the protracted honeymoon, while Carol, Seamus, Betty, and Zelda were taking the baths at Ojo Caliente, Alex and I rode our bicycles south on Ranchitos Road, through Los Cordovas, onto the sagebrush mesa. We pedaled along a dirt road to the edge of a cliff about two hundred feet above the Pueblo River.

"Well, ol' buddy," I said. "What do you think?"

"Helluva woman," he said, lighting his pipe. Though Alex does indeed look like something macho and prehistoric out of Sicily, he smokes a meerschaum.

"She's beautiful," I said.

"Can't argue with that." He puffed some more.

"She's a wee bit volatile," I said.

He nodded.

I said, "It's wonderful between us in bed."

He nodded again. "I should hope so. I envy you that. The broad is a real looker."

"I never met a woman who's as funny, wacky, alive, intelligent, and vivacious," I said.

Alex stooped over, located a small stone, straightened, and pitched it out into the air. We watched it dive in a graceful arc down to the smooth water of a long, placid pool in the river, where it made a little trout-sized splash.

"Do you think I should jump off this cliff right now," I asked, "or wait awhile and see what happens?"

Alex replied, "What do I look like, a soothsayer?"

Later on that afternoon, Alex, who is very discreet and not normally an intrusive person, asked me, "Just to be curious, Roger, why did you get married? I thought you had the perfect bachelor existence."

So I told him. At least as best as I could figure it out, I related the tale.

Here's the gist of that story.

My life had gotten complicated. I was working on two film scripts at once, including one of my own third novel, *The Catacombs of Luray*. The other was an hour show for the Zane Adams TV series. I was also humming along way ahead of deadline on my latest Sidney Bard sci-fi detective thriller, *Return of the Perseid Meteor Thugs*.

I don't want to delve into my stuff here, but by now I have earned a living at it for almost twenty years. I don't think the books are great art, but I do admit that Sidney Bard has become a minor underground cult figure along the lines of Kurt Vonnegut's Kilgore Trout. Sidney is a detective who meanders through the galaxies at the end of a psychic silver thread, solving space crimes through soul travel while his actual body sleeps in a flotation tank in a split-level ranch palace in Beverly Hills.

The thing that makes Sidney interesting (to me, at least) is he used to be a professional hockey player of the same caliber as Wayne Gretzky. And he's still a distinguished lepidopterist reknowned for discovering the Sidney's Hairstreak, which was named, of course, after the great intergalactic sleuth himself.

So: for starters, I was a very busy man.

To boot, I had a handful of quasiserious relationships going: with Gretal and Christie, Megan, María Teresa, Sandra, and, of course, Zelda.

Long ago, after Bonnie and I divorced, I had sworn never again to be monogamous. But it wasn't easy to live that philosophy. First of all, I'm not a real handsome guy, nor am I the world's greatest stud. But I'm full of energy and I love women, I really do. I mean talking and relating, as well as the sex. I really pay attention to women. They fascinate me. I listen. I do the dishes and cuddle and I enjoy foreplay. I like goofing around with their kids, who adore me because I'm warm, I'm zany, I'm funny. I know how to function on their level. I laugh, I think life is a great big bowl of cherries. I'm upbeat. I really have fun. So people have always sort of flocked around because they like my cheerful optimism.

Okay: I had longstanding relationships with several women. It was all on the up-and-up, no lies, no sneaking around. They had other boyfriends also.

The glitch was, we sort of loved each other. We had

great adventures together. Yet often Megan asked, "How can you be so loving with me, then go love somebody else?" And although Sandra never said a word, one day I discovered that she hadn't screwed another guy in over a year. When I asked why, she said, "I don't *want* to." Gretal rarely hassled me after our initial blowout when Christie stole me away, but she (Gretal) had revealed recently that for years she'd felt a sexual loyalty to me because I was so understanding about the cancer.

Christie's attitude was, "Just so long as you give me your undivided attention while we're together, I don't give a hoot in hell what you do on your own time."

And María Teresa lived in Buenos Aires, so aside from our semiannual get-togethers, she wasn't really much of a factor.

And then there was Zelda.

Zelda was the most recent, the most complicated, the most exciting. An angel, a devil, a quixotic cock teaser. She was the funniest also, a real comedienne. She made me laugh. She was the most glamorous woman I'd ever gone out with. She had chutzpah and daring with clothes, with her wild dark hair, with her sassy no-holds strut. She had that diminutive but perfect hourglass body right out of the 1950s girlie magazines; fanatical jogging and aerobics and Jazzercise kept it that way. She looked a lot younger than her real age; and like I said earlier, she would have offed anybody who had the audacity to reveal her true years.

Most especially, Zelda's eyes sparkled. I mean *sparkled*. When she turned them on, she could slaughter with those eyes. All the time we were courting, those liquid brown orbs literally sizzled with a tantalizing light.

Her effervescence, effortlessly, slew me.

Of course, when those eyes went cold, they could make a lion shudder and curl its tail between its legs.

Zelda loved to order stuff from Night N Day Intimates and Victoria's Secret. She wore that style for me, and for the world. Every male out there with hormones couldn't help but want to grab her.

Zelda liked attention in public. She adored the squealing of brakes, the thud of guys colliding against walls, the wolf whistles. When Zelda clickety-clacked along the sidewalk, men broke their necks—Snap! Crackle! Pop!

The show stopped wherever Zelda swaggered.

Oh, Zelda had flair, she had panache, she had outrageous hubris, she had rapacious energy. She was an honest-to-God sex symbol. She always made a grand entrance, even in the morning, in our kitchen, for breakfast. Zelda was constantly on stage, the life of the party, the It girl.

So at first it sure didn't jibe with me that above all else Zelda wanted to be married.

I said, "You've been married twice, both disasters."

She answered, "I'll keep doing it until I get it right."

I said, "Any man would sell his soul to the devil for just one night in your arms. You could have any stud you wanted. You could have adventures galore with the glitterati. Who knows, maybe even a spread one day in *People* magazine. Why harness yourself to the marital wheel?"

Apparently, Zelda couldn't live without the security of a badge.

"I believe in true love, Roger," she explained. "I am not a shallow human being."

Nor am I a person without depth.

I mean, it wasn't just cheap sexual allure that had bonded

me to Zelda. It was her energy, her electric mind, her complexity. She had a thousand beguiling faces.

Unpredictable Zelda was always talking, laughing, teasing, flirting, arguing, joking, smooching.

"That's why you like me," Zelda often smirked coquettishly. " 'Cause I'm not an easy read."

I was enchanted by her quicksilver darting moods as she barreled full steam ahead.

Always Full Steam Ahead.

"I'm like Pancho Villa," she liked to brag. "My only direction is forward. I'm fearless, I never learned how to retreat. I was born to attack."

My bewitching Zelda had never finished college, but she had read a million books and seen a trillion films. She had references galore and held a zillion opinions.

Oh yes, more than any woman I'd ever known, arrogant Zelda had opinions.

Opinions burst from her like fireworks after a home run in a domed baseball stadium.

"Ronald Reagan is what happens when you cross a bottle of Geritol with a can of Spam."

"I hate people who think they're hot stuff because they own two Amado Peñas, one R. C. Gorman, and a Fritz Scholder lithograph of a dog."

That went for me, too—double.

In bed, Zelda and I had made love and talked, and talked and made love again, and kept on talking. Since the day of our initial meeting, we had been infinitely fascinated by each other.

Topics leaped off Zelda's tongue, they tap-danced about our coverlets, they cavorted in joyful abandon. Antonioni's *La Notte*, the career of Jeanne Moreau, how to breed registered chows, the philosophy of Robert Bly. In the next breath it could be Matisse, Monet, and Helmut Newton, varieties of tulips and mushrooms, the latest Hite Report, memories of the sixties' Haight-Ashbury, and the sad fact that houses in America no longer had attics where children could rummage among the family treasures.

Zelda hated George Bush, despised Frederick's of Hollywood, loved Coco Chanel and Colette, mocked all rainforest chic, admired Muhammad Ali, thought Gloria Steinem was a jerk, and would have crawled on her belly for a mile over sharp rocks just to kiss Diego Rivera's (or Frida Kahlo's) feet.

She wasn't neutral about anything.

Zelda had opinions about the stock exchange, the capitalist system, stupid beer ads on TV. She definitely knew the difference between "sexy" and "tacky." "I dress sexy," she informed me, "but *never* tacky. Everything I do has class. There's a way to kill 'em without appealing to their prurient instincts."

Marilyn Monroe was sexy; Dolly Parton was tacky.

No electric-blue spandex bodysuits for Zelda; no checkered pedal pushers with lacing up the thigh. She believed that character both dictated, and reflected, style.

"I will never look like a hooker," she swore. "Nothing cheap. Nothing overt. Nothing *easy*. I like a more subtle eroticism, defined by a soupçon of innocence and playfulness. No way will I ever come on too strong."

"Like a *Playboy* playmate with brains?" I suggested.

Zelda snorted, "Those dumb twits couldn't hold a candle to my flesh."

Long ago she had warned: "Don't you ever dare try to cheapen me, Roger. I'm the kind of woman who makes a man immortal. You should be open to the possibilities."

At one candlelight dinner during our courtship days, I teased, "You're too cocky, Zelda. You better tone it down or you're headed for a fall."

She plucked a strawberry from her champagne, popped it into her mouth, and grinned like a miniature female Kirk Douglas:

"What are you talking about, Roger? I *always* win."

"Oh yeah?" I immediately pulled out a Bic pen, wrote the date and *I always win* on a napkin, and ordered her to sign it.

"Gladly."

Zelda scribbled her name with a bold flourish.

I bought a picture frame at Wal-Mart, inserted that napkin, and hung it on my wall.

In her arms, inside her body, watching us in the mirror—oh, Zelda had held me in her thrall.

She once murmured, "Only the dancer can change the dance. Only the dreamer can change the dream."

"What is your dream?" I asked.

"I want to discover love," she said. "Don't laugh. I want to realize the *promise*. So what if I failed twice? I'll keep trying until I get it right. It doesn't just happen, though. You have to push it. Take risks. Be daring. You can't be afraid of confrontation. A miner can't tunnel down into the heart of a mountain without using dynamite. You have to destroy in order to create. I want to rise above all the petty self-indulgences people use to bore each other to death. I want to float a thousand miles above the grunting Warthogs of Apathy who control the planet. I want my partner and me to feel like magic. I want to manifest an intimacy that's as radiant for both of us as summer evenings after rain. I couldn't bear being a cliché."

I chuckled and lightly brushed her cheek. "Vey, vey, such an idealist."

Zelda cast a thoughtful gaze in my direction, then paraphrased Robert Browning.

She said, "A person's reach should exceed their grasp, or else what's a heaven for?"

She added, "I'm not stupid, Roger. I have bubbles in me

like Einstein and Bette Davis. My mind is quick like a hummingbird."

During our courtship, Zelda had one other heavy guy in her stable of sycophants, a big-time realtor down in the capital, where she lived, an hour south of here. He was hot on her tail. His name was Douglas Morgan.

She told me and Douglas, flat out: "Whichever one of you bozos asks me first, him I'll marry."

Well, that was an interesting challenge.

I said, "Don't you love one of us more than the other?"

Zelda laughed and kissed the tip of my nose. "I love each of you in a different way, and each way is valid. I'm just not going to be jerked around by some asshole who's nothing but milk and honey but never makes a commitment. I'm not interested in being anybody's flashy hooker. If you want to dance, you've got to pay the band."

Now, as I think I sort of intimated earlier, all was not well with Roger's Harem Theory of Existence. Truth is, by the time Zelda and I had logged close to a year of commuter dalliance, I was sort of frazzled from trying to balance her and the other women. Multiple loving is complex, it requires a lot of time and concentration. It also entails downright baroque logistics.

Too, I was beginning to sense that everybody, including yours truly, was not all that cool. Maybe this is a common flaw at forty-five, but I found myself starting to be *in love* with Christie and Megan and Sandra ... and with Zelda and even María Teresa, too.

Not to mention Gretal.

Like, it seemed as if I was beginning to care too much

about my lovers. I had a weird itch to settle down with each one of them. God knows from whence this conscience derived. "Conscience"? Perhaps "homing instinct" would be closer to the truth. A lust for security, Jeeves?

Whatever the case, I had begun to feel that all of us were hurting because of that withheld Final Push. And the whole situation wasn't fair, somehow. Just possibly Zelda was correct and my sexual politics stunk. Even if everyone involved was a consenting adult.

I also knew that Christie was leaning toward another guy, Tom. And Megan seemed to be vascillating somewhat between me and a cowboy named Harry. Hey, we were all of approximately similar ages, in the midterm of our lives. Plus, I suppose there is a traditional point where the Eternal Rut inevitably defers to a more genteel and contemplative sexuality.

In the final analysis, I became confused. I concluded that with marriage life would be more simple. And the Simple Life would enable me to concentrate more on my work.

I give you Flaubert:

Be regular and orderly . . . like a Bourgeois, so that you may be violent and original in your art.

Or maybe the urge to get married was like the impulsive gesture of a suicide. A day or a month on either side and it never would have happened.

Certainly all of the above entered the equation. I'd gotten to running too fast, and Zelda had made it sort of a contest anyway, and she certainly acted like a prize. Much more so than any of the others. Too, Zelda was the only one who was insisting on marriage. And maybe that schmuck Douglas Morgan was about to pop the question.

So suddenly I asked Zelda to marry me (before he did), and she said, "Bingo—you win!"

Simple as that.

41

Victory.

It is only now, in retrospect, that I often ask myself: Did Douglas Morgan the real-estate tycoon really exist? Or was he merely a figment of Zelda's diabolical imagination?

Lest you suspect that I ignored my family whilst contemplating this momentous decision, let me set your mind at rest.

I'm no fool. I know the kids are supposed to get along with a new mate. So I asked Woody his opinion of Zelda.

"She's neat," he replied.

"Do you like her better than Christie?"

"No. I like Christie okay too," he said.

"Do you like Christie more than Megan?"

"No, Megan is pretty cool," he answered. Woody is terrified of being trapped by adults.

I said, "But not as cool as María Teresa, right?"

"Who's María Teresa?"

I then mentioned Sandra.

"Yeah, she's a pretty righteous dude," he opined.

"And Gretal?"

"Her too," he said. "Can I go now?"

When I asked Kim who she liked best of all my girlfriends, without hesitation she said, "Zelda." I asked why. Kim said, "Because she's groovy. She's funny. She never hassles me. I like her perfume."

"What about Christie?" I said.

"Yuck. One stupid disaster after another," my cruel offspring answered. "Her karma stinks. She drives a VW Beetle. I hate Cazzie."

"What about Gretal?"

"Too old."

"And María Teresa?"

"Who's María Teresa?"

"Okay, tell me about Megan."

"She's grody. And uptight. And she has no sense of humor."

"Sandra has a sense of humor."

"Sandra brushes her teeth with organic toothpaste."

"What's wrong with that?"

"If you don't know," said my teenage daughter with a bored sigh, "I hardly think it's up to me to set you straight, old man."

When I told Bonnie that Zelda and I were headed for the altar, she burst into tears. She said, "I'm so happy for you" and "I hate you" all in the same breath. She asked, "Will you still talk to me?" and I replied, "My God, of *course*. Nothing is going to change."

And then I married Zelda.

Now you know.

So return with us again to the exciting days of the extended communal barn-raising honeymoon.

Alex and Betty and Seamus and Carol and Zelda and I were seated at the kitchen table drinking Kahluas and cream and noshing on guacamole and low-salt organic bluecorn chips while discussing the nature of relationships, marriage, commitment.

Zelda's rabid reaction to Bonnie's phone call and to Christie's dilemma was the topic under discussion.

"I'll admit I acted childishly," Zelda said. "But I had a reason for acting childishly."

It would turn out that Zelda always had a reason. She positively *never* lacked an explanation.

"In a marriage there are no secrets," Zelda said. "Trust is the name of the game. Secrets only encourage paranoia. We should be able to share anything, including the good, the bad, and the ugly. In a marriage, two people become one. That's the purpose, and the incredible beauty, too."

Carol gave Seamus the evil eye while intoning, "Amen, sister."

Seamus rolled his eyeballs to heaven.

I asked Alex, "Is that the way you and Betty function?"

Alex opened his mouth, but Betty jumped all over his lines. "I don't want to know everything," she said. "Jesus Christ, life's bad enough without looking for trouble."

"That's why you guys are always at each other's throats," Zelda explained.

I stated the obvious. "Well, I told you about Christie's problem, and you abruptly had a megaconniption."

Zelda said, "You were talking about smothering this marriage in a ton of dysfunctionals who used to fuck you, so who *wouldn't* have a conniption?"

I whined, "But how can I be open with you, baby, if every time I tell the truth, you knock my block off?"

"You can't expect that just because it's the truth, I'm supposed to fall on my knees and grovel," Zelda explained. "I have an unconditional right to be honest, also, in return."

Carol sighed, "Amen, sister."

Seamus rolled his eyeballs to heaven.

"If Roger feels he can't share things with me, that's a lack of trust," Zelda said. "It's evasive. It's actually passive-aggressive."

Seamus disagreed. "Everybody needs privacy, even in a marriage."

Carol said, "Don't listen to him. Seamus likes privacy so he can mess around. But it's not a two-way street. He's a jealous pig. He pokes his nose into everything *I* do, then he screams if I call *him* to account."

"What about mail?" Zelda said. "Do you guys read each other's letters?"

"My mail is not exciting," Carol revealed. "The only person who writes is my mother."

"They're dumb epistles," Seamus said. "Boring. I never read 'em."

Carol said, "At least I get mail. Seamus never receives a single letter."

"They send me the bills," Seamus informed us. "Money, money, money."

But Zelda was already cruising after Betty and Alex.

"Betty hauls in a lot of mail," Alex said. "Sometimes she shares, sometimes she doesn't."

"If it's not too personal, fine," Betty said. "Otherwise, I keep it to myself. Alex only shares business and family stuff. He keeps the love notes from his students to himself."

"That doesn't bother you?" Zelda asked.

Betty shrugged. "I figure it's his business. You can't own another life. And it's dishonorable to pry."

Zelda said, "Roger gets millions of letters from teenyboppers on the make. He loves that kind of stroking."

"I don't get millions," I protested good-naturedly. "And the authors are rarely on the make. Plus, don't forget that's how we met."

"Oh my, *there's* a low blow." Zelda's eyes changed from cheerfully inquisitive to sardonically predatory.

I have a funny habit of always obsequiously wanting to score points with people, hoping they'll like me better, I suppose. So:

"I've got nothing to hide," I said rashly. "I certainly don't mind letting you read my letters. Why shouldn't two

45

people who love and trust each other be able to share each other's mail?"

Alex cast my way a look of dire puzzlement.

In bed that night Zelda hugged me to her quivering bosom.

"God, I was so proud of you at supper, Roger. I *love* what you said about trust and sharing the mail. You make me the happiest person on Earth. I feel sorry for Alex and Betty, they're such regressive sticks-in-the-mud. The whole world is so cynical and sophisticated. I am so glad we refuse to buy into that trap. Go ahead, name your thrill, what do you want me to wear?"

Zelda has an iridescent purple skin-tight one-piece bathing suit that shines, in the candlelight, like salmon sperm from Alaska.

Two days later our community honeymoon finally ended. We played the final tennis game, painted the last cabinet, went for a good-bye hike. For the sake of auld lang syne we drank our ultimate bottle of champagne. Then Betty and Alex caught a plane for New York, Carol and Seamus returned to L.A.

Suddenly the house was empty.

Zelda and I faced each other, slightly hung over, a trifle startled.

Zelda said, "Okay, let's clean up this mess."

I wanted to make love first.

She was wearing a pink bando top, white short-shorts, and high-heel sandals. Her skin was cinnamon brown. Her eyes shimmered like backlit diamonds. The veins (or were they arteries?) in her neck throbbed seductively—

We floated onto the Two Grey Hills rug in the middle of

the living-room floor. Home alone at last. Oh God, what a luxury—the empty house!

Now *real* married life would begin.

It was to be an idyll beyond belief; and it lasted almost a week.

But oh, what a week!

To me, I suppose marriage was like a great big sanctified monogamous orgy—of bodies, words, emotions, intellects. It was a goofy happy carnival that I didn't want to analyze. I just wanted to have *fun*.

To Zelda, marriage was a sacred trust. It was an opportunity to forge a downright mystical connection between us by boldly breaking apart old restraints, facing the issues, demanding accountability.

She just *knew* we could soar beyond normalcy, like Tchaikovsky and Nadejda von Meck, Gaston and Mrs. Lachaise, Yeats and Maud Gonne, or even Hume Cronyn and Jessica Tandy.

Zelda poured out her soul to me.

Each decoration, each plant and rug and mirror in our house, was part of a deliberate effect. "Every touch should be meaningful," she said. "There *is* an overall scheme. We can weave around ourselves a perfect net. Presentation molds the soul. If you make each detail important, invested with care and love, you can build a sensational tapestry."

She lit a tapered candle, fluffed up the centerpiece bouquet of asters, rosehips, and milkweed pods, and put real silverware on the linen tablecloth. Then delivered a platter of deviled eggs and caviar on toast, and poured two glasses of wine.

Her outfit would have made Phyllis Diller desirable.

We clinked glasses. Zelda sang out brightly, "L'chaim."

47

* * *

Never in my life had I felt more alive. It seemed as if our relationship was some fantastic climax stage of pure, unadulterated *energy*. We were totally absorbed by each other and by how the world at large touched us in our togetherness. We were extremely eager to share all things with each other. Our marriage was going to be one of constant discovery.

On Monday, when an odd bird landed on the feeder, Zelda raced for a Peterson guide to look it up so that when I came in from the tower she could tell me: "A Williamson's sapsucker visited!"

On Tuesday, I brought in two monarch butterfly cocoons attached underneath a milkweed leaf, and we put them in a large jar to germinate.

On Wednesday, while I worked, Zelda taped a National Geographic Special on rain forests so we could watch it, together, later.

On Thursday, in the middle of chopping wood, I noticed a split log whose interior had been riddled by voracious bugs; their lacework eating-trail mazes were beautifully intricate. I carried the prize inside.

Zelda actually kissed the wood, then she placed it on the windowsill in front of her typewriter, "Forever."

Speaking of fuel for winter fires, once, during that exquisite time, we drove our truck into the nearby mountains for a load of sleaze wood. My wife had fixed a picnic of caviar and crisp round toastettes, cucumber slices and white wine, smoked frogs' legs and lite mayonnaise and anchovy paste.

Zelda tugged on a pair of gloves and vehemently set to work gathering slash. She wore a knitted cap, a faded lumberjack shirt, tattered jeans, and sneakers. It was late in the afternoon and cold. Belligerent jays scolded as we dragged old logs downhill and flung branches into a pile.

Building a load of wood is great therapy. "It's like manna from heaven!" Zelda rejoiced. In about an hour the bed of the old Dodge was filled to the brim. I had no gloves and my hands were frozen. Zelda leaned back against the truck and told me, "Slip your hands up under my shirt and cup my breasts. I promise that'll make 'em warm."

I obeyed.

If there is another sensation as blissfully perfect as frozen hands melded around the contours of an ample bosom glowing with megawatts of female heat, I have not yet experienced it.

Zelda squinched her eyes, gritted her teeth, and shivered. We laughed.

When my hands tingled with restored feeling, she pried them off, dug out a satchel, shed her shirt and jeans and sneakers, and put on a skimpy low-cut thing held up by black spaghetti straps, a tight little skirt, and fuck-me pumps. Then she attacked her hair with a plastic cake cutter until it (the hair) was deemed acceptable and applied fresh lipstick. After that, she lit a votive candle arranged in a saucer on the dashboard.

We ate, radiating contentment.

"You love me because I am inventive," Zelda cooed.

Yes. Oh yes, indeed.

"I want to write a novel," Zelda said. "But I guess I need a real job."

During our year of courtship, Zelda had been simultaneously employed in multiple capacities. She had waited on tables at an upscale restaurant twice a week; acted as the personal secretary to a famous painter on Mondays and Wednesdays; and sold cosmetics at a May D & F every Friday afternoon.

Seldom had she earned much more than minimum wage. Consequently Zelda was always broke, robbing Peter to pay Paul, begging Visa and Mastercard not to throw her in jail.

Daddy Warbucks said, "Baby, take a vacation. I got money. Write your book."

"Honest?" Her eyes expanded to twice their normal size, exuding oodles of little-girl ingenuousness.

"I would love you to write a novel," I said. "I bet it would be a best-seller."

"Oh Roger—" Zelda wrapped her arms around me and lightly kissed my lips. "You're too good," she said. "You're like a saint to me."

Did I blush? Did I toe the earth in humble servility? Did I say, "Aw shucks, it's nothing"?

Hardly. I simply reached for my gal (who sighed voluptuously at my touch) and fed her a bit of the old python.

Postcoital Zelda cooed, "You're the best human being I ever met. I don't deserve you, Roger. Why are you so sweet to me? How can I ever repay you?"

And that very night she began her novel.

"It's going to be a love story," Zelda said. "About a woman born with a cleft palate who nobody can stand to look at. But she's beautiful inside. During her childhood she's a victim of incest, but survives. She's terribly shy. She reads voraciously and writes poetry and paints. Her father, Burt, the abuser, works for the FBI. Her mother, Janie, is an alcoholic beauty who used to act in B horror films. Claudia—that's the heroine—adores her mom, even though Janie has failed her terribly. In high school Claudia meets a kid, a guy named Geoffry, who's a kindred spirit. But

Geoffry is a jock, a big-shot football player, a major cheese. So naturally they can't do stuff together openly. But Geoffry comes to respect Claudia a lot. Yet he always asks the cheerleaders and the vivacious sluts to the proms. He gets a lot of ass, too, but it's meaningless. And he never touches Claudia. They watch VCR movies together and read books and talk. He falls in love with Claudia, but she's so ugly he can't make himself go out with her, or kiss her, or anything like that. Until suddenly, in the front seat of his Thunderbird at the drive-in during a Friday-night triple creepy creature feature, Geoffry rapes her. And he's so ashamed, he never speaks to her again. Naturally, Claudia is devastated. Her heart is broken. About eight months later, Geoffry commits suicide. But the way it happens, people think it's murder. He props himself up in front of a baseball automatic pitching machine and gets fastballed to death. The rumor mill whispers that he was gay. Naturally, Claudia is beside herself with grief. She's also very fat, almost at term. She attends Geoffry's funeral and, in front of everybody, throws herself on the coffin. Then she goes totally bonkers. She rips off all her clothes and starts humping one of the coffin handles. Her dad, Burt, the FBI agent, is so mortified he pulls out his .357 magnum and plugs her. But his wife, Janie, has had enough, so while all the other mourners are sprinting for cover, she takes off one of her spike heels and bangs it into Burt's noggin from behind. He croaks. Then Janie pulls a metal fingernail file from her purse, cuts open Claudia's belly, and pulls out the baby while it's still alive."

Zelda paused to catch her breath.

Gingerly I said, "Are you serious?" I mean, she almost sort of *looked* serious.

But my wife couldn't pull it off. A mischievous light flooded her eyes, then she melted against me like a spring thaw in the Klondike and burst out laughing.

"Dear Roger," she cackled happily, cuddling into me

with a heartbreaking little-girl kind of affection, "You are the biggest idiot I ever met . . . but I love you!"

I remember one night we were sitting in the hot tub, beleaguered by cheerful bubbles.

Zelda was flushed. Her hair was all pinned up, but dabs and tangles of it flared off wet and sexy in many directions. Beads of sweat had gathered along her upper lip.

She said, "Oh gosh, Roger, I'm so happy we're together. I adore you like a god. I want to dance for you."

So saying, she climbed out of the water, turned her back to me, and began to move in queer, childlike undulations that were so special and vulnerable they almost made me cry.

Zelda loves ballet. She can talk all night about Nijinsky and Diaghilev, Martha Graham and Alvin Ailey, Jacques d'Amboise and Girodais. . . .

Now, as I watched, my wife posed wistfully in front of the full-length mirror in our hot-tub room, assessing her perfect yet aging body. Slowly she twisted her right hand with the delicate grace of a Balinese dancer. She assumed hieroglyphic Egyptian positions. She bent over in a sorrowful arc and whispered, "Sometimes I wish I could kill myself with beauty."

Quietly, while on tiptoes reaching for the ceiling, Zelda told me, "Everybody's so teeny-weeny nowadays. By the time they reach thirty, they've already given up. They don't care anymore. They turn into blobs. But I want to be larger than life, for you. I want to be lithe and tempting like this when I'm eighty."

I forget the movie, I saw it eons ago. But there's a scene where an old man watches a young woman disrobe in order to go skinny-dipping in a Hollywood swimming pool. The girl is totally unself-conscious because the guy is so ancient he's entirely out of her purview—neither threat nor possible seduction. There is an agony of longing and of simultaneous acceptance visible in the codger's face. The memory of his air of tenderness and erotic yearning has always made me pause.

I'm not sure exactly how, but Zelda and I, at this moment, reminded me of that poignant tableau.

And then, in accordance with the laws of nature, everything changed.

On Tuesday, Zelda drove down to the capital to have lunch with a former boss. I was free, so I went to the hospital to see Gretal, who was not exactly in perfect fettle. Truth is, the cancer had metastasized every which way but loose. So it was back to radiation therapy. With chemo shots to follow. Unless they opted for an operation. Gretal said, "Dammit, Roger, I hate this shit."

I held her hand and stroked it. "I don't blame you."

"I'd like to take a bath," she said. "Will you help me?"

Sure. Of course I would. I had helped her a million times before.

Gretal was feeble. She stumbled a little, trying to walk. "Excuse me," she said, "but it hurts."

I never know what to say when people I love are in pain. So I told her, "Hey, quit being silly, don't apologize."

She sat on the toilet shivering while I drew the bath. She told me which skin beads and bubble concoctions I should use to lace the steaming water.

Gretal asked, "Do we ever get to make love anymore, now that you're married, or is that all over?"

I said, "You know I can't do that. It would be a betrayal of the marriage. Being married doesn't work unless you're monogamous."

Gretal had always had a blunt way about her. "Fuck your

new wife, Roger. I hope she chokes on a chicken bone. I'm gonna miss you."

I helped Gretal off with the robe, then held her arms and guided her gently into the tub. Talk about awkward. I was shocked at how old, suddenly, she appeared. Pain'll do that to you. She was kind of pudgy-bloated, but her legs were skinny. She'd never had much bosom to speak of, but now her thin breasts sagged miserably. She was wearing too much makeup, also, and the mascara made her face seem extra gaunt. I didn't say anything, however.

Gretal slid into the bubbles with a sigh. I worried she might sink all the way under, and kept touching her arms to make sure I could grab quick if that happened.

She said, "I like it when you touch me."

"I love you. You know I always will."

"Careful. A lightning bolt launched by Zelda the Terrible might strike you dead."

"She isn't terrible," I said gently.

"Spare me the treacle, Roger, okay?"

I sat on the toilet and talked to her while she soaked up the warm water. "I look like a hag, don't I?" Gretal said.

"No, you look beautiful." She did, too—like Anna Magnani and Irene Papas and Indira Gandhi—that sort of haunted dazzle.

Gretal started to cry. "I'm gonna lose all my hair again," she said. "I hate it when that happens."

"I'll buy you a couple of wigs," I said.

"Thanks, you're a fucking prince."

"I mean it, seriously."

"Zelda wouldn't allow it," she said mournfully.

"Of course she will," I assured her. "Zelda is not a monster, Gretal."

"Oh, shut up, Roger. God, I hate men."

* * *

I have mentioned that the last time Gretal had lost all her hair, she bought herself a platinum-blond Dolly wig. It really turned me on. When she was worst off, Gretal liked playing the hooker. When she was on death's door, her theater had always made me extra horny.

Seeing her in the tub almost made me cry. She seemed old and tired. We had certainly shared a lot of bawdy times together. Once we actually made love in an elevator of the Empire State Building. On another occasion we screwed in the bathroom of an Amtrak train somewhere between Lamy, New Mexico, and Flagstaff, Arizona. In 1982 we had spent a week on location at the Fontainebleau Hotel in Miami Beach and wound up balling in a stretch limo traveling swiftly through the heart of Liberty City.

During her rambunctious younger days, Gretal had had a brief affair with the Brooklyn gangster Joey Gallo. Shelley Winters had once chased her with a butcher knife through all the tables at Luchow's. She'd lived on the island of Ischia for eight months with a one-legged billionaire who owned a racehorse that had won the English Derby.

Gretal had participated in orgies and she had gambled in Monaco. And she once sailed up the Amazon River collecting spiders for the Peabody Museum of Boston.

"Go away," she finally said. "I hate you seeing me like this. I hate your new wife with her perfect little body and ravishing tits. Your happiness makes me wanna puke."

At that moment my happiness made *me* feel guilty, also terribly sorry for Gretal and at a loss on how to be sweet and compassionate with this friend I had once loved so well.

It also gave me a premonition of doom.

* * *

And sure enough, the next morning's mail really upset our apple cart. It contained a letter from one of my longtime pen pals, Ginger Mancini, and another from my ex-girlfriend Christie. Zelda picked up eight envelopes in all at the post office and left them on the kitchen table sort of fanned out like a poker hand so I could see she had noticed the return addresses.

Then she drove to the spa for a Jane Raines aerobics workout.

When I came in from the writing tower, my heart glitched. Forget the lull caused by our precious week of marital nirvana, that pair of letters from Ginger and Christie really stood out. In fact, they were glowing like small lethal heaps of radioactive snake shit.

Yes, I receive a lot of mail. Much of it comes from women who simply adore my transmigrating intergalactic detective, Sidney Bard. Apparently he has that combination of machismo and sensitivity which clobbers them between the eyes. Most of the letters are sincere, also very laudatory. Contrary to Zelda's belief, only rarely are they flirtatious. I like to correspond with women and men out there whom I know I'll never meet. It's fun. They tell me all about their lives. I tell them about mine. The fact that we're strangers, separated usually by many miles, makes it safe to spill almost any kind of beans.

Enter Ginger Mancini. She lives with her sickly mother in Cherry Hill, New Jersey. She's fourteen years younger than me, and for the past four years has been working toward a Ph.D. in psychology at Temple University.

Mostly what we write to each other about is sex. Ginger is a late bloomer. I learned all the gory details of her first true love affair in a blizzard of ten-page single-spaced elite-size typed letters. She asked me for advice on orgasms, how to handle men, what is erotic to us, and so forth. I was only too glad to oblige, using examples—in detail—from my own experience.

I enjoy being candid with strangers. And although we'd never met, Ginger and I had become pretty close over the years.

During our courting period, I told Zelda about this woman. In fact, I had shared with Zelda some of Ginger's juicier epistles. Back then, Zelda had remarked that a relationship like the one I enjoyed with Ginger seemed "utterly wonderful and free." Often Zelda had urged, "Read me another passage from one of Ginger's fascinating adventures."

Well, on the Wednesday in question, I was now a married man. And one of the letters was from Ginger. And in a flash—instantaneously—I suspected that Zelda would not be as amused by its contents as she might have been prior to becoming my legal guardian.

Naturally, Ginger hit the first page full tilt, galloping like a Thoroughbred. "Dear Roger," she began, "let me tell you about this transvestite megastud I picked up last night in a queer bar called Caligula's—"

And the other letter, from Christie, was thick enough to require two stamps.

I needed almost half an hour to read it.

Basically, Christie thanked me for the five quid. Again and again. She said Cazzie was doing okay in the Wigwam Group Therapy Center for Wayward Adolescents down just outside the capital.

Then she wrote, "I don't care if you're married or not, Roger, I'm gonna hold you to that promise we made ages ago never to quit fucking each other no matter what happens, remember?"

Following this statement, for about ten pages Christie ran

57

down, in astonishingly accurate and lurid detail, most of the high points in our sexual shenanigans together over the past six years.

By the end of this saga I had already leaked so much jism that I decided I'd better finish myself off, and it took only five strokes.

"Oh no!" I cried. "Not *already*!"

You see, I had violated a promise to myself that I would not, repeat not *ever*, masturbate during this marriage. Previous experience had taught me it is a bad sign when I start getting the urge to genuflect toward Onan. It's the beginning of the end. It means I am horny, and this monogamy ain't cutting the mustard.

Zelda disliked masturbation. "I think it's sad," she told me shortly after the wedding. "It makes me real antsy if I do it. I hate feeling incomplete. I want to be *with* you. Sex only feels good if we're together. I need you inside of me to feel complete."

Implicit, I think now, was the idea that if I ever jerked myself off, it'd be a betrayal.

Suddenly my path was strewn with land mines, punji pits, and other sorts of booby traps too numerous to mention.

The dilemma I faced on the morning we are talking about was this: Zelda knew too much already about Christie and Ginger. She didn't need to know any more. But in a fit of misguided altruism one night during the barn-raising honeymoon with our friends, I had promised she could read my mail.

Yet in a split instant I had perspicaciously deduced that

Zelda was not likely to emerge from a reading of either of those letters with her equanimity intact.

I sat there for a while contemplatively fingering the envelopes. I experienced an uncomfortable squeeze inside. I knew I was committed to making this marriage work. I said, "Roger, if you don't let her read these letters, it will arouse her suspicions."

I replied, "Buddy, if you do show her those missives, it will arouse her Vesuvius."

Already I felt like an adulterer for jerking off to Christie's life history of our combat in her erogenous zones.

By way of procrastination, I opened the other letters addressed to me. All were relatively harmless. My agent, Don Perry, politely reminded me of upcoming deadlines. My editor, Bill Witherspoon, politely reminded me of upcoming deadlines. My daughter Kim asked me for a signed copy of *The Catacombs of Luray* to give to her English teacher. There was also a ballot from the Writers' Guild and a check of $59.60 for royalties from a Danish sci-fi detective book club.

I left that bunch on the kitchen table, in open invitation for Zelda to browse.

Ginger and Christie went out to my little writing tower and disappeared into a file cabinet where Zelda would never be able to find them.

But I couldn't concentrate on Sidney Bard that afternoon. I fidgeted uneasily. The writing came out flat.

I was waiting for Zelda to flare.

The good thing about Zelda, also the bad thing, depending, is you never have to wait for very long.

She brought it up at cocktail time. We had jogged up the road and back three miles. Now she was guzzling a Kahlua and cream while I worked on a Blackjack and Coke. We had the usual hors d'oeuvres—smoked oysters, smoked clams, kielbasy, Swiss cheese. I was engrossed in the sports section, Zelda was perusing the *NYTBR*. Already this had become an established end-of-the-day ritual for us.

"Anything of interest in your mail?" Zelda asked off-handedly.

I shrugged, indicating the envelopes still arrayed on the table. I said, "Not much, mostly routine stuff. See for yourself, if you want."

How exactly can I describe this? Immediately the room went gelid. Why? Obviously because I had told a monstrous lie and betrayed my wife. And even though my wife did not twitch or change expression, suddenly she became an almost titanically hostile enemy.

Yet absolutely nothing happened. It's one of the most amazing transformations I've ever experienced.

I continued reading, drinking, downing those greasy little shellfish.

Zelda did the same.

We discussed the day's news in an outwardly friendly manner. Zelda mixed me another drink. Then I went outside and pissed on the lawn, feeling so angry I could hardly see straight, so guilty I could hardly see straight, and so bewildered I could hardly see straight.

When I returned, Zelda was in the bedroom reading a Colette novel. The door was closed.

I led the dog onto the porch and pulled cockleburs from his fur. I talked to him softly, telling him what a sweet boy he was—which is true.

Then I moseyed on over to the tower with my third drink in hand and started composing a section where Sidney Bard is soul-traveling through the Crab Nebula, looking for a Perseid Meteor Thug named Marvin Stravletovich Tolstoi, a real creep.

* * *

About midnight I went to bed. The lights were doused. Cats curled up on the comforter peacefully purred. But Zelda was not asleep. She lay in the dark, staring at the ceiling. I wriggled in beside her and also stared at the ceiling. Hell hath no fury, I thought. For the past three hours I had not been able to write a single coherent word.

"How'd it go?" Zelda asked.

"So-so," I replied. "You know."

"No," she said. "I don't know."

I said, "What's that supposed to mean?"

"I figure if you don't know, it certainly isn't my business to tell you."

I clammed up. We stewed for about an hour in silence until finally Zelda exploded. She sat bolt upright, clicked on the bedside lamp, and let me tell you, her face was flushed. Like almost beet red.

My wife said, "If you think I'm going to stand for you carrying on with that pair of sluts right under my nose, then I am going to divorce you this instant!"

I said, "I didn't ask them to write me letters."

"Bullshit! You *love* it. You encourage it with everybody. You flirt with every god damn literary gold-digger in this town. Your ego couldn't live without it."

I said, "You're crazy."

"Why did you hide those letters from me, you liar? You insult my intelligence."

That did it. *I* exploded. "Because it's none of your business! What makes you think you have a right to destroy all my privacy in life? That's not trust or sharing togetherness. That's *slavery*!"

In reply, Zelda ran down almost exactly the same sexual history Christie had just rehashed in her blistering letter. She also reiterated the life story of Ginger Mancini, including a recitation—word for word—of every letter about every sexual issue that I'd ever shared with her when we were courting.

She flattened me with evidence, most of it verbatim.

"You even wrote about *our* personal life to that nudnik, you said so," Zelda accused.

"Well, you asked me to say what I wrote," I blubbered, "and like a total idiot I told you the truth."

Zelda said, "You wouldn't know the truth if it took a leak in your back pocket."

I experienced a chill the way you do in a horror movie when you know the monster with razor-sharp needles for fingernails is crouched behind the door that the perky teenybopper at summer camp is about to open.

My new wife had a photographic memory. Nothing that I had ever said to Zelda in the past, or might say to her in the future, would ever be forgotten.

I was being convicted ex post facto. Or do I mean habeus corpus? Or should it be double jeopardy?

I tried to get a grip. "Zelda, those people are my friends. They're important. They're part of my support system. I care about them. I—"

"First," she said, "they aren't 'people.' Most of them are 'women' you used to screw. And if they are more important to you than me, then you married the wrong person. And what about me, anyway? Where's *my* support system? You made a commitment to *me* at that wedding, not to all your ex-lovers or your scatology groupies. Or have you already forgotten?"

By the end of her blast I felt so guilty and browbeaten that all I could do was wilt, give in, surrender, be repentant.

"I'm sorry," I said. "I understand what you mean when you say it's an intrusion on the marriage. I'll write those two women letters cutting them off tomorrow. If you want to read the letters before I mail them, you're welcome."

"No need," she said, suddenly all sugar and maple syrup. "I have no interest. That's your business. I didn't say you had to go to the extreme of cutting them off. That's your decision, darling, not mine. I would never presume. I just want us to be open and honest with each other, that's all. Now come here, you big lug."

Then Zelda crawled all over me like Joe DiMaggio on his fifty-six-game hitting streak, delightfully immortal and unstoppable.

I have an odd and touching friend, her name is Margaret. She's a painter who used to be terribly shy and reclusive and terrified of men. About ten years ago she approached me with the following proposition:

"Roger, I don't want to be a crazy old maid. I want to be normal and snag a husband and have a child. But I don't know anything about making love. The bar scene is scary, I couldn't ever pick up a guy. I wish you could go to the spa and rent different kinds of male bodies by the hour for sex, but you can't. So would you be willing to help me out, please?"

Margaret is a delightful plump little person with bright blue eyes and a super-intense expression. Nothing about her physically had ever really turned me on, but I liked her a lot because she was an intelligent and zany and compassionate human being.

So it seemed like a sort of comradely duty, and we tried. We fumbled around for a couple of weeks, but no dice. I failed. I wound up impotent simply because the chemistry wasn't there. My deficiency hurt her feelings. I tried to explain it wasn't personal, attraction is a mystery nobody can

John Nichols

explain. And in the end, we wound up caring for each other much more than previously.

Eventually Margaret tumbled for a nice guy, Peter, who fell in love back. She got pregnant and had nonidentical twins: Libby and Debby.

At the time of our story, Libby and Debby were five years old. They looked like pretty Christmas sugar cookies covered with rainbow sprinkles. Talk about cute squared. I was their godfather. Peter, a construction worker by day who built solar houses out of old tires and beer cans, played a mean blues guitar at night. Margaret had never for a minute stopped painting, and now she was selling landscapes at a regular clip.

Margaret and the twins were in the Benedictine Café, interacting with Moe Bubbles and Susan Dice and Susan's five-year-old kid, Leroy Shanti Bogdanovich, when I walked in and sat down at their table and opened my big fat mouth.

Leroy Shanti Bogdanovich, by the way, is the original Nightmare Kid from Hell. Susan lets him run roughshod. If you yelled at Leroy for shooting his BB gun at the cat, he'd walk over to the irrigation ditch, siddown, take off his million-dollar pump-up Reeboks, and toss them into the fast-flowing muddy water.

Moe once told me he'd like to feed that minimonster a Ritalin brownie the size of the *Webster's International Dictionary*.

The twins were playing "Chopsticks" on the café piano. Leroy Shanti Bogdanovich was torturing a pickle by sticking toothpicks into its vulnerable places.

Zelda's buddy Weezie Bednarik was sitting in a corner, downing a bowl of lentil soup. Adrian the hand puppet, believe it or not, was holding the stupid spoon.

"What's the matter?" Margaret asked me. "You look like death warmed over."

64

Susan joked, "You would too if you were getting laid eight times a day by Chiquita Banana."

I said, "Bag it, Susan, I'm not in the mood."

Moe Bubbles affected a Popeye accent when he asked, "What's troublin' yer, sonny?"

I blurted, "If you guys were married, would you make your spouse write letters of good-bye to any member of the opposite sex they had loved?"

Margaret said, "Roger, you're the twins' godfather. Of course not."

Susan said, "When I was married to Derrick, he threatened to kill me if he ever caught me even thinking about a former boyfriend."

"How did you handle that?"

"I kneed him in the balls."

"Ouch. Then what happened?"

"He slugged me."

I flinched. "Hard?"

She pointed at her mouth. "Honey, you of all people should know that half of these are false."

Margaret said, "The first year's always the hardest. After that, it's relatively easy sledding."

"Suppose you don't survive the first *month*?"

Susan warned, "If you let her push you around now, sweetie, it'll be Hell-to-Pay City later."

Words tumbled clear of me on clouds of woe. "It seems as if anybody of the female gender I ever cared about is a threat, an affront, or an intrusion. It's like that whole part of my past life was wrong."

Margaret leaned forward and circled her arms around me and squeezed in a gentle, affectionate manner.

"You'll live," she said. "I promise."

Not if those adorable twins kept playing "Chopsticks."

* * *

And not if Zelda could help it, either.

As soon as my wife heard, she came directly to the point. She said, "I really think it's out of line for you to discuss our private travails with every tramp in town."

"Excuse me?" Per usual, I hadn't seen it coming.

"I feel completely humiliated." She appeared near tears. "It isn't fair for you to go in town and ridicule me behind my back with your ex-girlfriends and your chauvinist-pig drinking buddies."

This early in the game, I was still a trifle slow on the draw. I said, "What are you talking about?"

"You know what I'm talking about."

"No I don't."

"Then you're stupider than I thought."

"Zelda—" I grabbed her wrist.

She yanked the hand away. "God damn you, Roger," she blurted, "you have no sense of honor, or of fair play. You have no respect."

"About fucking WHAT?" I yelled.

"YOU TOLD YOUR ARTIST BUDDY AND SUSAN DICE AND MOE BUBBLES THAT I MADE YOU WRITE LETTERS TO ALL YOUR OLD GIRLFRIENDS CUTTING THEM OFF FOREVER!" she hollered.

"What?" I don't know what startled me more—the noise, or the fact that Zelda had such information.

"Who told you so?" I whimpered, already acknowledging defeat.

"Never you mind. It's true, isn't it?"

"Who told you?" I repeated.

"Everybody tells me," she moaned. "This dumb town is one great big gossip mill set up to keep me informed of anything and everything that could possibly hurt me to the bones."

"Everybody lies," I said. "You don't have to listen."

With that, I realized it *had* to have been Weezie

Bednarik, storm trooper par excellence of our local Gossip Gestapo!

All the blood drained out of Zelda's face. I don't know what her emotion was inside. True rage? Jealousy? Sly hysteria? Fear, insecurity, and trembling? Or maybe utter scorn for the mouse I had become in her eyes?

Zelda said, "I pity you, Roger. I really do. You're going to lose the most precious thing you ever had in your life."

For some reason, all at once her declaration seemed so funny and absurd and so much ado about nothing that I cracked a goofy grin and said, "Oh please, *when*?"

Zelda didn't think that was funny.

She stood up, marched outside, got into her Subaru, revved up the engine, threw it into reverse, and, wheels spinning, slammed backward smack into my old basketball pole. The ancient pine viga cracked in half, and the backboard and hoop crashed atop the Subaru as Zelda gunned forward in a cloud of pebbles and clutch smoke, heading down the driveway.

Halfway to the paved road, the backboard fell off, leaving a major dent the length of Zelda's roof, and a cracked rear window.

From the kitchen I watched the Subaru skid onto the pavement, nearly sideswiping a Jeep Cherokee, which veered, almost tumbling into the Pueblo River.

Zelda leaned on her horn, flipped off the moron, and laid down thirty feet of rubber accelerating toward Armageddon.

Wow.

This time I refused to give chase. I poured myself a triple bourbon instead, and worked on *Return of the Perseid Meteor Thugs*. A wonderful calm lay over the house and grounds, but I could not lose myself in the book. Sidney Bard, who was trying to apprehend a gaggle of nomadic

John Nichols

Kite Killers from Galaxy B, kept running into Zeldas. Angry Zeldas, shouting Zeldas, insulted Zeldas; also dancing Zeldas, poetic Zeldas, fucking Zeldas. My heart was in turmoil, my thoughts were scattered. I had a hard-on that lasted all afternoon, desperate to make love. I was confused and frightened, angry and inept. I got up and wandered about, scratched the dog, drank a dozen cups of coffee to sober up from the whisky. In the same breath I fantasized about getting a divorce from, and having a baby with, my terribly beautiful Zelda.

Soon enough a peaceful night fell upon us. I deserved a short break from literary hiatus, switched from coffee back to bourbon, and fed the dog and the cats. I watched a little news, then returned to the space-time hustings.

I was still seated fruitlessly at the laptop when her Subaru jounced home at midnight. Zelda knocked on the writing-tower door. I called, "It's open." Zelda turned the handle, advanced just inside the jamb, and halted. Having feigned enough indifference, I looked up at last.

My wife was naked except for a black velvet choker around her neck and a pair of high heels. Across her belly, in red Magic Marker, she had written:

COME
AND
GET
IT!

I don't think it's necessarily the worst fate on Earth to become a slave of sex.

Zelda led me by the hand into the house. My body relaxed, woozy from relief now that the fight was over. That airiness in itself felt like an orgasm. Zelda lit candles, then floated onto the bed in a whisper of skin and shiny material. Every place I touched her at sent tiny

68

electric slivers up through my fingertips. We moved slowly. It was dreamy and thrilling. We dawdled. Whenever I twitched urgently, Zelda stayed me with a nearly imperceptible hesitancy of her groin. Silent and terribly, terribly gentle. I couldn't hear us breathing. Almost immobile, she brought me to a climax. I couldn't hold back. I said, "Wait." She said, "Please go ahead." It was so emotional and potent that I whimpered and, for the first time ever, began to cry.

Zelda lay beside me shy and wide-eyed. Delicate, yet earthy. Totally surrendering, but in control. Her skin gleamed like peach mist. She had fairy-tale creamy features. Her beauty stunned me.

I just stared at her, mortally wounded and loving it.

Did I write the letters? What, are you kidding? Of *course* I wrote the letters.

I couldn't believe I was doing it, though. I had never even met Ginger Mancini, but I penned her a six-page pathetic pusillanimous missive trying to explain that because our bawdy literary intimacy offended my new bride, I couldn't correspond anymore.

I employed Zelda's reasoning to justify the letter. Intrusion on the marriage and all that. I felt ghastly, but reminded myself: I *live* with Zelda. I only write to Ginger once every couple of months, that's all. And anyway, now that the raunch was barred, what could I reveal to Ginger in a letter that wouldn't be a betrayal of Zelda?

In retrospect, I have often wondered—why did I do it?

I have concluded: Fear.

Pure and simple.

* * *

The letter to Christie was harder to write.

I kept ripping up pages. I couldn't believe I was doing it. On several occasions I put the letter aside, determined not to go through with it. Then I rummaged through a manila envelope filled with sexy photographs of Christie and decided to burn them all. I was terrified that one day, while snooping, Zelda would discover the collection. Already she had busted an artery over the dedication in a book—*Quiet Days in Clichy*, by Henry Miller. Christie had given it to me. On the half-title page she had inscribed it: *To my favorite Henry Miller, with so much love from all my pertinent orifaces . . . Christie.*

I don't know how Zelda "accidentally" picked that particular volume out of the ten thousand paperback books on my shelves. But she had an incredible nose for that sort of perfidy.

For example: The day after our tiff over my conversation with Margaret and Susan in the Benedictine Café, Zelda just happened to knock from the kitchen wall a framed photograph of Woody and Kim in their freaky skinhead outfits flipping off the photographer, yours truly. And among the glass shards Zelda discovered another snapshot that had been slipped between Woody and Kim and the cardboard backing. It was of Christie in a bikini, a froufrou lace apron, and high heels. She was pretending to be a sexy cigarette girl, offering up an enormous chocolate chip cookie (with a candle in it) on her tray, at my birthday party two years ago.

Cazzie and Woody and Kim were cheering in the background. They had all helped bake that wonderful monster cookie.

Zelda left the photo on my desk with a yellow Post-it stuck over Christie's smiling face:

> *I presume you want to keep this in*
> *your X-rated porno collection?*

OOXX
Zelda

My heart sank. Naturally, I destroyed that picture also, hating myself for leaving it someplace where Zelda could miraculously track it down.

When I asked how the frame had busted, she said, "I bumped it off the wall." An accident. I said, "I'll get another frame. I love that photograph of Woody and Kim."

"Actually, Roger, I don't want them on my kitchen wall."

"But they're funny," I said. "They make me laugh."

Zelda replied, "I really don't need your kids giving me the finger in my kitchen. Maybe to you it's cute. I think it's obnoxious and disrespectful."

"They're not giving *you* the finger," I started to explain, "they're—" Then I realized. "You're right, I'm sorry, of course."

Zelda hugged me and gave me a sweet little kiss. "I'm sorry," she said gently. "But we're *married* now. Did you think that things wouldn't change?"

"No, of course not. It's just—"

"Just what?" She gave me one of her dazzling smiles. Yet at the same instant both her eyes assumed an edgy glitter that would soon come to paralyze me every time I caught the slightest hint of it in those brown enchanting orbs.

"You're right," I said. "Of course. Things change."

So: I penned that farewell to Christie. Another good-bye lament. Before the month was out I would have written about a half-dozen such letters. Jeez, Louise, when I deliriously asked for Zelda's hand in marriage, I never thought it would entail so much *dismantling*.

I once had a friend, an Edgar Cayce freak, who jumped off the Nantucket ferry hoping to separate his soul from his body. The blissful dude was eager to advance on to his next incarnation.

Before the jump, he wrote letters to his family, bidding one and all adieu. He said don't worry, I'll be fine. Didn't say where he was or where he was going. Nothing. Just headed for the old void—adios.

Somebody saw the splash. They backed up the boat, hauled him out, and threw him in Taunton State Hospital for a couple of months. Then he wound up in Aspen for two years living on brown rice and doing astrological charts in his office (and living quarters), a bread truck.

Now he's a three-piece Brooks Brothers Manhattan lawyer who negotiates L.B.O. deals offshore to avoid U.S. tax penalties.

Encouraged, by this memory, to believe that there *is* life after death, I mailed both letters. Good-bye Ginger, good-bye Christie.

I begged Christie not to write back. Because if Zelda picked up the mail, she'd recognize the handwriting, or the return address. Even if it was a typed generic envelope, Zelda would know. Zelda could be standing in Anchorage, Alaska, and smell a skunk in Tierra del Fuego.

Christie sent her reply in a large manilla envelope, with cutout *Playboy* playmates taped all over it, and the nickname "Long Dong" inserted in place of my middle initial.

Thank Christ that on that day I hit the post office before Zelda.

Inside was a photograph of Christie, nude, astride a motorcycle, hefting her papayas.

I reinserted the photograph in the envelope, which I slipped under the filthy old rug in my writing tower, figur-

ing that's a place where Zelda would never think to rum-
mage.

Megan, on the other hand, took her medicine like a trouper.
She sent a brief note in reply to my long turgid apologetic
good-bye letter. She said it surprised the heck out of her
that I had decided to tie the knot. She wished me good
luck. Then she signed off. Forever.

Hey, wait a minute!

I pored over the curt epistle for about ten minutes. I reread it a half-dozen times.

Megan's reaction was exactly what I thought I had
wanted. But I did not like it at all. Why so little emotion?
It made me feel creepy. Then angry. Then humiliated. How
dare she retire so gracefully? My letter to her had been a
sniveling, heartfelt single-spaced four-page number. Full of
loving protestations, gratitude for sexual fulfillment, guilt
for having to withdraw, best wishes for her future, and so
forth ad nauseum.

I almost fired off a retaliatory dispatch, asking how could
she pen such a cryptic au revoir after all the passion we had
shared?

Fortunately, I still possessed just enough class to resist
that temptation.

But I felt empty and unresolved about Megan.

For an hour, rather desperately, I fantasized about all the
great times with Megan. They gave me an erection. Next
thing I knew I was on all fours on the floor of my office
jerking off to a memory of Megan in a sort of foxy business suit, her mouth gagged with panty hose, and her wrists
hog-tied to her ankles with my tie.

Soon I was deluged by other memories. Whenever we
played tennis, Megan had actually batted at the ball while
clenching a cigarette between her teeth.

Megan loved to frequent country-and-western bars, where she had taught me how to two-step.

We used to pull weeds in her garden, and I remembered rolling around in the dirt together, squealing in delight, copulating among the cucumbers. . . .

Yo, Roger, stop for Pete's sake—*get a grip*!

Three days after I had hidden the photo of Christie under my rug in the writing tower, I returned home from playing tennis with Ed Griffin and confronted that same rug hanging over the garden fence being aired.

Zelda had gone in and scrubbed the place!

"No wonder you have allergies," she commented dryly. "Mix water with all the dust that came from your rug, and you could build an entire adobe mansion."

She kept mum about Christie on the motorcycle. The picture had evaporated, and it never showed up, either.

For whatever pathological reason, I couldn't bring myself to ask about it.

I waited, however, for that blow to fall. Zelda must have been wallowing in glee at all the points she had garnered. You can't imagine how manipulative a silence like hers, about a cheesecake photo like that, could be.

The kicker is, I hated *Christie* for setting up the predicament.

I wrote her back.

I believe I actually told *her* to grow up.

Christie sent another envelope. In it was a photograph I had taken of her posing almost nude on the front fender of my pickup.

Nobody plays fair anymore, do they?

* * *

Certainly nobody in Hollywood, that's for sure.

As I mentioned earlier, I'd been working on a script for my second Sidney Bard thriller, *The Catacombs of Luray*. Now, I'm not saying it was a project as distinguished as an *Alien* film, or Kubrick's *2001*. But a joint Zeppo Rosenberg–Alan Cavett production is not to be sneezed at. Those dudes flex muscles. Rumors had Jack Muncie interested in the lead *if* my treatment held water. So a fair amount of k-fuffle surrounded the movie, even at this early-development stage.

All I needed to do was write a winner and deliver it by February fifteenth of the coming year.

My contract guaranteed me the right to write chez moi. I hate L.A. I figured home is peaceful, bucolic, familiar, qué no?

It wasn't even an exclusive, the *Catacombs* deal. Hence, nobody had a problem with me also scripting the Zane Adams thriller I'd taken on back in June, desperate to pay my taxes.

Too, I had a January first deadline on *Return of the Perseid Meteor Thugs*. The novel. On which I had so far accumulated one hundred twenty-seven moderately up-to-speed pages.

Multiple projects of that ilk may sound like a lot of toil, but believe me, I type fast. When I can concentrate, I jam. I'm known in some circles as the Speedy Gonzales of sci-fi. A few of my friends call it "the blam method of writing."

Then Don Perry (my agent) called and said, "Roger, I just got a buzz from Faye Crane at Zeppo–Cavett. They want to know how the script's coming along."

"Great," I lied, sipping on my first Campari and soda even though the Catholic church bells had barely tolled the noon hour. "All eight cylinders are cranking overtime. So far it's been a smooth ride."

"Translate that for me into finished pages," Don said in

his phony-baloney English accent. Don's a good guy, but he was raised in Greenwich, Connecticut, and went to Choate. He made all-American playing lacrosse at Johns Hopkins. He's thirteen years my junior and about a hundred times richer. He wears Abercrombie & Fitch shirts, Brooks Brothers slacks, Bostonians' loafers. He's married to the novelist June Dundee, who's had a best-seller her last three times out of the barn. Her work is a cross between Erica Jong, Joan Didion, and Francine du Plessix Gray.

By and large, if you jerk Don's chain, he doesn't flush. So I ponied up.

"Actually, I'm having a bit of trouble, Don. Marriage is a trifle more complicated than I anticipated."

Don said, "Faye says Peter Wykopf, Jack Muncie's agent, asked her for pages. I know you're not obligated until February fifteenth, but according to Faye, Jack needs an indication now about whether or not to even *think* about committing in February. He's read the book, of course, and loves it. Faye thinks maybe sixty pages would be okay. Naturally, there'd be a preview fee."

My nose twitched. I asked, "How big?"

"Five K. The hitch is that half would be deductible from the option when it's up for renewal in January."

"Ask for five G's, straight up, no deduction, and I'll get them the pages," I said. "But only forty-five, not sixty." To date I had approximately eighteen on disk.

Don said, "I'll buzz her and get back to you. By the way, they're talking November fourteenth, max. They'd love November first."

Hey, wouldn't we all?

Zelda asked, "What's the matter?"

I told her.

"Those bastards!" she exploded. "How dare they put you under the gun like this?"

I backpedaled a little. "If I couldn't stand the heat, I shouldn't have entered the kitchen."

"You always do that," Zelda said.

"Do what?"

"You always take the opposite side from me. Even if you started on my side, if I agree, then you start to disagree."

I didn't exactly follow. I frowned at her, semidumb-founded. I sensed an altercation coming on and wanted none of it. I said, "I don't understand."

Zelda smiled. "Remember when you said Moe Bubbles was an incorrigible womanizer, and I agreed, so then instantly you said actually he *wasn't* as bad as all that, and we had a little tiff?"

No, I did not remember.

"Well, do you recall that conversation about *People* magazine, when you said it was High Art just like James Joyce, but when I told you I thought the *Weekly World News* was better High Art, you started arguing that *People* was actually cultural fast food without any relevant vitamins of social value, like an Egg McMuffin?"

No, I did not remember our famous *People*-as-Egg-McMuffin dispute.

Zelda never runs out of examples, however.

"What about that time you ridiculed Weezie Bednarik for being conversationally dependent on a hand puppet, and I agreed, telling you about the time Adrian got jerked into the garbage disposal, so a plumber had to take apart the entire sink to perform a rescue, whereupon you started defending her, saying we shouldn't be too cruel, because she had a 'good heart' and did all those singing-clown benefits for hospitalized kids—remember that?"

No.

I did not.

* * *

We are in bed. Hesitant rain is tinkering about the tin stove-pipes on that gray September afternoon. I lie on my back, my head on the pillow. Zelda is bent over, lazily sweeping my chest with the tips of her hair. I suck on three of her fingers. My hands are laxly arranged against her hips. We are sorrowful and aroused.

Zelda lowers a bit more, and her breasts settle against my body. Their subtle heft is like no other gravity-caused pressure on Earth. From toe to shoulder, I quiver at the blunt sting of that gelatinous weight. How can mere flesh be so provocative?

Zelda's breath trembles against my chin. Her lips are faintly clicking at my ear. She kisses shut my eyes. We are in synch, in a virtually liquid harmony. Zelda whispers that I am the sex fiend she has yearned for all her life. In a faint lazy voice she praises my love, my patience, and my man-hood. She thanks me for all the small favors and for all the big ones, too. She remembers every one of my kindnesses and generosities. She tells me I have rescued her like a knight on a dashing white charger.

Gingerly, Zelda begs for absolution.

"I married you 'cause you're a compassionate man," she says. "I hope you can forgive me."

I ask her forgiveness in return.

For our wedding my friend Margaret had given us one of her lithographs, a black-and-white drawing of a simple adobe house surrounded by snow-laden plum thickets in which a couple of magpies perched. The drawing beauti-fully evoked our valley during its hibernal season.

Zelda wanted to frame the picture and hang it in our

bedroom. Margaret had not yet arisen in a sexual-jealousy context, although I seemed to recall that when Zelda and I were courting, I'd regaled her with that fiasco. Though who knows for sure? Zelda is the one with the memory, not me.

In any case, my wife thought it a lovely print. We decided to have it framed. The only question was: What sort of frame would look best?

I said, "White. Or frosted silver."

Zelda made a face. "You got to be kidding. This scene has to be in a black frame."

"Black incarcerates," I said. "The picture can't breathe. Your eye keeps traveling to the frame instead of to the drawing. It's like putting Buddy Holly glasses on a face."

Zelda grinned. "Since when did you become the world's greatest authority on packaging art?"

"I'm not. But I believe what I just said makes sense."

Not to Zelda. "White is stupid. It's wimpy. It lets the picture melt outward, it makes it weak. A black frame actually draws attention, it sucks you directly into the picture, helping to focus the subject matter. Interference from outside is eliminated."

"It clobbers you over the head," I insisted, really feeling strongly on the matter. "Black gives you no choice. The print suffocates. This is a soft picture, a gentle mood, a bucolic scene. Black is much too bold. Totally overbearing."

I suggested we let a framer at the Craft Gallery help us reach an informed decision. Zelda preferred doing business at the Redoubtable Framing Company. I balked. My pal Sandra earned a living slaving for those bastards. But Zelda, adamant, is like a tornado in a Mississippi trailer park. So I prayed for it to be Sandra's day off.

No such luck.

On the surface Sandra is Any Woman, U.S.A.: vaguely pudgy, brunette, cheerful, freckled, polite. Underneath, however, she is a twisted human being, delightfully kinky, passionate, perverted, off the wall.

Sandra demonstrated how black would look, then frosted silver, then white. Zelda cocked an eyebrow and intently rested her chin between thumb and forefinger.

"Oh, all . . . right," she said after a while. "I guess I see your point, Roger. Let's go with the frosted silver."

Caught totally by surprise, I actually felt a triumphant surge inside, but was careful not to let it show on my face. Zelda looked real pleased with herself. She kissed me and held my hand on the way out.

Sandra called, "Adios," but we ignored her.

While circling toward the back parking lot, my wife stopped near two silver garbage cans, pushed me through some dry hollyhock stalks and up against the wall, and kissed me fiercely while negotiating aggressive power moves with her right hand on my nether regions.

Yessir, we got into it.

Suddenly I flung her tummy down over the garbage cans, flipped up her pleated Mexican mariachi skirt, and drove home the old bacon.

"Come fast," Zelda giggled.

"What about you?"

"Forget me, indulge yourself. But make it snappy, before some jerk turns that corner."

I counted aloud each thrust:

"One . . ." Bam! "Two . . ." Bam! "Three . . ."

On eight, I bailed.

Both of us stifled guffaws.

Zelda straightened up, adjusting her skirt. Being a bit groggy, I lost my balance, tumbled backward into the hollyhocks, and crumpled into a sitting position with my eyes all cockeyed and my semitumescent cock poking out of my fly like a puzzled chubby newt.

Zelda ran away, laughing, and disappeared around the corner.

I thought: It doesn't get any better than this.

In the truck, Madame Lafarge remarked, "She's fat. And dumpy. And banal. I'm surprised at you, sweetie."

Oh.

Margaret's poignant adobe house, nicely complemented by its frosted silver frame, hung in our bedroom for exactly one week. Then it disappeared.

"What happened?" I asked.

"I put it in the shed."

"Why?" I asked.

"I didn't like it," Zelda said.

"Dare I be so bold as to elicit some rationale behind this abrupt change of heart?" I joked lightheartedly.

"It reminded me of your charity love affair."

Oh, again.

Bonnie called, sobbing and hysterical. Zelda banged on the writing-tower door. "Your ex-wife is on the phone," she snarled, then spun around and stalked away in a royal twit.

Heart sinking, I traipsed to the kitchen, picked up the receiver, and said, "Hello?"

"I hate that person you call your wife!" Bonnie blurted. "She's a total cunt, Roger. You ought to have your brains put through dialysis. You should get a marrow transplant in your cranium. I can't believe you married such a harridan. What does she eat for breakfast, tenpenny nails and razor blades? I hate you, Roger, I really do. How do you suppose this is going to affect our children, huh? Did you even think about that before you decided to get married? Did you even—"

"Hey, yo, *Bonnie!*"

My scream startled her. Then the floodgates really

opened. "They ripped us off again," she boo-hooed. "They actually put chains around the bars of the kitchen window and yanked them off. They stole the stereo and the TV, the VCR and Kim's bike." Then she wailed, "And they grabbed her computer, also! She needs it in school, Roger. She's doing a paper on Henry David Thoreau. It's due the day after tomorrow. Kim is hysterical. She—"

"*She's* hysterical? C'mon, Bonnie, take a deep breath, get hold of yourself."

"What is it with her?" my former wife babbled tearfully. "Does she get off on being rude? How can she hate me so much when she doesn't even *know* me? I haven't even *met* her yet. What did you do, Roger, you married a porcupine? Where does she get off being so snooty? Who gave her a license to be so—"

"I'll send money," I interrupted. "Just tell me how much. I'll replace the computer, don't worry. Did you make a police report? If not, call 'em right away. You'll need it for the insurance. You didn't let the insurance lapse, did you? Is Kim there? Lemme talk to her, I'll explain about the computer. Don't worry, everything will be all right."

"No it won't be," Bonnie sobbed. Then she corrected, "No it *isn't*!" and slammed down the phone.

I checked in all directions for Weezie Bednarik, then sidled sideways into the Redoubtable Framing Company, my imaginary raincoat collar upturned, my invisible fedora brim tugged down low, an inessential cancer stick planted between my Bogey lips.

"Listen, about the other day," I apologized to Sandra. "I didn't mean to be aloof."

"Then why were you?" she asked.

"That was Zelda," I explained. "My new wife."

"Really? You don't say."

We stood about six feet apart, staring at each other.

Finally I spoke up. "I came by to apologize for being impolite."

"That's okay, Roger. I'm a woman. I'm used to it."

"What I mean is I never would have had that picture framed here if Zelda hadn't—"

"I know what you mean," Sandra interrupted. She added, "Ever since Adam and Eve."

I hemmed, I hawed, I mumbled. "Zelda's a pretty jealous person. I have no idea why she deliberately chose to come here and—"

"Then you're the only ignoramus within a thousand square miles," Sandra said.

"You're not making this any easier," I complained.

"Oh. Pardonnez-moi, je vous en prie."

What happened next is probably as bizarre an experience as I've ever had the displeasure of witnessing.

It all begins as I'm grappling with Sidney Bard in the writing tower.

Zelda is at the Ojo Caliente hot springs taking the baths for the afternoon.

A large, ornate Harley-Davidson motorcycle driven by a statuesque redheaded woman wearing a Lone Ranger mask and a black leather outfit comes roaring up the driveway.

She is followed by a white Cadillac, circa 1957, trailing colorful crepe streamers taped to the rear trunk and bumper.

The motorcycle chugs to a stop in front of my office door.

The Cadillac draws up alongside it.

In masking tape, on the luxury vehicle's side door, is written: GO FOR IT, ROGER!

The woman dismounts the Harley and bangs on my glass door. A guy with a guitar, another guy squeezing an accordion, a third guy aiming a camera, and a heavyset woman in a white-fringed cowboy outfit rattling a tambourine all debark from the Cadillac.

They, too, wear masks.

Somewhat taken aback, I open the door. On this cue, the redhead turns, snaps her fingers, and says, "Hit it, boys."

The guitar, accordion, and tambourine go nuts, launching a raucous burlesque striptease melody.

Then up, like the right arm of Dr. Strangelove, goes the right arm of the tambourine lady, and lo and behold, it's our old friend Adrian, the prurient talking hand-puppet parrot.

Who scrawks, "Hey, baby, take it off! Take it *all* off!"

The motorcycle lady obligingly segues into a professional bump and grind.

Yup, I gawk.

The camera nerd pushed the shutter button and a flashbulb pops.

Immediately sensing a devious plot, I throw up one hand. "Hey, wait a minute!"

"C'mon, baby, shed 'em," calls the parrot. "Look at this lollapalooza, Roger. Ain't she a humdinger?"

Well, yeah, sure, but—*Jesus!* Who put them up to this— Christie? That, that, that unprincipled little . . . devil! Just wait until I—"

The flashbulb pops again.

"Hold on a sec!" I cry.

The black leather jacket lands at my feet, followed immediately by the pants.

"Ooo, wee, lookit them hooters," Adrian exclaims.

"Go away, you people," I blubber. "You got the wrong address!"

The stripper is a very statuesque person whose body I do not recognize.

"Hubba hubba, dig those crazy melons!" the parrot chatters. "Wouldn't you like to squeeze 'em, Roger? Wouldn't you like to pump that rump?"

Presto! In less time than is required to relate this, the stripper is in front of me, bare breasted, shimmying her chest just inches from my nose, while the photographer gallops back and forth, capturing the event—and my astonishment—for posterity from every possible angle.

"Hey cut it out!" I cry. "Put your clothes on, ma'am." *Ma'am?* Yet even as I gather up the leathers and shove them toward the strip-o-gram lady, she's stepping out of her thong and into history.

"Oh wow, baby, shake that thing!" chortles the hand-puppet parrot.

I drop the clothes, and, shielding my face from more paparazzi candid photos, I retreat into the tower and slam the door.

Our undauntable stripper presses her tits against the glass panes. They flare out—ploomph. Then she pushes her groin up on a window. The others quit playing music, rush the door, and stick their lips in splayed-out lascivious kisses to the glass. They wiggle their tongues obscenely.

"Open the door!" hollers the stripper, stepping back. "We won't hurt you."

Explain, please, why I open that door?

A lemon-meringue pie clobbers me square in the face.

Then, hooting and cackling and dancing and hee-hawing, the little troupe piles into its Cadillac and onto the motorcycle, and roars off in a cloud of illicit and mocking energy.

I wonder: How will I ever explain this to Zelda?

Forget it. Not in a million years would I tell her.

But of course, she'll find out anyway. Weezie Bednarik is her friend.

Or some bastard will mail her the photos.

Who is trying to wreck my marriage? Christie? Gretal? Megan? María Teresa?

There is nothing to do but confess.

I creak down onto my hands and knees in the driveway,

and the dog trots over and obediantly licks the pie off my face.

I called Weezie. Adrian answered the phone. "Adrian," I said, "lemme speak to Weezie."

"Weezie's not here," Adrian said.

"Weezie," I pleaded, "grow up, would you please? I am not talking to that fucking puppet on the telephone."

"Oh my, feeling a little testy, are we?" the parrot scrawked in its gravelly voice. "Did you take your stress tabs today, Roger?"

"Weezie, who put you up to that disgraceful show this afternoon? I'll kill 'em."

"Sorry," the parrot squawked, "Weezie ain't in."

"Just gimme a name, that's all I ask. I can do the rest. Who did it? Who paid you to frame me?"

"I'm sorry, sir, but the client asked for anonymity."

"You set me up. I want those pictures," I growled in a menacing way. "If you don't give them to me, I'll sue."

"Tut tut, Roger," said the stupid parrot voice. "That's not a very friendly way to address your friends."

"You don't understand," I pleaded, trying a different attack, a hurt and vulnerable tone. "My wife will kill me."

"Did you like that hot broad, Roger?" the parrot chortled. "Didn't she have wonderful buns? Couldn't she shake that thing?"

"So how was your day, sweetie?" Zelda asked innocently enough that evening as we opened a tin of no-salt-added sardines and a box of low-salt Wheat Thins.

I shrugged. "Oh, you know . . ."

And for a millisecond my brain told me: Lie, Roger, this

is a no-win situation. Equivocate like a fucking professional mug-wump.

But the other side of my brain promptly cried: Are you crazy? Don't even *think* about it!

So I blurted, "You won't believe this, but some asshole hired that schizo buddy of yours with the moronic hand-puppet parrot to send me a strip-o-gram this afternoon. They also hit me with a pie in the face."

Zelda delicately dropped an entire sardine into her gorgeous throat, swallowed, and said, "Oh. Did you enjoy it?"

Why didn't it surprise me more that she did not seem surprised?

"I was too scared to enjoy it," I admitted.

"That 'asshole' was me," Zelda confessed, smiling demurely.

"Excuse me?"

Zelda enunciated more clearly this time around: "That—asshole—was—me."

I said, "Oh." Then I asked, "Why?"

Chipper as a little old tweetie bird, she answered, "Why not?"

I was failing to grasp the concept, I could not find the key, I was floundering. I said, "I don't understand."

Zelda slipped in the knife as smooth as quicksilver. "It's simple, Roger. I love you. You love that kind of stuff. I wanted to please my man."

In my head I exploded. I screamed, *Why you no-good low-down uptight conniving double-crossing sarcastic fork-tongued deviant mocker*, I HATE YOU! *How could you be so cruel? What's the opposite of misogynistic, mistersogynistic? That's you, Zelda, from top to bottom! That stripper was a total insult! A megahumiliation! I oughtta knock you for a royal loop, you ditsy psychopath!*

Aloud, I said, "Excuse me, but I don't think it was a very funny joke."

Zelda's eyes went misty, changing moods, and she cocked her head in a cute coquettish way, then licked her tantalizing lips.

I melted.

Anybody would have melted.

Yeah . . . it was wonderful.

Zelda wanted us to be totally original together. "This is the most incredible sex of my life," she said. "I hate it that it's not as special for you."

"But it *is*," I contradicted. "Jesus, baby, this is like the . . . the nuclear war of sex . . . the, the Mount Everest of erotic. This is incredible. I love this sex. It's unique, original, funky—"

Zelda was crying. "Oh for God's sake shut up, Roger, would you do me the favor, please?"

I gestured in clumsy disbelief. I never knew where the ambush was coming from.

I remembered back to those halcyon days of our courtship when I had glibly revealed to her—at her command, mind you—so many of the lurid details of my life with Christie and Megan, Sandra and Gretal, María Teresa and others too numerous to mention.

How could I have been so stupid?

You didn't know you were gonna get married, taunted a still, small voice.

"This sex feels new to me," I swore. "It's wonderful, exciting, turbulent—*good*. Of course this is original. Shit, Zelda, you are one of a kind. When She made you, God broke the mold—"

"Cut that 'She' crap, Roger, you male chauvinist pig."

My jaw fell.

"I want this to be a great love," Zelda said earnestly. "It is going to be *the* great love of our lives. I want you to be as obsessed with me as I am with you. I want to be like Gaston Lachaise's wife for you. I want you to feel an erotic passion for me that drives you crazy, I'm not kidding. I want everything to be as if it was The First Time. I couldn't stand a relationship that was mediocre."

"Zelda," I pleaded passionately, "the romance in this marriage is *anything* but mediocre."

I meant it too.

Like, let me describe a typical day of ours during that time.

We wake up, roll into each other, start screwing. This lasts about an hour. We dawdle a lot. I like to climax early in the morning when I also have to pee like crazy—the pain heightens the sensation.

Eventually we crawl out of bed, fetch the newspapers, and loll about the kitchen, drinking coffee, nibbling on toasted Essene bread and bran muffins. After that I start working and Zelda sits down in front of her Selectric to write another chapter of her own novel.

About eleven I glance out the glass door of my tower and spot Zelda crossing the driveway in high heels and a pink silk camisole that covers only half her buttocks. She's carrying a lettuce leaf to the garbage can.

I jump up, bang out the door, and chase her back into the house.

After that it's time for lunch.

Lunch makes us sleepy; time for a little lie-down. My balls are starting to ache.

So we both nap for about an hour.

Around five we jog. Then we sit at the kitchen table and eat hors d'oeuvres and have drinks and talk about our day, which means we talk about The Relationship. Endlessly we talk about The Relationship. Zelda enjoys analyzing every minute aspect of our progress, or lack of same. I do too. But by now I have discovered that all syntax is treacherous. I never know what might set us off.

For the occasion, Zelda has changed from her jogging outfit into more comfortable rags: a black teddy and fire-engine-red fuck-me slingbacks.

In that outfit my wife acts as if nothing at all is tantalizing, until finally I go bananas, grab her, and fuck her up against the refrigerator.

Then I crawl out to my tower and start scribbling, while Zelda goes to bed, where she is reading her eleventh book by May Sarton, who is one of her idols.

Social life? Congress with other of our fellow human beings? What, are you kidding? Zelda and I were obsessed with being obsessed with *each other.*

Hey, we were learning about our respective *souls*!

To be truthful, I used to think I had a lot of energy ... until I married Zelda.

Like, growing up, I drove my cohorts in crime crazy because I was always diddy-bopping close to out of control. I was a wiseapple, a class clown, a manic athlete. I couldn't sleep, so I read for hours under the covers using a flashlight. I inspired clichés. My mother was always telling me, "Slow down, Roger, don't gobble your food, you'll choke to death." Teachers admired my fast mind and quick wit, but they constantly barked, "For God's sake, Roger, quit jiggling your *legs.*"

I was always in motion. I ran and ran and ran. When I finally learned how to get laid, relatively late in life, I had a prodigious sexual energy.

I loved juggling a dozen balls in the air at once.

I knew I was indestructible.

Then along comes Zelda, we tie the knot, and—*bam!* Welcome to the old Irresistible Force vs. Immovable Object Syndrome. When it came to energy, Zelda would pit her Fat Man against my Little Boy any day and demand change on the deal.

We fucked our brains out, we chattered, we drank, we stayed up all night talking. Inevitably I yawned before she did. Zelda never wanted to stop.

By now our lovemaking regularly evolved into impromptu wrestling matches. We groaned and laughed and flip-flopped all over each other, exuberant in our wanton folly and jubilation. I tried to pin her but usually failed. Yes, Zelda was tiny, but she bucked and screamed, yanked at my hair, pummeled my chest, and bit me, *hard.* She heaved me up against the wall, then sank one heel into my gut and propelled me backward off the bed ignominiously onto the floor.

Pound for pound, Zelda was like a little ant that could carry an object weighing twenty times its weight.

We formalized our tussles. Whoever could throw the other off the bed won a prize. The reward was often sexual: a blowjob, lingering foreplay, a certain tear-away outfit.

Zelda was strong. She amazed me. Her power, when straining against me, seemed nearly masculine. "Don't mess with my chi," she chortled.

One morning Zelda caught me off balance, kicked hard, and I landed on the floor, clonking my head against the edge of our small gas heater.

"Hey," I whined, "you don't have to be so rough."

Zelda, kneeling on the bed, her lush teeny-weeny atomic-bomb body achingly poised to repel any counterattack, impishly growled, "But I love kicking your butt." She pointed to that framed napkin on the wall and bragged, "I always win."

"Don't you ever get tired?" I asked, genuinely puzzled by her fierce and intractable chutzpah.

Zelda pulled out her poetry six-gun and fired at me a quote from Nikos Kazantzakis:

" 'I tell my body to obey my soul, and thus I never tire.' "

In fact, when we weren't running, jumping, eating, drinking, smoking, wrestling, arguing, fucking, or otherwise procrastinating big-time, Zelda was churning out the fiction pages, probably ten to every two I managed to conceive. But when I asked her what they were all about, she blanched and made a face.

"Oh no you don't, Roger. I'm not gonna open myself to ridicule from you."

"I won't ridicule," I promised. "I love you."

"You're a professional," she pointed out. "You won't be able to help it. You'll lose all respect for me. I'll want to commit suicide."

"Really, my dear, I do think you exaggerate."

She relented a bit. "Well, when it's ready, if that time ever comes, *maybe* you can take a look. But until then, if you ever dare read my work, I swear I'll kill you in horrible ways that have never been tried before."

Needless to say, my curiosity was piqued. So one day while Zelda cavorted at the spa, I betrayed her trust, tiptoed into our bedroom, and opened the unlocked file drawer where she kept her manuscript pages. Seldom in my life have I felt guiltier, yet still I persisted. I filched out a few pages and, with my heart palpitating, began to read.

Who knows what I'd expected? But the writing was wonderful. In the passage I had selected, a jive-talking narrator named Samantha was about to parachute from an airplane for the first time, strapped to the front of her new boyfriend, Geoff, a professional sky diver, who had a hard-on she could feel against her butt through the rough cloth of a spiffy new jumpsuit. Samantha had just learned she was pregnant by another guy named Dave, and she was suffering terrible morning sickness and plotting an abortion. Likewise, sheer terror easily described her attitude about skydiving, but the lady had sworn to jump in order to impress Geoff. Meanwhile, Geoff's pal Mel was tinkering with his video camcorder, preparing to leap and film Samantha and Geoff on the way down. Just as the three of them bailed, Samantha vomited all over Geoff's goggles, blinding him. And suddenly their free-fall became real traumatic, because without earthly reference Geoff could not judge when to pull the rip cord.

I thought I heard a noise outside, quickly jammed back the pages, closed the file drawer, flopped backward on the bed, and pretended to be taking a nap. My heart thundered alarmingly. I had a slight vertigo attack caused by guilt. I presumed Zelda would divorce me for invading her private turf, or maybe she'd plug me in the testicles with her thirty-eight.

The noise, however, was a false alarm.

I waited a moment longer for the coast to clear, then scurried out to my writing tower—*safe!* I couldn't work, though. Partially, I felt weak from the fear of being caught. But also I was impressed by Zelda's zany prose. If she could sustain it, I just knew the book would sell.

My wife was a natural-born storyteller!

Perhaps I never wholly comprehended Zelda's insecurity because she was so incredibly beautiful.

I mean, in my eyes she had everything.

But maybe that was a curse worse than death.

It fascinated me, the way Zelda took care of her face and

her body. She spent hours in the bathroom, bathing, shaving, plucking hair, applying makeup, brushing her nearly black tresses. She put bubble beads and skin beads and wrinkle elixir in the steamy water. She massaged her features with vitamin E oil and other compounds of mysterious youthfulizing powers.

About once a week Zelda smeared on a weird green mud mask, and if I entered the bathroom while she was lounging in pink foam reading a book with that Hopi mask on, she'd instantly say, "Don't make me laugh."

So of course it was an irresistible temptation to try and induce a laugh, cracking the mask.

I loved to stand in the doorway and watch her scrub down her rosy body with a sponge called a loofah. It was shaped like a big piece of corn on the cob.

Often she let me apply the loofah. I couldn't do it without getting a hard-on. Her body was so . . . so *luscious.* Zelda's skin was wondrously smooth, no cellulite anywhere. People often pegged her as ten, maybe fifteen years younger than her true age. And believe me, my wife worked hard to create that illusion.

Each morning she put on exercise tights and did stretches for half an hour. Sometimes she exercised to a Jane Fonda workout video. For variation she had a Victoria Principal workout video. For her birthday I gave her a Richard Simmons workout video, which she unwrapped and threw directly across the kitchen into the garbage.

Zelda always executed two hundred sit-ups before breakfast.

I had bought her a Finnish exercycle upon which she usually spent at least forty-five minutes a day, reading *The New Yorker* or one of those body-beautiful rags put out by the Joe Weider conglomerate.

Zelda taped pictures of women with perfect bodies to the refrigerator door so that she could see them whenever hunger drove her to reach for the handle.

Then, of course, she swam at the spa at least twice a week. She wore that purple one-piece bathing suit to die for. Same as Marilyn Monroe posing nude on a velvet blanket, those togs left little to the imagination.

My friend Ed Griffin once drooled, "Roger, excuse me for being crude about your new wife, but please take this as a compliment: That is the most fuckable woman I have ever laid eyes upon."

When I told Zelda, thinking it might boost her ego, she replied, "Ed Griffin is a slimy grub you'd expect to find hiding out in a rusty snail shell."

Zelda rubbed lotions all over her body. She ordered unguents that came UPS from Hawaii. Skin creams, hand-care lotions, beauty powders, shampoos, and hair conditioners. She used special antiperspirants made from organic gubgub trees in Polynesia.

Zelda painted her exquisite fingernails and toenails Passion Pink. If a nail broke, she glued on a false one and shaped it to match her others.

Zelda applied mascara and eyeliner and lash enhancer and lip gloss and pancake makeup. After the bath, the loofah, and the hair rinse, Zelda balanced a hand mirror on the window ledge above the tub, and with her hair in a towel turban, she stood in the empty tub working on her face with all that daylight shining directly upon it.

She washed her hair daily.

And spent half an hour fluffing it with the noisy electric hair dryer.

Every day, during some point in these ablutions, Zelda used dental floss. Her impeccable white teeth sparkled like forbidden ivory.

In total awe, I watched Zelda put herself together. The routine was incredibly sexy. She was like a goddess of allure. Enchanting feminine secrets revealed! The intimacy was a bodacious turn-on. She liked country and western for background music, and often hummed along. Her favorites were Tammy Wynette, Patsy Cline, Emmylou Harris.

"God, you're the, you're the most, the most beautiful woman I've ever met," I stammered.

Beyond that, words failed me.

Figure this, however: "No I'm not, I'm ugly," she replied.

To show you how little I knew about life way back then, I thought Zelda was joking.

On a Monday in mid-October I entered my bank to cash a check. I walked up to the first window on the left, cosigned the back of the check, and pushed it across the counter while doing the mathematics of subtraction on my stub. I never looked up.

"Hi there, big boy," said a familiar voice. "How're they hangin'?"

My heart dropped into my shoes and bounced.

"Jesus Christ, Christie, wh-what are *you* doing here?"

"I used to work in back, in accounting, remember? Well, they put me up front. I love it. I meet people all day long."

She was wearing the type of tight fuzzy jersey that would've gotten her stoned to death in Saudi Arabia. A perky black velvet bow decorated the left side of her flouncy hair. She looked good, like a voluptuous sugar cookie.

"What's the matter?" Christie asked, wiseapple, yet also quasiconcerned. "You look as if you saw a ghost."

"You can't work up front as a teller," I said, feeling totally desperate.

"Oh yeah? Why not?" Christie plumped one little fist against her defiantly jutted hip.

I explained the obvious. "I bank here, idiot. *We* bank here, I mean. It's a joint account. As soon as Zelda realizes you're a teller, she'll go berserk. She'll say I did it deliberately."

Zelda had never met Christie, but we all know she had seen pictures. And believe me, Zelda would tip. Her nostrils would flare the instant they got a whiff of perfume just inside the door. And the second Zelda's eyes fell on Christie, no matter how demure the little sex kitten happened to be habilléed that day, all Zelda would be able to see, probably, was Christie naked, hanging upside down from a chandelier, being buttfucked by guess who.

Helplessly I told my ex-girlfriend, "I've been banking here for sixteen years."

"I don't get it," Christie said, chipper as all get-out, pretending to be an imbecile. She opened her eyes really wide, like a dumb ingenue. "What's the problem?"

"Oh cut me some slack, kid. *You're* the problem, obviously. Now I'm gonna have to deposit all my money at First State, and I hate those vultures. I can't believe they put you up front."

"It's a break, Roger," she explained as if to a retard. "I earn more dough. It's more fun, too. All my ex-lovers come in to make deposits and withdrawals."

Very funny.

She added, "Well, honey, I guess there's just no justice in this vale of tears we live in."

I glanced around wildly, wondering if the morals posse— a.k.a. Weezie Bednarik—was closing in. Who had seen me talking to Christie and would report it on the six o'clock national news, then again at ten?

"I hate it," I groused. "Everything is conspiring against me. It wasn't funny, that letter you wrote. Or the pictures you sent. You could get me killed."

Frisky as a speckled pup, Christie said, "I thought it was hilarious. I laughed until I cried." Then she counted, "Ten, twenty, thirty, forty, and—*here.*" She slapped down the final ten-spot with fetching oomph. "One to grow on."

"This new job is . . . permanent?" I mumbled.

"Nothing in life is permanent, sugar. But hey, I got my fingers crossed, and I sure hope it lasts long enough to fix that fucking Volkswagen. I reckon you can't bail me out anymore, can you?"

Christie sounded abruptly sad. I stuffed the money in my pocket and kept avoiding her eyes.

"Why are you avoiding my eyes?" she asked.

" 'Cause I feel weird, okay?" Not to mention terrible for writing the letter that shot her down. Basically, I flat out didn't enjoy this predicament. It also irritated me that she was so obnoxious. And I wanted to sink to my knees and apologize.

"Oh, Roger," Christie whispered, sort of mocking, yet not without a dash of pity, "I miss you. What have you gotten yourself into?"

"A big pickle," I moaned, and scooted for the exit.

"Cazzie's doing great," I heard her chirp 'ere I'd scuttled out of sight. "Thanks for asking!"

Naturally, I did not wish to be caught sneaking around, not by Zelda. So whenever I visited Gretal, I always mentioned it to my wife. She would have found out anyway. Weezie Bednarik was a bit like the town crier in that respect. No day passed when I did not bump into her about the village at least once. I suspect Weezie was always wired and operating a miniature Minox camera hidden in her free palm. She probably had a clandestine CIA-funded private-detective dealership and, from a two-way wrist radio broadcasting through that irritating hand-puppet parrot, was sending to Zelda quarter-hourly APBs on my whereabouts whenever I was not at home.

After the latest of my hospital visits, Zelda said, "I bet she's just pretending to be sick, the hypocrite. You're a fool if you can't see that."

In other years I had observed Gretal on a half-dozen death-beds. I had been there when they opened up her back, cut lumps from her forehead, removed tissue from her neck and throat. I had seen cross sections of her tumors on slides projected against a screen. I'd stared through lead-lined windows while she lay strapped to a couch getting zapped with beta rays or gamma rays, or whatever you call them: rads . . . tiny little rads. I had watched all her hair fall out on no less than three different occasions.

So I said, "No, she's really sick. Gretal doesn't lie about stuff like this."

"Then you're more gullible than I thought when it comes to women," Zelda said. "I can't believe you're so naive."

It worked. Guilt oozed through my veins. I grew increasingly self-conscious about seeing Gretal. "Your relationship with her has changed," Zelda explained patiently. "You have to take my feelings into account now, you know."

"It's strictly platonic with Gretal," I said. "She's my friend."

"If she could knife me in the back, she would," Zelda said. "Any person conversant with first-grade psychology would understand that."

I told the invalid what Zelda had said. "She's right," Gretal informed me. "Of course I would stab her in the back. She's a royal asshole. You're a royal asshole for marrying the bitch. I feel sorry for you. You're going to hell in a hand-cart."

"Worry about yourself," I replied a trifle testily. "You're the one at death's door."

Gretal laughed, an effort that made her flinch in pain. "I

wouldn't be so sure of that," she said. "Go find me a cigarette."

I was shocked. "You don't smoke," I said.

"I used to, and I'm in that kind of a mood," she insisted.

Fair enough. I went and bought a pack of Kool Filter Kings, came back, balanced two between my lips, lit 'em, gave her one, and sucked deeply of the other.

She looked at me weirdly. "Since when did you start smoking, Roger?"

"Age of fourteen. But I quit when I reached twenty-one."

"So what are you doing now, idiot?"

I explained, "I'm in that kind of a mood."

She said, "Roger, you put that out right now. Those things will kill you. You've got enough problems."

I ignored her. I inhaled again. It made me feel incredibly dizzy. Also in solidarity with Gretal. It felt good. It felt suicidal. It felt appropriate.

When I left, Gretal said, "Ciao, bello—arrivederci."

Zelda is a master of psychology.

When, in fear and trepidation, I lit a Kool in front of her (during one of our cocktail ritual intimate conversations about children and extended-family obligations) and inhaled brazenly, her face did not change expression. I couldn't believe it. I had expected a torrent of recriminations. I had planned on defending my lunatic gesture tooth and nail. I had presumed that she would threaten to divorce me that instant if I failed to grow up.

No such luck.

Zelda merely rose at an appropriate pause in the conversation, located a glass ashtray in a cupboard, set it down in front of me, and continued talking.

Next afternoon, when I returned to my writing tower after a short siesta, a carton of Kool Filter Kings lay on the desk. It was wrapped in a red ribbon. A frilly pink heart said *I love you, Roger.*

When next I tapped out a cigarette and set it between my lips, Zelda beat me to the punch, striking a match. She smiled with genuine love in her eyes while I puffed away.

I could stand it no longer. I said, "I don't understand why you're so amenable to me smoking cigarettes."

She said, "Do you want to smoke cigarettes?"

I nodded, puzzled. "Yeah ... I guess so."

"Then what right have I got to impose my disapproval on you? It's no worse a habit than a million others in the world. If you enjoy it, more power to you."

For a minute my pea-sized brain labored to ascertain her ulterior motives. Simultaneously, that same brain was trying to understand *my* ulterior motives. Even as it was also struggling to comprehend why her answer not only disappointed me but made me angry, too, and into the bargain it gave me a great sense of relief.

Next morning I opened each pack of Filter Kings in the carton, drenched the innards with water, and threw the soggy remains into the garbage can.

About two hours later, halfway through a difficult paragraph in which Sidney Bard was maladroitly seducing a Velcron maiden with twin vaginas located in her kneecaps, I experienced a desperate hunger for nicotine.

I went to the garbage can, extricated a soggy pack, marched into the kitchen, set a frying pan over a gas burner, delicately extracted two cigarettes, warmed them in my frying pan until they had dried out, then smoked them both with relish.

That scared me. So I retrieved from the trash all those waterlogged cancer sticks, pissed in a mayonnaise jar, and poured urine from the jar into each pack of weeds, tainting them beyond recall.

Three days later, listen to this. I was inordinately flustered. Zelda had just informed me that she never again wanted to see a letter addressed to Gretal in our mailbox. "You told me it was over with her six years ago," she said. "It's sick the way your ego must cling to these petty assurances that you're still a stud."

Okay, fair enough, but how to tell Gretal? Naturally, Zelda was correct. Why hadn't Gretal rented her own box? Quién sabe? Maybe inertia. Also, it had been a connection. I enjoyed delivering her mail. Often she brewed a cup of tea and we chatted. Sometimes we indulged in a fast little boff.

Well, no more quickies, of course. And I sure could see Zelda's point. Explain, then, please, why I resented the ultimatum?

Had our roles been reversed, I would have demanded that Zelda put the kibosh on her ex-lovers' letters, I think.

I guess my hincty mood derived from the knowledge that Gretal was in rotten shape. It would be a lot more humane to wait until she was back on her feet again before breaking the bad news.

Then I saw a Marlboro lying on the sidewalk, a fresh one, still pretty long. In fact, it was lit and languidly smoking.

I picked it up and took a hit, inhaling deeply.

The rush made my knees rubbery. My heart started to fibrillate.

I sat down on a bench and breathed deeply. Soon, however, I copped another puff. The smoke punched my lungs like Oscar Bonavena clobbering Dick Whipperman, way back when.

By the start of the following week I was up to a pack a day.

Gretal, lying in a mound of pillows, her withered hair

framing her sallow face, said, "You hypocrite, give me a damn cigarette."

Like the weak-kneed, lily-livered, sniveling guppy I had become, I complied. I actually lit it for her, too. Gretal exhaled the way Marlene Dietrich used to exhale a torch song. Closed her eyes, held it forever, then let the smoke drain out sort of by osmosis. Very sensual. She murmured, "Mmmm, that's real coffee."

It made me sad.

Gretal was like a frail girl among all those pillows. A tough little kid with gray hair and cancer in half her vital organs, sucking on a coffin nail.

Calls came in regularly from my professional connections and business associates. Don Perry never makes much of a fuss. In fact, for an agent he's remarkably gentle. He does yoga. He jogs. He plays a lot of tennis.

But he also gets rich by keeping tabs.

"How's it goin', cowboy?" he asked. "Are we still on target for the fourteenth, if not the first? Or maybe the seventh?"

I disliked that possessive "we." But of course I answered, "On target? Could William Tell hit an apple on a kid's head with an arrow?"

I get that way sometimes under pressure. Real glib. Manic. I set up smoke screens. I know a thousand ways to avoid fibbing while not exactly answering a question truthfully, either.

My editor at Cross and Merton, Bill Witherspoon, checked in every now and then for a progress report. Unfortunately, *Perseid* had already appeared in the spring catalog because the previous deadline had been August first.

A deadline which, needless to say, did come and go, nattering about Michelangelo.

John Nichols

Bill and I had been through hell together. In the old days, before Sidney Bard became a minor celebrity, there was a lot of flexibility in my deadlines.

But now that Sidney had become a marketing phenom, apparently "we" had to produce, in order to sustain a bottom line predicated on my success.

Bill is a gruff, sardonic, white-haired survivor of God knows how many publishing wars. Some people thought him a trifle dour. I'd always considered him wise.

When he asked, I said, "I'm trying, Bill. I'm a little under the gun right now with the *Catacombs* script, but I should be able to pull out *Perseid* close to the revised deadline we agreed upon."

"Don't lie to me," Bill said. "When can I read it?"

"What's the deadline?" I asked.

"You know it's January first."

"There's your answer," I replied.

Bill said, "You're jerking me off, Roger."

"Bill," I whined, "honest to God, I'm trying. I just tied the knot. There's a bit of turmoil here. We fight, we argue, we screw our brains out. It's a time of adjustment. Still, I work eighteen hours a day. I'm a professional. You know that."

But they always get down to the nitty-gritty. "Like, how many pages?" Bill asked.

"Two hundred and twelve." I was only hedging by sixty pages. The average Sidney Bard novel comes to about four hundred and ten manuscript pages.

"You're hallucinating," Bill said. "I can hear it in your voice. You sound like Dick Nixon saying 'I am not a crook!' "

"Bill, I'm *trying.*"

"Try harder," Bill said. "Marty"—the publisher—"is champing at the bit."

104

* * *

Zelda said, "I don't understand how you can let those creeps walk all over you."

I explained, "I signed contracts, baby. They're business people. They also keep me—correction, us—alive."

"You're an artist," Zelda said. "You don't have to punch a clock."

Her nose I would've liked to punch. Instead, out of habit, in a daze, I started fondling her left breast. "Oh *no* . . ." I whimpered.

"Oh *yes* . . ." my glamorous mate replied.

I think it was either Emile Zola or Balzac or Victor Hugo who said, every time he had an orgasm:

"Oops, there goes another novel!"

The trouble with sex is, the more of it you're getting, the harder it is to abstain.

Calls also kept arriving for me from Argentina.

Collect.

From María Teresa.

María Teresa Olguín y Caramillo, a hairdresser from Buenos Aires.

I had met her on the set of the first Sidney Bard movie— *The Universe and Dr. Feinstein*—which had been headquartered in Alicante, Spain, in August of 1984.

When the film wrapped, we had spent a week on Formentera in all the usual throes of debilitating and wonderful sexual rhapsody.

María Teresa had one of those raspy Latin voices that's like a raven crashing around in a boudoir full of silk lingerie.

And, yes, I must admit, we had had a lot of fun together.

But Argentina is a far piece from the southwestern United States.

About once a year she conned a friend who worked for Avianca into a free ticket, and we'd meet in Atlanta, or New York, or maybe St. Louis or Kansas City. Somehow, those destinations were always cheapest.

When Zelda picked up the phone before I could get to it, María Teresa said, "Let me speak to the man of the casa, por favor."

Zelda said, "Who the hell are you?"

María Teresa replied, "I am María Teresa Olguín y Caramillo, and I want to espeak to Roger."

"I am his wife," Zelda said, "and Roger can't come to the phone right now."

"Why can he not do this?" María Teresa said.

Zelda hung up on her and lit into me. "Tell that rude bitch I don't ever want her calling my house again. I can't bear people who are obnoxious and have no sense of manners whatsoever. She never even said please."

Then Zelda launched a tirade against *all* my friends who called. If they did not identify themselves at first but simply asked for me, Zelda always queried back icily, "And who shall I say is calling?" Then she lambasted me for their discourteous behavior. They had not chitchatted in a friendly manner. She demanded esteem. She wanted to be acknowledged as mistress of the house. She deserved a certain deference and she'd be damned if she would tolerate inconsiderate people on the telephone.

Fair enough. I dropped notes to all my friends, to my children, and to my ex-wife, begging them to be polite on the telephone if Zelda answered so they wouldn't hurt her feelings or, more to the point, get me in dutch.

"Feelings," Bonnie said to me while I was surreptitiously talking to her from a booth in Rexall's on the town plaza, *"what* feelings?"

* * *

I began to have cold-sweat terror spurts every time the phone rang. If Zelda reached the receiver first, I'd die, thinking, Oh God please no, don't let it be rude Bonnie or sullen Woody or whiny Kim or some pugnacious ex-girlfriend emerging from the woodwork.

Then always, after I'd spoken on the phone, Zelda would enter the kitchen and rattle around. It was understood I should tell her who had called. I resented that assumption, but the alternative was worse—The Cold Shoulder à la Zelda.

So I always fessed up.

"That was the Argentine nudnik," I admitted. I'd taken to disparaging my imprudent friends. I'd taken to disparaging my ex-girlfriends. I'd taken to disparaging my own children. I'd taken to disparaging anybody who I figured was even remotely on Zelda's shit list.

Zelda said, "I thought you explained the lay of the land to that hussy."

"I did. But María Teresa is stubborn. She doesn't fluster easy."

Zelda said, "Frankly, I think old girlfriends calling you up every other day is an intrusion on this marriage. You keep it up, and we're headed for disaster."

"*I* don't make the phone calls," I said.

I wrote María Teresa another one of my famous Fatal Bullet letters, all in grammatically butchered Spanish. Her fifteen-page reply said I was the passion of her existence, and Latins don't give up easy, and no two-bit jealous wench who I'd chosen to marry in a fit of bourgeois American guilt could change the beauty, or take away the passion, we had shared together.

I left the open letter on the kitchen table, secure in the

knowledge that Zelda could not read a word of any foreign lingo.

Unfortunately, Weezie Bednarik is fluent in Spanish.

A blistering English translation of María Teresa's letter appeared tacked on my office door on the morning of October twenty-fourth. At the top of page one, my wife had written:

FYI
OOXX

Zelda

"I am not ashamed to be a jealous person," Zelda bragged. "It just means that I am passionate. It's proof that I care. It's a normal part of the human condition. What do you want, some old hag who doesn't give a damn? You'd be bored, and patronizing a whorehouse within a week."

I said, "I hate jealousy. The worst sensations I've ever had in my life were feelings of jealousy. It's the most uncomfortable emotion I know."

"If you were honest, you'd admit that you're jealous, too," she said.

"You weren't jealous when we were courting."

"See what you do?" she said. "You do it every time."

"Do what?" I asked.

"You shift it back from yourself to me. You avoid the issue. You refuse to answer the question."

"What question?" I muttered.

"I said, 'If you were honest, you'd admit that you're jealous, too.' "

"And—?" I stared at her, frowning.

"And so—?" she replied.

Was she crazy as a loon, or was I? I said, "I don't understand."

Zelda reiterated. "You didn't answer my question. You switched it right back to me."

"Switched *what?*" I mumbled, totally bewildered.

"The onus of jealousy."

I gaped at her. I wanted to cry in frustration. I said, "I don't understand."

Zelda said, "I asked you about *your* feelings of jealousy, not mine."

"You didn't ask a *question*, Zelda. You made a *statement.*"

Her turn to gawk. She said, "Roger, it's perfectly legal for a *statement* to be accepted as a *question*. That's the unwritten understanding."

I didn't remember what the hell we were talking about, and I told her so.

Zelda moaned, "Roger, why are you so deliberately obtuse?"

And then she buried her face in her hands.

"The hell I wasn't jealous when we were courting," Zelda said.

That caught me by surprise. "You didn't act that way."

Zelda made an interesting observation. "I didn't have the right."

Why? "Well," she explained, "you had other girlfriends, I had other boyfriends. It was a different situation. It had different rules."

"I loved that situation, Zelda."

"I hated it, Roger."

"I *married* you because that was such a wonderful situation," I said. "We were so open together. And free. No jealousy. I was not afraid of you, nor you of me. We could joke about anything. I never had more fun in my life. What do you mean, you hated it?"

109

"It was horribly callous, without meaning. There was no commitment. It humiliated me when you made cracks about Douglas. I hated fucking you when you were fucking other women. I thought the whole thing was tacky as hell. I detested your cavalier attitudes. I abhorred all your other women. You had the sexual politics of a newt. You were the George Lincoln Rockwell of male chauvinist pigs."

Stunned, I asked, "Why didn't you say something?"

She smiled, reached down, and began to tinker at my fly. "Where do you think *that* would have gotten me?"

I was speechless. But before I found my voice, she had put on a low-cut skin-tight blue jersey tube (purchased for a buck at Goodwill) and a pair of black high heels.

My knees became jelly. Zelda had a bunch of sexy outfits in that vein, secondhand jobs she called her tear-away numbers. I was encouraged to shred them at will. We had even shopped for them together, which was oodles of fun.

Zelda knew exactly how to shake my nerves and rattle my brain.

"Oh Christ, baby, let's fuck," I blubbered.

Whereupon, yet again, Zelda caught me by surprise: "Sorry, Roger, but I don't 'fuck' anymore," she said.

Naturally, she had to be joking. But I was learning that with a person this volatile, it's better not to jump to conclusions.

So, instead of forthrightly grabbing my wife, throwing her to the floor, and laying on a bit of the old timber, I said, I am sure with a totally silly shit-eating grin on my face, "Say what?"

Zelda said, "I'm tired of you calling it 'fucking' all the time. I'm bored with your crude nature."

I leaned forward, tilted my head, and peered at her the way a field zoologist might inspect a living specimen of a bottlenose Madagascar lemur long thought extinct.

Finally I said, "You're kidding, right?"

"I couldn't be more serious."

"We've *always* talked about 'fucking,' " I said, still thoroughly bewildered. "We *love* fucking."

"Maybe with one of your other tarts," Zelda said. "But not with me anymore, no way, never again. I am not a low-class broad."

I said, "Excuse me, but have you gone bonkers?"

Zelda patted my cheek affectionately. "No, dear, I just do not wish to be placed in that crass category inhabited by your former sluts and oversexed teenyboppers."

Alarmed, yet still jocular whilst trying to play left field even though I had lost the ball in the lights, I gasped, "You mean we're not gonna screw anymore?"

Exasperated, Zelda said, "Why don't you try saying 'make love' just once in your life? Did it ever occur to you that I might think that was nice?"

Increasingly puzzled, I blurted, "I say 'make love' all the time. The words are interchangeable. 'Fucking,' 'balling,' 'screwing,' 'loving,' they all mean 'making love.' "

"Do you feel the same way when you call it 'fucking' as you do when you say 'making love'?"

I was starting to be aggravated. "Fucking-A, of course. It's all sex, by whatever name. And it's always wonderful."

"Is that a generic 'wonderful,' or should I be flattered that you're talking about us?"

¡Ay Dios, sálgame de aquí!

I opened my mouth to defend myself, but Zelda interrupted. "I hate it when you say 'fucking,' Roger. It sounds so crass."

I pointed out the obvious. "You never used to hate it."

"Bravo, Roger." She clapped her hands sarcastically. "You're finally learning about female psychology."

"What am I learning, Zelda?" I had grown positively edgy.

"Things change." Zelda flounced away, heading into the living room.

I'll say this about me, I'm a quick study. Hurrying after her, I said, "Hey, baby, do you wanna make love?"

Bingo!

Zelda stopped in her tracks, turned around to face me, grasped the hem of her jersey tube, and—upsy daisy!—she skinned the cat.

Her breasts wobbled like quart Baggies filled with vanilla custard negotiating a speed bump.

Zelda and I could do gentle sex the way milkweed fluff and dandelion seeds might copulate in midair if such an exercise was warranted by their genes.

Zelda could insinuate beatific perversions with her lips. She could mouth my male member with an almost derisively soft expertise both voluptuous and silkily kinky.

Zelda knew how to touch me exactly as I wanted. In a subtle yet playful manner she could laxly tinker my equipment into a real dither.

I could kiss Zelda the way raindrops cling to a leaf.

I could touch her intimate places like Michelangelo's *Pietà*.

Zelda taught me to scrape my damp lips quietly against her throat as if they were simultaneously sharpened steel and gelatinous bulbs of honey.

My fingers whispered at her snatch like Marilyn Monroe singing "Happy Birthday" to President Kennedy.

We would lie for hours, barely moving, gazing into each other's eyes, kissing, fondling, murmuring. Both of us were totally captivated by the mysterious juice that drove us.

Our sex was heavenly infatuation.

* * *

Sometimes, when the theme of a story is Problems of a Marriage, you tend to forget that most of that marriage was spent in a state of conjugal bliss.

I.e., Zelda and I shared countless ecstatic adventures together.

For starters, we were making love every day, and usually two or even three times at that. And what other activity in life is more wonderful?

Physically we sure clicked, and we had a ball. So no matter what happens to me for the rest of my life, I'll always have that astonishing erotic affair with Zelda to remember.

Plus, let me make this perfectly clear. However volatile our interactions, I'd never had such an intoxicating, such a thrilling, such a tantalizing relationship in all my born days.

Zelda was, is, and always will be hands down the most exciting person I have ever met.

But she is also gentle, considerate, and very loving.

For example, Zelda was always giving me things.

She gave me gifts like little Joseph Cornell-type boxes. She filled them with bits of lace and feathers and rose petals and tiny metal milagros in the shape of hearts or arms or eyeballs. She found small rodent bones out on the mesa and glued the tiny bones to ruby ribbons or bits of ultramarine silk, and added them to her colorful nests for me.

The boxes were small cheerful poems, kaleidoscopic fantasies, love letters from a whimsical clown.

They were beautiful.

They might show up on my desk beside a vase of fresh-picked wildflowers.

They might appear in the refrigerator on top of my jar of lite mayonnaise.

They might be waiting on the seat of my truck when I climbed behind the wheel at noon.

Once, when I came home after the town chores, an orange crepe streamer had been unraveled from the truck's parking space in our driveway over to the woodpile. At the end of that paper ribbon I found a pair of her panties with a paper heart-shaped *I love you* pinned to the crotch.

On another occasion, as I left the tower and headed toward the house for more coffee, I spied a yellow crepe ribbon on the front walkway. I followed it inside and through the house to our bedroom, where Zelda lay nude upon a lime-green sheet reading *The Colossus of Maroussi.*

A delicious bean-sprout and avocado sandwich often appeared miraculously on the writing-tower stoop just at that moment when my stomach had begun to rumble. Sometimes, when I bit into it, I would find a piece of paper in the gooey innards. Once it said:

You are my everything.

Another time, after a little spat between us, the paper read:

Go fuck yourself, you amoral dunce!

A day later, mayonnaise-stained, it was an entirely different story:

Roger, I care for you more than
J. Paul Getty loved money.

Zelda said, "It's a hoot to surprise you. I want to always catch you off guard. Never be predictable. I hope you stay interested in me forever."

* * *

Zelda gave me a book about Tina Modotti: It was called *A Fragile Life*. On the refrigerator door she taped an Edward Weston photograph of Tina full length, lying on her back, naked.

I took a picture of Zelda in an identical pose.

My wife practiced mime. She put on a black elastic outfit and painted her face white with a big rouge dot on either cheek. I clicked the camera while she made forlorn airy gestures across the garden, clenching a yellow zinnia between her teeth.

Zelda collected wildflower seeds along the road. Sunflower, chicory, golden and purple asters. She sprinkled the seeds around our house. Her eyes, like opalescent gems, intensified their gleam.

"I'm so excited," she gasped, fluttering fingertips over the ground where her seeds had fallen. "I can't wait until springtime! I bet I expire in February from holding my breath."

Zelda thrived on suspense. It made her glow like a wild fox.

And that made me happy, too.

Unfortunately, things soon reached a head re Gretal.

The mistake I made that launched a thousand angry quips was to confess to Zelda that on several occasions I had helped Gretal take a bath.

Wrong move, Dagwood!

Zelda went into her Ice Maiden routine. The sparkling eyes went *click!*—instantly dead, bland, icy. Zelda could shut down her ebullience as quickly and as emphatically as Fat Man had shut down Hiroshima.

I can't exactly explain it, but it was scary. Whenever it happened, my heart would dive into my toes and I would feel almost faint from apprehension.

"I bet that gave you a thrill," Zelda said, referring to Gretal's bath.

I fumfered. "Well, um, not exactly. She's in a lot of pain."

Zelda said, "I'll *bet* she was in a lot of pain."

"We don't make love," I said. "We haven't in a long time."

"Who said anything about making love?"

"Oh," I blundered, trapped again. "I . . . uh . . . thought that you were implying—"

"I hate it when you put words in my mouth, or thoughts in my head, Roger. I hate it that in your eyes everybody else is the good guy, and I'm the bitch."

"I'm sorry," I fumfered. "I didn't mean to be offensive. You're right, it's wrong to project. It's just that—"

"Does she still have a good body?" Zelda asked.

I shook my head. God, I felt uncomfortable. I didn't want to tell her anything more about Gretal, because it was a violation of Gretal's privacy. But I couldn't lie, or refuse to answer, either. Plus, like Charlie Brown kicking at Lucy's football every autumn, I kept thinking that maybe this time, "The truth—"

"No, her body's sort of ravaged," I said. "Puffy in places, drooping in others. It's sad. She used to have a lovely body."

Zelda smiled icily. "Have you ever noticed how all your girlfriends always had 'lovely bodies'? What a guy. A real lothario."

I shut up. It really did seem as if I had done one more terrible injustice to a person I loved—in this case, Gretal.

Why couldn't I keep my mouth shut?

Zelda stood up, leaned over, kissed my forehead, hooked up her tight skirt, straddled my lap, unbuttoned my fly, gave me the magic touch, then settled down, releasing a long, tantalizing sigh as I entered her body.

Somehow, the sex always seemed sexier when I was in a quandary, off balance, confused, and guilt ridden, not knowing whether to love my wife or hate her or commit suicide because I couldn't figure out *any*thing.

So there I am, seated in the Benedictine Café, revising a chapter of *Return of the Perseid Meteor Thugs*, when a shadow falls over me, and before I can look up, Adrian the hand-puppet parrot sticks his beak into my face and squawks, "Hello, Roger. What's a nice guy like you doing in a sleazy joint like this?"

I can't help it, I refuse to talk with the damn parrot.

"Weezie, please remove that thing out of my face, okay?"

I try not to be too caustic, however, because Weezie and Zelda are bosom buddies, and I wouldn't want to ruffle the feathers of Zelda's friend now, would I?

"What is this I hear about you fucking a crippled ex-girlfriend in the local cancer ward?" the scratchy-voiced parrot continued. When Adrian talks, Weezie always keeps her eyes on him, never on you. I asked Zelda once if she'd ever had a normal conversation with Weezie. "All the time," Zelda said. "But without the parrot she's a total space cadet."

"Don't you ever grow tired of the parrot?" I asked.

"I ignore the parrot," Zelda said. "I pretend it's Weezie. It *is* Weezie."

"When Weezie goes to bed with men, does the parrot do all the talking and grunting and groaning?" I asked.

"That's really a crude question." Zelda tossed her flamboyant curls. "Why don't you lift your head out of the gutter just once?"

"Weezie," I say, struggling to hold my temper. "I am not fucking a crippled ex-girlfriend, repeat *not*. Do you copy?"

Weezie made the parrot's beak twist in imitation of sarcastic incredulity. Then Adrian said, "The whole town is talking about it. It's killing Zelda. You really have no right to treat her like this, you cad. You should be loving and supportive. You should—"

I reached over and grabbed the parrot's head and crushed it.

Weezie Bednarik shrieked, *"Ouch!"*

Sad, genuinely contrite, Zelda said, "Roger, I'm sorry. I don't know what gets into me. I understand Gretal is a lovely human being. I also realize she is not a threat to me or us, and she is an important person in your life. I know you two love each other, it's platonic, and you should. Deep inside, I respect that—honest. In fact, I envy you the closeness you guys have shared. Also, I love you with all my heart, which means I care for the important people in your life. All the rest of it, when I flare, is bullshit. Vestigial crap. I don't know why I can't stop myself, but I can't. It just boils up like the Creature from the Black Lagoon, impossible to derail. I can't fathom what's wrong with my brain. It's like a monster from my heart scrambles the circuits inside my skull."

She kissed me so tenderly I almost swooned.

I kissed her back.

The moment was as nice as silk.

To tell the truth, however, by then my thoughts were pretty scattered. In particular, the work was going nowhere. In my more lucid moments I realized that I had arrived up Shit Creek without a paddle.

The IRS hungered for its bread. Only by a miracle could I finish *Perseid* by January first. Zane Adams was due December tenth. The entire *Catacombs* first draft had a February fifteenth deadline. And the minute, and I do mean the exact minute—12:01 A.M., November fourteenth—that my preview pages were due for Jack Muncie's perusal, Don Perry and Faye Crane and God knows who from Zeppo–Cavett would be on the phone, calling in those chits.

And those chits are the kind you had better deliver if you ever wanna work in Hollywood again.

But this was starting to happen. I would be sitting at the laptop, working on *Catacombs*, when suddenly I'd realize that Zane Adams had been spouting dialogue for six pages. Or a Trogon from *Perseid Meteor Thugs* would appear in *Catacombs* and promptly sabotage three pages of what was less than stellar prose in the first place. Or some minor dwidget, like Peraclifuss, the Aeleron Dwarf from *Catacombs*, would begin writing an irate letter to Zelda about her grotesque friend Weezie Bednarik.

I threw up my hands and screamed.

The dog came snuffling around the office door, whining and scratching, wanting to make sure I was all right.

I told him to shut up, leave me alone, go away.

He slunk off into the night.

Soon enough Don Perry's cheerful ersatz-English-aristocrat voice was saying, "Hey, Roger, guess what day tomorrow is?"

This is the truth: I hadn't the foggiest.

"November first," he informed me.

I said, "Oh." My guilt meter clicked through twenty-seven different obligations and deadlines, but came up empty-handed. So I added, "It's the day before the Day of the Dead."

Don said, "Correction, friend. It's the day Jack Muncie would love to see those pages."

I said, "You said November fourteenth."

"At the latest," Don reminded me. "Faye Crane called this morning. She said Jack's on pins and needles. Lorimar just came up with a killer project they're filming on the French Riviera. You know Jack, he's been a sucker for those frogs ever since his affair with Jacqueline Monet during the *Monaco Moonlight* shoot. Lorimar is flexible, but Jack needs to know. He thinks Sidney Bard could out-Connery Sean Connery of James Bond fame *if* it clicks, but you know how fickle this industry is. What've you got that's showable?"

"Let's compromise," I begged. "Gimme eight more days."

"Six," Don said.

"Seven, I'll throw in a pair of hedge clippers, and that's my final offer."

"Sold," he chuckled, and we had a deal.

Zelda proclaimed, "You're letting them kill you with stress."

"Baby," I said, "if we weren't fucking six times a day, having an extended brawl every week, and talking it all out at least five hours a day, meeting any one of these deadlines would be a lead-pipe cinch."

"Oh, that's a real low blow," she retorted. "Blaming me for your professional shortcomings. I haven't put any demands on you that you haven't asked for. It takes two to tango. You know you're free to do as you please."

"I'm sorry," I said, reaching for her neck. "I'm a little edgy, that's all. Don't take it personal."

She smiled and reached for my crotch. I pried off her fingers. "Uh, listen, sweetheart, not now. I better go out to work."

"Just five minutes," my wife entreated. "I'll miss you so much when you're gone."

Three hours later I typed:

FADE IN:

EXT. SHEA STADIUM, FLUSHING MEADOWS, N.Y.

The Trogon starship begins lowering down for a landing directly upon the pitcher's mound.

Then I pushed aside the laptop, folded my arms on the desk, laid my head on that pillow, and vociferously began cutting Z's.

"Wake up, Roger." Softly, Zelda jabbed my shoulder. "It's okay, you're only dreaming."

I opened my eyes. It was later afternoon. I had been taking a nap. Zelda said, "Listen to this from Marge Piercy." And she went positively glassy-eyed with rapture:

> *This morning we must make each other strong.*
> *Change is qualitative: we are*
> *each other's miracles.*

Zelda closed the book and said, "What do you think of that?"

"It's beautiful. I love you."

"How much between one and ten?"

Without hesitation I said, "A thousand."

She kissed me and hugged me, then nuzzled her head

into that space between my neck and shoulder, saying, "Te quiero one thousand, too."

Inevitably, we had our final toe-to-toe concerning Gretal.

This one commenced at three A.M., when I was sound asleep. Zelda shook my shoulder. She jabbed it hard, and shouted, "Wake up, you cocksucker!"

My eyes flew open, I rolled out of bed, ran to her dresser, yanked open the lingerie drawer, grabbed a loaded thirty-eight revolver Zelda always kept hidden under a dozen Brazilian-cut panties, dropped into a crouch by the window, and barked, "What? Who is it? Where?"

I had the distinct impression a burglar was looting the kitchen and our house was under siege.

Zelda said, "Put that away, you idiot. You were talking in your sleep."

"Oh." Long pause. I returned the weapon to its hiding place. "What did I say?"

"You said, 'Gretal, I can't steer this boat.' "

I climbed back into bed. "What do you suppose that means?"

"It means I've had it with that sob-story hypochondriac," Zelda said. "I think it's an insult the way you two carry on. I'm humiliated in the eyes of this whole town, and I won't take it anymore. The next time you visit that woman, I'm calling Douglas to arrange a date. Two can play this game, you know."

I said, "Zelda, she's crippled. She's been a dear friend over the years. There is no hanky-panky, nothing. Gretal is even too sick to eat half the time."

"I don't care," said my wife. "It's high time I changed my ways to jibe with your constant breaches of faith."

That irked. "I don't give a fuck *what* you do," I replied, "just so long as you let me sleep."

Zelda bounced from the bed, threw off her shorty night-gown, tugged on a pair of jeans, knee-high boots, and a tight pullover, and headed toward the door.

"Hey," I mumbled, "Where do you think you're going?"

"You don't give a fuck," she tossed backward, "just so long as you get some sleep."

Boing! I catapulted into a wide-awake state. And listened to the car door slam, the engine start, and the usual furious wheel wrenching and tire spinning as she maneuvered to turn around. *K-blomp bomp!* went her underside, banging against the high center of our driveway as Zelda yet again displayed her anger by ricocheting violently off into the blackest night.

For about an hour I lay awake reading her a massive riot act in my head. But I was deep in morphinic ruminations by the time Zelda returned and crawled in beside me, glued her lips to my male member, and made me climax, still half asleep, into her marvelously convulsing gorge.

Gretal moaned, "I can't believe you're letting her do this to us."

"You and I are not an 'us' anymore," I explained. "Zelda and me are the couple, now. We're the 'us.'"

"We have a longtime friendship," Gretal said. "Doesn't that mean anything to you?"

"It means everything to me," I assured her. "But if we keep it up, it'll wreck my marriage."

"Fuck your marriage," Gretal said. "I can't believe you're turning into such a toady."

"I live with her," I explained patiently. "I spend all my days with her. She's my lover, my future, my main emotional and intellectual and sexual investment."

Boy, that sounded trite.

John Nichols

Gretal said, "I can't believe we can't remain good friends."

I said, "I'll always love you, you know that. It's just that things change. Maybe when Zelda feels more secure, she'll lighten up. But until then—"

"I hate it when you parrot that bitch," Gretal hissed. "When did your spine turn into Jell-O? I thought you had more character than this."

"I am not parroting her," I said. "It just makes sense, is all. Picture yourself in her place. This is my town. It's my house. You and I lived together in that house. Bonnie and I lived together in that house. Megan and Sandra and Christie and all the others spent time in that house."

"Spare me the rogue's gallery, okay Roger?"

I ignored that. "So she has to claim the house for her own," I explained. "And I don't blame her. It's her way of eradicating the ghosts. Establishing her own identity. If you or I were in her position, I bet we'd act the same way."

Gretal said, "What happens if you kill off everybody you loved? What about Bonnie? What about your kids?"

She made me real uncomfortable. I didn't want her to be a confidante anymore. What if, in a fit of pique, Gretal called up Zelda or wrote her a letter detailing how she and I had analyzed the marriage together?

"This is a new love," I explained patiently. "Time marches on. We can't cling to the past. At some point it's healthier to let go. The past is an intrusion. You have to quit playing old tapes."

"I am *not* an old tape." Gretal stared out the window for a minute without speaking.

Then she said, "I thought you would always be my friend."

"I will," I said. "This'll blow over. In the meantime, you know I'll always love you."

"How?" she asked. "You won't deliver my mail anymore. You made me get another box. You can't come and

124

see me. We're not allowed to have dinner together once in a while. So what's it gonna be, connecting with each other by ESP?"

I said, "As soon as she gets her sea legs, I'm sure Zelda will quiet down. You won't be a threat anymore."

"Did I ever ask you to butcher any of your other friendships?" Gretal asked.

"You told me you were a one-man woman and expected me to be a one-woman man in exchange," I said.

"That was just about fucking, Roger. Nothing else. Did I shit all over Bonnie?"

"No. You were real friendly." Then I remembered, "But you wanted to be married. You made me divorce Bonnie."

"Did I push marriage after you got cold feet?"

No, not at all. But she sure had gone bananas when Christie showed up and spirited me away.

"A woman's allowed to fight for her man," Gretal said quietly.

"I guess that's what Zelda is up to," I replied.

"When it was over, after Christie won, did I keep on beating a dead dog?"

"No ma'am, you didn't."

In an odd, remote mood, Gretal said, "I feel sorry for both of you. It's funny to hear myself say that, but I do. I feel sorry for Zelda. She's only going to wreck it in the end."

The way Gretal said this wasn't bitter or vindictive, it was poignant and melancholic.

"Now, get out of here, Roger. I don't ever want to see you again." Her eyes were bright with tears.

I hesitated. I told her I loved her. Gretal turned her head toward the window and waved me away with her hand.

I felt creepy, discombobulated. I wanted to say something mean. Like remind Gretal that she'd had five husbands, a zillion lovers. She'd walked out on a lot of people. She had always done it her way.

But I said nothing. I simply slunk away, leaving my pal forever. I can't explain how weird that made me feel. Fragile, embarrassed, also self-righteous. Gretal was no innocent in the game of love. Game? War is more like it, don't you think?

Things weren't stressful enough, so Kim came for a visit.

She took a bus up from Bonnie's house in the capital.

As soon as my daughter walked through the kitchen door, her eyes went lubbering around the room, then her face screwed up into one of those pained adolescent pouty spoiled-rotten sneering expressions I have learned to loathe, and she whined:

"Hey, Daddy, where's all the stuff that was on the fridge?"

The "stuff" consisted of about three dozen funky snapshots of the Little Fur Family in various stages of our usual demonic pranks, making goofy faces, hugging each other drunk at birthday parties, dancing to heavy-metal sado-masochistic punk-rock music, and so forth—use your imagination.

After Zelda had finished with the fridge (during our honeymoon barn-raising week), not a fingerprint or a tape mark remained.

I explained to Kim, "Ah, that crap was so curdled, a dozen spiders and silverfish were living in it."

Kim asked, "Where's that picture of me and Woody giving you the finger?"

I said, "Hey, Kim, lighten up. Things change. It was time to clean up this place."

"What happened to Big Al?"

"We set him free."

"Good. I hated that yucky spider. Where's my glamorous graduation photo?"

"It's outside in the writing tower."

"You don't work in the house anymore?"

"Zelda and I *live* in the house, sweetie. Now gimme a hug."

As we embraced and Kim said, "I love you, Daddy," Zelda walked in.

"Hi Kim," Zelda said in a chipper, frosty tone that made my scrotum shrivel.

"Hello Zelda," Kim answered, equally icy.

I reached for the Maalox bottle.

At her first opportunity that night, Zelda said, "I suppose it's none of my business, but don't you think Kim is a little old to be calling you Daddy?"

And the next thing my wife said was "Frankly, watching you two together is almost like observing incest in action."

I said, "Excuse me?" I wasn't sure I had heard correctly.

Zelda said, "It seems you two have a sexual thing together. She crawls all over you. Frankly, it's a little embarrassing."

I still couldn't twig. "What do you mean?"

"I mean, and I know you may not be aware of this, but it appears as if she wants to fuck you, and vice versa."

I said, "We've always hugged each other in this family. I like physical warmth. I grew up in a puritan Hell where nobody touched. I shook hands with my stepfathers. I called them 'sir.' "

"I know all about your puritan upbringing, Roger, thank you very much."

"Well, I don't understand." I was stalling for time. When

127

Zelda had me flustered, my brain shut down, hence I always wound up stalling for time.

She said, "Kim is fifteen. It's different at fifteen than it is at ten. Maybe it's time for her to grow up. At some point she *has* to grow up. We all do. Right now I think you mollycoddle everybody. You let them manipulate you. Sometimes you seem afraid to mature out of your own adolescence. And, in a family, that can make for mixed signals, emotional confusion."

I said, "I've always had a comfortable relationship with my children."

Zelda backed off a little, mellowed her tone, and tried a different tack. "Roger, please don't tense up. I'm not blaming you, honest. I'm trying to give you observations that might be helpful, that might help *us*. Don't you see?"

Her eyes got a truly sincere, pleading look. I could tell she was trying desperately hard to reach me.

"I want to be part of your family," Zelda said. "And I want you to be a part of mine. I want us all to relate to each other. I want us to understand and *care* about and *value* each other."

Here's an observation I have made about people and language, hearing and interpretation, the Art of Communication. You will be face to face with your spouse or with somebody important—a Significant Auditor—trying to "explain." You will make a superhuman effort to be compassionate, articulate, and intelligent as you speak about things very crucial to both of you. Of course, the subject matter is controversial. The person facing you will hopefully and lovingly strain forward, eager to accept and understand your words. These words will exit from your mouth like a flock of tiny, dazzling butterflies, shimmering with good intentions. In almost a dreamlike fashion, they will flutter across the space between you, heading toward your Significant Auditor's ears. But at the last instant before the insects actually enter those ears, something incredible happens. The butterflies transform miraculously into slimy newts, fat toads, and feces-covered salamanders, and they zip down the Significant Auditor's ear canals out of sight.

The Auditor's eyes adopt a somewhat puzzled, slightly abandoned look. And though you, the Speaker, sort of understand what is happening (or *not* happening, as the case may be), you can't quite believe it. So you fire off more butterflies, sometimes entire migrating flocks of the pretty little rascals, but not *one* escapes that Kafkaesque metamorphosis that inevitably occurs at your beloved's ears.

Finally, he or she—the Significant Auditor—starts explaining back to you. And you marvel as his or her words, in the shape of flower blossoms, rubies, and autumn maple leaves, start on their simple voyage toward your compassionate brain.

Unfortunately, these treasures enter your head as little pieces of bat shit, stale bread, and pit-run gravel.

You can actually *see* it happening.

But no matter how hard you try, you cannot *do* anything about it.

Well, right now that was happening between me and Zelda. I know she wanted me to comprehend, accept, learn, give positive feedback. But all I could hear was the word *Incest! Incest! Incest!* repeated repeatedly in my fuddled noggin.

Finally, I interrupted my wife.

I said, "What do you mean, 'incest'?"

Zelda looked perplexed. " 'Incest'?"

"You said Kim and I were like 'incest' together."

"Actually, Roger, I said, 'Watching you two together is *almost* like observing incest in action.' "

"There," I said. "See what I mean?"

Zelda said, "I didn't mean actual incest, sweetie. I was just making a point."

"It sounded like actual incest to me." I said. "You *said* the word 'incest,' didn't you?"

Zelda's shoulders slumped. "But I didn't mean *incest*, Roger. It was only a figure of speech—"

And we continued like that, parrying each other's salamanders, bat shit, and pit-run gravel, well into the wee small hours.

The discussions between Zelda and me were like quicksand. They sucked us under. They built a momentum of their own. Often they were rich, complicated, exciting. Sometimes they weren't.

"At least I don't kid myself about my mistakes," Zelda said.

"Bonnie wasn't a mistake," I said. "Nor are Woody and Kim. Just because things don't work out like Pollyanna doesn't mean they're mistakes."

Zelda said, "You told me that a year after you got married you were secretly buying *Playboy* magazines and jerking off on the sly. You used to wander around New York staring into the windows of topless go-go joints so horny you could die. You admitted the two of you were so afraid of confrontation that you never showed anger to each other, you just let everything fester inside. You told me—"

Suddenly, I sneezed.

Zelda suggested that I was being dishonest for sticking up for Bonnie and my kids and for caring for Megan and Christie and Gretal and all those other "bitched" relationships I'd enjoyed. She thought I was in denial; she felt I had a lot of repressed hostility.

I told Zelda that Bonnie and I had a code: Never speak ill of the other in front of the children. We really felt a loyalty toward each other.

Zelda pricked up her ears. "But that's so phony," she said, "don't you see? It's such a hypocritical loyalty."

"Why should I speak ill of Bonnie if I don't *feel* ill toward her?" I said defiantly.

"You were walking around lusting after go-go girls, that's your idea of loyalty?"

I asked, "How come you always twist everything I say?"

"Twist? I'm just repeating what you told me."

"But you change everything," I fumfered helplessly. "You make my whole past life seem . . . tacky or something. You make me not want to be honest with you ever again."

When she caught the full impact of the pained look on my face, Zelda abruptly softened. It's hard to describe the effect of those sudden transformations: they were almost apocalyptic. I have been in snowstorms when all at once the sun began shining. I have been sweating terrified inside storm-tossed airplanes when they skidded into a totally calm atmosphere. And I once found myself, five minutes after a Times Square New Year's Eve hullabaloo, gently kissing a lazy girlfriend in an otherwise empty Park Avenue penthouse to the strains of a João Gilberto–Stan Getz record.

Zelda gave me a funny, melancholy little smile and clasped my hand between her palms.

She said, "Oh Roger, you poor baby. I'm sorry, don't look so hurt. I appreciate the honesty, I really do. I know you're trying hard. I must be impossible."

"I feel like you're always attacking me," I whimpered. "I wish you'd cut me some slack."

"I feel like *you're* always attacking *me*," she stated quietly. "And where's *my* slack?"

That surprised me. I said, "But I never attack you. I'm not volatile like you. I mean hardly ever. Or at least . . ."

Gently, Zelda said, "Roger, there are as many different ways to attack a person as there are stars in heaven."

131

* * *

I told Kim, "Listen, baby, I'd really appreciate it if you would call me Dad or Pop or something like that. Daddy sounds pretty childish, don't you think?"

Kim regarded me with a wise, hurt expression.

Then she said, "How can you let Zelda tell me what I'm allowed to call you?"

"It's not Zelda, sweetie, it's me. It's my idea."

"I wish you wouldn't call me 'sweetie,' *Dad*," Kim replied. "It's so totally puerile."

Now where had she learned a word like that?

When Don Perry is concerned about something, he doesn't beat around the bush. The second I picked up the phone, he said, "Hi Roger. Today is November eighth."

The cold harsh fingers of guilt closed tightly around my heart.

I said what I always say: "Oh dear."

Don said, "Send me the pages, *now*."

"Okay, okay, you got 'em."

"How many do I 'got,' Roger?"

"Thirty-five, polished."

"The agreement was sixty."

I said, "Don, I'm sorry, I think I'm having a sort of amateur nervous breakdown."

"Oh I'm so sorry," Don said, all heart. "I'll call Faye Crane and Jack Muncie and Bill Slobin at Zeppo-Cavett and explain your predicament. I'm sure they'll understand."

I groaned, "Sarcasm is the sign of a petty mind. Also a poor imagination."

"If I had imagination, I'd be creating art instead of selling it," Don said.

I rounded up a manila envelope and sent him the pages.

"If you weren't such a patsy," Zelda informed me, "you would tell people like Don Perry where to get off, instead of it always being vice versa."

Wearily I said, "Zelda, do me a favor, fuck off."

She unbuttoned the top three buttons of her green silk blouse, pushed the material down off both shoulders, untucked her breasts from a black French lace bra, squeezed them together, and coyly batted her eyelashes at me.

Oops, there went another novel!

The next time I entered the bank and Christie was at a window, she reached under the counter and handed me, along with my money, a card in a sealed envelope.

I asked, "What's this?"

"I've been saving it for days," she said, "waiting for you to come in. I do miss you, Roger. I miss all the laughter. I'm sorry we can't even be friends. How's it going with the Dragon Lady? Still a barrel of monkeyshines?"

She tilted her head in a funny insouciant mock-innocent way, both teasing and very appealing. Today's outfit was a form-fitting yellow number that gave her cute body a sort of gooey elastic tension. Vaguely I wondered how Christie could get away with that in a bank.

"She's not a dragon lady," I said, leaping to Zelda's defense. "She happens to be a wonderful human being."

Christie nodded, tapped numbers into her computer, smiled demurely, and cracked her gum.

"You don't have to be bitchy," I whimpered.

"Well, I hate this," she grumbled cheerfully. "I'm supposed to pretend I don't know you or something? After all we've been through? Don't forget, you promised. And now you act like I've got leprosy, and that bugs me. It isn't fair. You don't even act civilized with me anymore. Take your stupid money, then make like a breeze and blow. You give me indigestion right *here*."

She placed her little hand fetchingly over her right breast.

I said, "Hey, I'm sorry, it isn't personal. I'm just trying to keep things on an even keel. I—"

I felt miserable. Why couldn't Christie and I remain cheerful friends? What gave Zelda the right . . .

Christie smiled vapidly and, glancing beyond my shoulder, said, "Next!"

I backed away, feeling humiliated, the consummate jerk. I couldn't tell who I was more angry at—me? Or Christie? Or Zelda.

In the truck I opened her card. Flowering hollyhocks ranged alongside an adobe wall. The message, in her florid, curlicued scrawl with big *O*'s dotting all the *i*'s, said:

Dear Roger,

This is an honest apology. I'm sorry about sending that letter and all the photographs, that wasn't very nice on my part. I know it must be difficult for you, trying to put a marriage together, and I don't blame you for being gun-shy. In your shoes I would act exactly the same way. So I promise, I won't sass you anymore. And I wish nothing but the best of luck to you. In my less-selfish moments I actually got my fingers crossed, kid, hoping you make it. You deserve the best, you really do. So, please accept my apologies, and listen: if ever I can help you, just as a friend, I hope you'll call on me. I will always care about you.

You're the best!

Christie

Explain this, please. I shoved that card back in the envelope and sat there fuming. What was this goody-two-shoes act, anyway? How could Christie be so reasonable? It made no sense. Was it all an act? For sure it was a much more clever and Machiavellian method of attack than any she'd previously essayed. What was I supposed to do, feel I should've married *her* instead of Zelda, and that way I would have avoided all these headaches?

Ha ha, nice try, Christie, but no dice.

I saw through the whole transparent scheme!

One day Zelda asked, "How's your friend Camille?"

"Camille?"

"The one in the hospital, dying of cancer."

I shrugged, aloof and disinterested. "I dunno. I quit going there. She has other pals who took over."

Zelda said, "I hope you realize that wasn't my decision. I didn't ask you to do that."

I said, "I know, I know. I just thought it was better that way. Less intrusive, if you know what I mean."

She said, "Wait just a minute, here." Zelda gripped my shoulders and looked me straight in the eyes. "She's your friend, and it's none of my business. It's perfectly okay by me if you need to see her."

"I know, I know," I repeated. "Don't worry. If I want to see her, I will."

Yeah, sure, right—and announce it in a full-page ad in the daily paper so Zelda could congratulate me for my humanitarian gestures toward the wretched of the Earth.

"It's just very important you don't have any resentments toward me," Zelda said. "I didn't ask you to cut it off."

"I know. I don't have resentments. I love you."

"It would be very dishonest if you resented me for something I didn't do," Zelda insisted.

"Sweetheart," I reassured, kissing her tantalizing lips, "I understand. And believe me, I don't resent you. In fact, it's kind of a relief, if you wanna know the truth. To be free of that yoke."

Zelda continued scrutinizing my eyes. Finally, very somberly, she said, "Honest—?"

"Honest to God. Cross my heart."

She remained partially unconvinced, however. Also melancholy. "I feel sorry for Gretal," she said. "She used to be a beautiful person. I'm glad you two shared such a wonderful love together."

Two days later, while Zelda was in town shopping for groceries, I dialed the hospital. Awash in guilt, you bet, but I called anyway. They said Gretal had been released. So I phoned the house. A friend of mine, Mimi Jeantete, answered. I identified myself and asked for Gretal.

"She doesn't want to talk to you," Mimi said. And added, "I don't blame her."

"Aw, c'mon, Mimi, quit playing games. Tell her it's me on the phone."

Mimi's hand muffling the receiver. I heard underwater glub-glubbing, then a fumbling.

"Who's this?" Gretal asked.

"Me, Roger. How are you feeling?"

"Roger who?" she asked.

"Excuse me?"

"Roger who?" she repeated.

"Hey, Gretal," I blustered. "Don't be stupid, okay? I want to know how you're doing. I've been worried. How do you feel?"

"Betrayed," she said, and hung up.

You get it coming, you get it going.
Then you die.

Don't forget, I'm a professional writer. I use words to communicate emotions and ideas. I am a pro at verbally stim-
ulating a stranger's imagination. I know all the tricks to
make literary drama serve interactive functions. My books
sell pretty well. People write me letters. They are touched
and intrigued and excited by my prose. Some of them even
consider me wise. Too, they laugh in all the right places.
They also cry on cue whenever I choose to punch *that* particular button.

Like I said, then, I am a professional writer. Words are
my métier. With every sentence I forge a clarity of intent.
That is what drives a story forward.

So please explain to me this: How come words continu-
ally failed me with Zelda?

Here's a phenomenon that started to drive both of us
crazy. I guess you would call it the Ersatz Argument About
Hypothetical Situations.

One I still remember all too vividly goes like this. Zelda
and I have just made love like Mickey Rourke and Kim
Basinger in *9½ Weeks*. We are satiated and happy and
glowing like a couple of little old fireflies in the dewy grass
of a childhood summer evening.

After a spell, Zelda murmurs, "Roger, I love you more
than Eloise adored Abelard. If you ever die, I would be
eternally heartbroken. I'd stay a widow forever. I'd never
go with another man."

I am happy, in love, exuberant, incredibly horny and
alive, and so I reply, "Aw, c'mon, baby, you couldn't live
like a nun. You're a magnificent sexual being. I would *want*
you to find another man."

Zelda replies, "What are you talking about? If *I* died, would you immediately start boffing another woman?"

"Well, not right away," I admit. "But my gosh, look at all the joy this physical hallelujah gives us. Now that we know it's possible, how could either of us live for long without it? There's plenty of fish in the ocean."

Wrong!

Zelda sits up. She is hurt and angry. She says, "You bastard. You mean I'm not dead five minutes, and already you're out there fucking other women?"

"Wait a minute, whoa!" I reach for my darling, drawing her close. "We're not talking five minutes, here, sweetie. Jeepers. Of course I'd be heartbroken. But hey, I've always been a sexual being. You too. It's an important part of our lives."

Zelda squirms out of my arms. "So how long a period of mourning *are* we talking about, Roger, before you turn into an oversexed goat? Ten minutes? Fifteen? Maybe half an hour?"

"Zelda," I blurt, "this is a stupid argument."

She actually has a teardrop clinging to the corner of one eye. She says, "I am humiliated. I can't *believe* you're already plotting to screw another slut the minute I am dead!"

I groan, "Baby, I'm not planning anything. This is a discussion about a hypothetical situation. I never even would've thought of it if you hadn't brought it up. I *love* you."

Too late! Zelda jumps out of bed, snarls, "Fuck you, Roger, you heartless male chauvinist pig," and slams the door on her way out.

"Jack passed," Don Perry said.

I heard the news with dulled senses operating, and dull reactions, too. Zelda and I had talked about our relationship from nine P.M. to three A.M. During the discussion we had made love twice. I had smoked thirteen cigarettes and probably imbibed six ounces of Importer's vodka and one beer. I had also eaten four baloney and Swiss cheese sandwiches (soaked in diet Miracle Whip), an apple, three plums, five carrots, and a half-pint of vanilla Häagen Dazs ice cream.

Interestingly, I was losing weight at the rate of almost a third of a pound daily.

The confab had ended in a stalemate. Basically, Zelda was convinced that I feared all intimacy. I was unwilling to "let go." I knew she was crazy. I did not see why we had to keep beating all these dead horses. Zelda accused me of evading true love. When I remarked, "If this is true love, it hurts," she replied, "No pain, no gain."

I told Don, "I'm sorry." I always remember that he works hard putting the deals together, and when I fuck up, he's out his ten percent.

Don said, "Me too. Fay Crane added that Zeppo-Cavett isn't going to renew the option in January."

The sinking feeling continued. I could have used that bread.

"Well, I guess that's the way the cookie crumbles," said yours truly, Mr. Nonchalance.

"And they're dropping the screenplay as of now."

Oh dear.

Aloud, I said, "They have to pay me off. Twenty-five G's."

"Correction, twenty cents on the dollar," Don said. "It's part of the fine print, section twelve, subparagraph six."

"How much is that?" I asked glumly.

"Five thousand dollars."

"Hmm," I said. "That's a bit less than twenty-five, isn't it?"

"My sentiments exactly."

"I should keep working on the script, though, right? Because somebody is bound to pick it up on turnaround?"

Don said, "I wouldn't bother. If I were you, I'd concentrate on Zane Adams and *Perseid*. Now you'll have more time to whip them into shape."

Miss Firecracker blew her usual fuse. "How can you let them do that to you? That's robbery! Why won't you sue? I can't stand how you let people walk all over you. What a newt. You're not a man, you're a helpless little bunny rabbit. You're a masochist. You *love* it when they trash you, don't you? You never put up a fight. You're like a spineless jellyfish, you *want* to lose. It's incredible. Why don't you sell our house and mail them the money? We can live in the truck and scavenge our food from the Dumpsters behind Safeway. We can butcher the dog and make canine burgers. We can stew the cats and eat them. We can—"

"Basta ya!" I finally flipped. "Fuck you!" I hollered. And though it sure felt awkward, I added, with a veritable spindrift of spittle flying, "Up yours, you no-good uptight bird-brained teeny-weeny witch slut!"

My wife's lower jaw dropped open.

We stared at each other in astonishment.

Then Zelda cracked one of her absolutely radiant and beatific smiles, flung her arms around me, and exalted, "Oh Roger, you tiger, *I love you!*"

At an early point in her life, Megan had been a near Olympic caliber platform diver. But she fractured her right leg badly in an accident and never again reached a comparable plateau. She hailed originally from Biloxi, Mississippi. And used to make us the most incredible oysters bienville.

In her teenage days, Megan had been a local beauty queen. She won a Miss Crawdad Biloxi contest and came in third in a Junior Miss pageant. Then she married young; the guy was a hotshot New Orleans lawyer. Her husband left her for a younger woman in 1976, and, mostly on her own, Megan raised a son, Buddy, and a daughter, Melissa, by tutoring special-needs children at the grammar-school level.

Megan had a rather subdued yet independent personality. She did not expect much from life, and never took a nickel from me or anybody else. She had a pretty spiffy trailer in an upscale mobile-home park; it was almost paid off. She owned a satellite dish, too, and was addicted to TV, especially the country-and-western music stations. Our lovemaking had never been very smooth. But a tension created by the awkwardness was fairly erotic. Megan worked hard to have a climax; in fact, her orgasms were rare, therefore special. In daily life we never became very close; in bed, we had a strong physical-emotional connection. Sometimes, of an entire evening, we would not talk at all.

I was in the Copy Center faxing tax information to my accountant, Al Fasullo, down in the capital, when Megan came through the door.

I nodded hello, she acknowledged me back. Megan always seemed a trifle pained, and that had always turned me on.

She was wearing a shiny silver blouse, a pleated blue skirt, and sandals.

"I'm sorry about your accident," she said, handing a bundle of papers to Harry Suazo, the kid behind the counter.

"Excuse me? What accident?" I replied.

"I visited Gretal on Wednesday. She said you had been in a terrible head-on collision."

And then—get this, folks—Megan actually giggled!

When the balloon festival came, Zelda wanted to go up and float around the valley. I told her she was nuts. "Those things catch on fire," I said. "They hit telephone wires. They topple into rivers."

"Please spare me your paranoia, Roger. You talk like a little old lady. I married a church mouse."

We wound up in a balloon with Heckle and Jekyll the talking crows painted on it, sponsored by Moe Bubbles, owner of Bubbles Galore Pre-Used Foreign Autos.

In the basket were me, Zelda, Moe, Weezie Bednarik, and the hand puppet Adrian.

When I'm working and on a roll, I go to bed at four A.M. But balloons rise at dawn. Needless to say, I was exhausted. I couldn't stop yawning.

It was a frosty sunny morning. Moe was wearing an old bomber jacket, sun goggles, a sheepskin aviator's hat, and a silken ascot.

I had on a blue knitted cap, my Jordache Hollofill jacket, and a pair of TG&Y moon boots.

Weezie Bednarik could have passed for a Polish machine gunner on the Russian front in the winter of '42.

Zelda was resplendent in a pink ski cap (with tassles), Lolita sunglasses, a Levi's jacket over her white Scandinavian turtleneck sweater, skin-tight dungarees, knee-high high-heel musketeer boots, and psychedelic Peter Max mittens.

Guess whose balloon crew the *Sentinel-Argus* photographer, Cathie Moon, decided to feature?

I was scared.

But Weezie Bednarik was petrified.

Moe puffed on his cigar and sneaked little sips from a silver flask he kept in his back pocket.

Zelda blew a final kiss into Cathie's 80–200 zoom, and we lifted off.

Whenever Moe sent a blast up the balloon's innards, I shit a ten-pound brick.

Zelda giggled, seemingly fearless.

By the time we had attained an altitude of fifty feet, Weezie was hunkering in a corner, ashen-faced and babbling.

"I hate this," Adrian scrawked. "This is crazy. It's your fault, Roger, you forced me to come along against my will."

"Weezie, this was all Zelda's idea. She made me do it. I never even talked to you."

"You planned it," the parrot said. "You made her ask me. You love to see Weezie suffer. You're a cruel man and you're going to roast in Hell when it's over."

Moe passed the flask to Zelda, who touched the mouth to her pursed lips, allowing a trickle of elixir to enter her precious orifice. Then she said, "If I remember correctly, Roger, it was you who originally said we should go up in this balloon, right?"

"I never," I said. "You know I'm terrified of flying."

Our big garish bubble drifted along with about two dozen other big garish bubbles as Zelda replied, "Correct me if I'm wrong, Moe, but when we were at the movies last week and you mentioned the Balloon Fiesta, didn't Roger sing, 'Take me aloft, Moe, in your beautiful balloon'?"

"I was *singing*," I protested. "I was deliberately being stupid. Nobody could've taken me seriously."

Our basket lurched. I was terrified to move. I feared we might upset the gondola. Weezie Bednarik's eyes were squeezed tightly shut.

Zelda asked, "Why didn't you say anything then, Roger, when this was being set up?"

"I didn't want to spoil the fun," I admitted. "It was important to support something you wanted to do."

I couldn't look at Zelda, however. I was too busy being scared. By now I knew for a fact that we would soon bump into a neighbor, our lines would tangle, and we'd plummet screaming down to Earth, trailing two hundred feet of flame.

Moe hit the gas lever, I jumped out of my socks, and Adrian the hand puppet began reciting Ave Marías in Spanish: *"María, madre de Dios, ruega pa' nosotros pecadores . . ."*

Zelda removed her cap and sunglasses, leaned forward, and peered at me. "That is so *bogus*," she said. "That is so damn dishonest it's not even *funny*. See how you twist everything? First you suggest we go up in a balloon. But you're terrified. And you keep your mouth shut, which is the same as lying. And no doubt right now you're blaming *me* for your discomfort even though I had nothing to do with it."

Struggling to keep my cool, I said, "Look, sweetie, I'd just as soon not talk about this right here, right now, okay? I can't concentrate. I'm sort of terrified."

Zelda jerked upright, stamped her foot, and gestured angrily toward Moe. In fact, her arms began flailing. The gondola fluttered and swayed a bit. Weezie went *"Eeep!"* and vomited on my ankles.

Then Zelda hollered, "You heard him, Moe, you're a witness. You can't deny that it's wrong to keep quiet and then blame others for the consequences of your own reticence, can you?"

"Zelda," I whimpered, "please stop jumping around."

She barked, "I am not 'jumping,' Roger, I am just pissed off."

Feeling totally petrified and insane, I blew it completely. I screamed, *"I'll give you a million dollars in cash if you'll just calm down until we reach the ground again!"*

Meanwhile, Woody became a problem.

Back in October the lawyer had gotten him off with six

months' probation and ten hours of community service. But then Woody flunked four out of five midterm exams and decided to hell with it. So he came home. Not to Bonnie's pad down south, no sirree. Those two did not, repeat *not*, get along.

That left my happy domicile as his refuge of choice.

Correction, *our* happy domicile.

Woody was six feet two inches tall. But he weighed only about eleven pounds, even in his Doc Marten combat boots. The lad was scrawny. He had acne, and a Mohawk haircut dyed chartreuse. Day-Glo chartreuse. When in the presence of adults, Woody tended to communicate using pig grunts and other related noises.

I had always gotten along great with my son. Like I said, our house did not have many rules. Except you weren't allowed to play sadomasochistic heavy-metal punk-rock music at full volume if I was present and working or in any condition short of comatose.

Other than that, for years we had lived in a sort of anarchic paradise. I bought food; Woody and Kim fed themselves and came and went at will. Nobody washed dishes or cleaned house or made beds or put the records back in the album jackets or cleaned the tub after bathing.

Of course, by the time Woody slunk home to take up residence, the old humble adobe had been miraculously transformed by Zelda.

I picked the kid up at the bus station, and as I piled his duffel bags, paper sacks, filthy knapsack, cardboard cartons, and Stratocaster guitar into the back of the pickup, Woody sullenly pouted his angular frame into the front seat and folded his arms gloomily, stoically, grudgingly.

He was wearing a black leather jacket with a skull and crossbones and the Harley-Davidson logo in back. His shitkickers were falling apart. He seemed worn out, sapped of all energy. The way Sid Vicious might've played Quasimodo down on his luck.

Even before I started the engine, I said, "Listen, bro'— some changes have occurred at home."

He smiled and nodded like a senile teenage zombie.

"The house is all spruced up," I explained.

Woody smiled and nodded again.

"Spiffy rugs on the floor," I continued. "New tiles in the bathroom. The kitchen is all repainted."

He asked, "Are the spiderwebs gone?"

Real jocular, I said, "Of course. Are you kidding?"

"Even Big Al?"

Feigning comical chagrin, I smiled and shrugged. "Yup, even Big Al."

He smiled vapidly.

I got to the point. "Zelda and I feel it'd be an intrusion for us all to live together in the house. It's too small, and we need our privacy. So what we did is we fixed up one of the sheds for you. I bought a little TV at Wal-Mart. It'll make you independent of us."

"Except for shitting, pissing, and eating food?"

"Right. Of course, you can always pee in the field."

Woody smiled vacantly and nodded amicably.

"I know I don't have to say this," I said, "but Zelda likes things to be clean and orderly. She's not like we used to be, thank God. She wants people to respect each other, and I agree. Everyone must participate in the household chores. You know, like wash dishes, mop the floor, sweep, chop wood, stuff like that. Any sane family operates like that. It's called Being Grown-up."

Eyes glazed, idiotic grin frozen on his features, Woody nodded vigorously. "Sure, no problem."

My floundering boy lasted about three weeks before I had to give him the heave. I could see it coming about ten minutes after his arrival. He stashed his belongings in the shed, then hit the kitchen for food. Zelda and I were having our post-jogging drinks and hors d'oeuvres. Pachabel's "Canon" was on the living-room tape player.

Perhaps I should describe our kitchen after Zelda's redecoration efforts.

It was white and spotless and odorless.

The old linoleum had been ripped up. The wooden floors had been sanded, stained, polyurethaned. Spice racks over the sink bulged with bottles of herbs and delectable seasonings. The stove—? You couldn't find a smudge on it. Hanging wicker and macramé baskets held garlics and onions and little red potatoes. Everything had its proper place in the refrigerator, where an open box of baking soda suppressed vile odors.

An Irish linen cloth covered the table; a cut-flower centerpiece was flanked by two candles in pretty ceramic holders. Zelda adored flowers. I spent a fortune and loved every blossom.

In cheerfully decorated clay pots on the windowsills and counters grew chives, basil, aloe-vera plants, paperwhites.

The old indestructible metal chairs I'd had for a millennium had been replaced by fragile walnut lattice-back antiques. You would be shot, garroted, gassed, hung, or slowly dismembered by Zelda's rapier tongue if you ever dared to tilt back even slightly on one of those hooky-mooky chairs.

Mexican calaveras, Frida Kahlo retablos, and paper flowers decorated spaces on the walls and atop the refrigerator.

The once-tacky Formica countertops had been transformed by bright blue-and-white tiles imported from Italy.

Into this *Better Homes and Gardens* kitchen steps Joe Schmoe, the Homeless Mutant Serial Killer, otherwise known as my son Woody.

* * *

I'm sitting there in my sweats. Zelda is gorgeous in a mauve T-shirt, white short-shorts, and a pair of high-heel sandals.

Woody enters dressed like a nightmare creepy creature feature from Hell. He grunts in our direction, opens the refrigerator, and removes a beer. He twists off the cap, which clatters onto the floor. Then he proceeds to burglarize the fridge of everything in it, including Zelda's last carton of diet strawberry yogurt, her lone organic apple, and the final two slices of last night's spinach quiche.

Plus a half baguette soaked in garlic that I'd been planning to heat up for tonight's repast.

After that, Woody snags a newspaper from the table, mutters, "See you guys," and departs for the living room, where he can devour his winnings in front of our twenty-one-inch TV, instead of out in the shed where his tiny Wal-Mart special sits on a trunk at the foot of his bed.

Raucous strains from a zealous metal screamer on MTV reverberate into the kitchen, drowning out Pachabel's "Canon."

Zelda rises, bends over, retrieves the bottle cap, and drops it disdainfully into the garbage.

"Hey Woody," I call, "turn that thing down a little, would you?"

He shouts back, "Why? You're not working, are you?"

In the old days—? No sweat.

I would have screamed at Woody. "Hey, put that yogurt back, I'll kill you, it's mine! Don't touch that newspaper, I haven't read it yet! Pick up that bottle cap, schmuck, where were you brought up, in a barn?"

And so forth.

But somehow, with Zelda present, the atmosphere did not allow for that type of rowdy banter. It was *presumed* we would all act civilized. Woody had just committed about eleven cardinal sins in thirty seconds. The magnitude of his transgressions was beyond solution.

Actually, I was so embarrassed for the kid that I couldn't kvetch.

Zelda remained absolutely silent, reading every single word of a *New Yorker* article without comment. I did the same in a *Vanity Fair*. Woody soon grew bored, zapped the boob tube, said, "G'night, dudes," and shuffled off into whatever weird galaxy he inhabited.

I excused myself, followed him out to the shed, and tried to explain the situation.

Woody said, "If you didn't like it, why didn't you say something?"

"I should have, I'll admit. It's just that you're supposed to know enough not to be that rude in the first place."

"I've always been a slob," he said. "You have, too."

"I know, I know. But it's different now. You can't be so dense you didn't notice. It's not sauve qui peut anymore. It's a totally different atmosphere."

"I don't like it," Woody said. "Too harsh. It feels dumb. Like, grown-up."

That pissed me off. "Hey, Woodrow, it's my life, my wife, my house. I earn the money, I pay for everything. You're a guest. The free ride is over, kid. Soon as you get a job, you need to contribute to household expenses. You're not in college anymore."

"Whose idea was that?" he asked. "Hers?"

"No, actually, mine." Which was the truth.

"Bull-fucking-shit," Woody said.

I *hate* confrontation. "Hey, come on, it should be easy," I pleaded. "Watch your language, have a little respect. Wash the dishes every now and then, take out the garbage. Be polite to Zelda. Volunteer yourself. Ask her if there's anything you can do to help around the place. That's all it takes. Simple human courtesy."

"Okay," he grumbled. "I guess you're right. I'll give it a shot."

Bonnie called.

Zelda answered.

Bonnie said, "Lemme speak to Woody, please."

Zelda, who knew damn well who was calling, said, "And who shall I say is calling?"

"His mother." Bonnie sculpted all three syllables out of icicles.

Zelda banged down the phone, marched out to my happy little writing tower, and knocked on the door. "That rude bitch wants to talk to Woody," she said.

I glanced up, totally fuddled. Sidney Bard was at the end of a silver thread, dodging a flotilla of meteorites just outside the planet Zargnut's orbit in the Diatron Galaxy, on his way to solving yet another ridiculous, campy, interstellar gangster sub-plot episode.

The tone of my lady brought both yours truly and Sidney instantly back to Earth.

"Yell at him," I said. "He's probably out there watching *Deep Throat* on his VCR."

"You yell at him, Roger."

She stormed off to the house, ass twitching.

I hollered. Woody shuffled in to the telephone. Half an hour later he slouched back to his vile pad.

Immediately thereafter, Zelda appeared at my office door.

"We have to talk."

"Let's do it in the kitchen," I said.

The kitchen is where we keep the liquor. I poured a triple Blackjack and lit a cigarette.

"Okay, honey, shoot."

Neither Jimmy Cagney with a tommy gun, nor Michael

Jordan with a basketball, nor Wayne Gretzky with a hockey puck could have had a truer aim.

"I am sick and fucking tired of that 'person' calling up here and not even having the civility to identify herself or acknowledge my name," Zelda said. "Whether you or she or your son realize it or not, this is also *my* house, and I will not have it besmirched by that kind of discourtesy."

A sidebar: I could always see her point. I could also see Bonnie's point. I could even see Woody's points.

What I could not see was a way out of the situation.

I was beginning to understand why nations go to war, and why peace in our time is a ridiculous pipe dream.

What hurt most is I assumed it was all my fault. Somehow my ineptitude, my bungling, my emotional naïveté was responsible for this impasse.

I said, "Zelda, maybe if you went a little out of your way to make Woody and Bonnie feel comfortable, things would be easier."

"Why *me*, Roger? Why is it on *my* shoulders? Why not on *theirs*?"

I said, "You haven't exactly been all that friendly."

Wrong statement.

"Me?" I'm afraid Zelda actually turned purple. "Why am I supposed to grovel in front of you dysfunctionals? How come the onus always falls on me? What about you? What about your ex? What about that irresponsible slob you call your son? What is *your* obligation in all this? Have you asked her to be a little civil toward *me*, huh? Have you? Don't bother answering, you spineless jellyfish. Well, listen buster, and listen carefully. I'm telling you this for the last time. I am your wife. Not her. This isn't her house anymore, *I* live in it. I share it with you. And that kid hasn't lifted even one finger to help around here. So how come he gets all the benefit of the doubt? How come Bonnie gets all the benefit of the doubt? Huh? *What about me?"*

I wilted. I didn't blame Zelda one bit. She was correct. I put my hands over my face, blanked out, and just sat there in a miserable stupor.

Tick tock, tick tock, went the clock.

Then the refrigerator hummed.

Suddenly, incredibly, Zelda broke down and started crying.

I mean real crying.

I mean from deep down, from the heart, from wherever it is that all the defenses are totally flabby and you feel lost and so humiliated it seems the only logical solution is to die.

It sure caught me by surprise.

Zelda dropped all the masks, all the armor and chutzpah and hostility in about one second flat.

Her face went blank for a beat. Then it wrinkled up horribly like a time-lapse sequence of aging. Then Zelda bent her face over into her palms and began sobbing.

I stared in shock.

Then I touched her shoulder. "Zelda—"

I didn't understand those floodgates. I was embarrassed for her, and completely confused.

"Baby," I whispered. "Hey Zelda, don't cry."

Hers was a TV-news type of anguish: a widow from Beirut, an earthquake victim in Turkey.

Timeless and gut wrenching.

Awkwardly I put my arm around her shoulder. I said, "Please stop, Zelda. I love you. I'm sorry."

My wife didn't respond. Her hands were messy wet from snot and tears. Her body shuddered with each gasp. She did not look up, or push my arm away, nothing. Just wailed away like a person who's been in mourning for a millennium.

"Zelda, please, I love you with all my heart. I'm really sorry. We'll figure something out."

It scared me. I had never realized she could feel such pain. Zelda was crying like a person who's so damaged they're never going to quit the tears.

Meet Roger, the most useless man on Earth.

In the end I merely sat there, totally ineffectual, awkwardly leaning forward, keeping my arm awkwardly around her shoulders.

Maybe the cry lasted for a good ten minutes, then gradually subsided. Zelda got hold of herself and stopped. She pressed the heels of her hands against her swollen eyes, and sucked in fresh air. I rubbed my palm in nervous soothing circles on her shoulder.

"Are you okay?" I asked.

Talk about inane.

Zelda lifted the skirt of our tablecloth and wiped her face dry. In a dead, empty voice, she remarked, "I feel so lonely I could die."

Then she went to our bedroom. I followed and gently massaged her back. Neither of us could speak.

After a while Zelda fell asleep.

Next day I noticed that the framed *I always win* napkin had disappeared from its spot of honor on the wall.

All right, I confess, I did it again. I couldn't help myself. I thought maybe something Zelda was writing in her novel might give me an insight about her state of mind that would help me become a better husband. Thus, in fear and trembling once more (while Zelda was absent), I crept into our bedroom and opened the file drawer that held her novel, and removed the most recent pages.

They were so bizarre and sad and funny that I almost started crying. The narrator, Samantha, was wandering along a beach picking up seashells. Yet her thoughts dwelled exclusively on suicide. Though ridiculous, her plans were also quite touching. She contemplated ingesting a thousand marshmallows in a single day and dying of gooey congestion. Or running stark naked headfirst against a hornets' nest in order to trigger her bee-sting allergies. Then again, perhaps it made more sense to drive into a black ghetto dressed like a skank prostitute and start shouting racist epithets. Samantha concluded the chapter by deciding it would be easier to get roaring drunk and pilot her Mercedes at eighty miles per hour into a McDonald's restaurant full of Girl Scouts.

Sounds dumb, I know. But the writing was clear and funny and sorrowful, with a delightfully poignant edge. Zelda had a rich imagination, a great feeling for words, and a kind of vulnerable wisdom positively aching with a beautiful despair elucidating her haunting insecurity.

I slunk away from those pages in a state of confusion and alarm. And I swore *never* to intrude on her novel again.

"Bonnie," I said, "you have to make an effort to be friendly with Zelda. I can't deal with you guys hating each other anymore."

Bonnie started sobbing. "We were married eight years," she reminded me. "We had two children together. We've been friends for twenty-two years. In spite of the divorce, we raised the kids together. We never trashed each other. I always got along with your other girlfriends, they got along with me and the kids. You always got along with my other boyfriends, who always got along with you and the kids. No, we haven't screwed in twelve years, but I love you as a friend, and as a coparent, and that connection is important. I don't want to remarry you or fuck you or anything. So why is that woman so uptight?"

"Bonnie," I begged, "I know, I know. But she isn't a louse. She's merely insecure, and frankly, I don't blame her. Everybody is insecure, me included. And I need somebody to be willing to give a little here, that's all. Frankly, I think you are probably the most grown-up, so—"

"So why did you marry an infant?" Bonnie wailed. "Why couldn't you find another grown-up?"

"Bonnie, you're not hearing me."

"You're not hearing *me*, Roger. You're the husband. You're the father. You have rights. That's your house, for Chrissakes. And Woody's. You lived in it for sixteen years before she entered. You own it. You owned it way before she came along. You're generous with everybody. She doesn't even have a job. She should be grateful to you. She lucked into a fucking gold mine. And instead you just sit there while she shits on the mother lode."

"Bonnie, get a grip, okay?"

"*You* get a grip, Roger. I've had it. Good-bye."

Mr. Success. I hung up, grabbed another drink, lit another cigarette, coughed.

Sidney Bard would have zapped all four of us with his Zirkon Detective Special and then, after screwing one of those six-foot amazonian Garfunkle hooker babes from Telestar Z, he would've called it a day.

Nothing worked, however.

Woody was too big, too filthy, too surly, too clumsy.

Finally, he washed the dishes. Afterward Zelda held up a glass. "Look at this," she moaned.

I had to admit it seemed to have been smeared with Vaseline, then rolled through bits of leaves, gum wrappers, and dog shit.

Somehow, every time Woody threw a banana peel at the wastebasket, it missed, but he never noticed.

Instead of using my tube of Crest toothpaste, he always absentmindedly squeezed from Zelda's tube of Uncle Tom's Organic Dental Creme.

Invariably he left smudges of auto-mechanic grease on the tub, refrigerator, counters, and door jambs. And he wasn't even an auto mechanic.

Occasionally I called his attention to these transgressions. But mostly it felt too foolish to bring it up, like chastising a little kid. Zelda was right, he should have known better. Nobody is *that* oblivious.

Inevitably, I trudged out to the shed and said, "I'm sorry, bro', but you gotta split. It's not working."

He grumbled, "That's lame, Dad. I'm trying to stay out of the way."

"I know. But it seems everything you do makes it worse. Go find some buddies, rent a house together, you'll be a lot more comfortable."

"She makes me feel like I'm guilty just for being alive," Woody said. "I can't get motivated." And it broke my heart because I realized he was trying furiously not to cry.

I gave him a hug. And held it a long time. "I'm sorry," I said. "But she's my wife now. And you'll be out of our life pretty soon. You have your own life. You haven't been around much anyway, the past couple of years. It's time you were on your own."

Why did all that sound so pathetic?

Here's another tragedy. I wanted to give Woody a bundle of cash. But Zelda said that would just spoil him more than I'd already spoiled him over the past nineteen years, and I couldn't stand the flak from her if I coughed, so I didn't cough.

Plus I knew she was right.

But jeepers, I sure resented her for making me feel I

couldn't. I resented myself for not being man enough simply to do it on my own.

"He should learn to stand on his own two feet," Zelda said.

I couldn't argue with that.

Woody found a job, at four and a half bucks an hour, shoveling dirt for a gravel company. In about a week he located a crash pad with four other skinheads, and moved out of our shed.

The next day, at Smith's, I bought six bags of groceries and dropped them off at a semi-ruined house from Hell: the Pig Pen. I counted thirty-two beer bottles on the living-room floor before I turned away.

His voice distant and aloof, Woody called, "Thanks."

I felt like committing suicide.

Or maybe murder.

Or just possibly both.

Susan Dice and my friend Margaret the painter were coffee klatching in the Benedictine Café when I morosed in and ordered a sunset almond tea and a lemon square and sat down at their table with a desultory "Hi."

Libby and Debby, the nonidentical twins, in matching pink Communion dresses with butterfly bows in back, were seated at the piano playing "Chopsticks."

Leroy Shanti Bogdanovich was sailing sugar packets back and forth in a huge puddle of cream at the adjacent table.

"Hi yourself," Margaret piped cheerfully.

Susan merely chuckled. "Look what the cat dragged in."

"Not funny, Susan," I groaned theatrically. "Not funny at all. Life is dismal. I am not a happy person."

"What's the matter?" Margaret asked. Then she did this chummy little thing she often does. She reached out and gently pinched my cheek and jiggled it, and said, "Tell Mama everything, my little bubalu."

Can you believe it? Boom! I burst into tears. I mean *burst*. Like all of a sudden, totally of their own volition, hundreds of fat droplets of salty water began splattering from my eyes. Naturally, my features screwed up like Buddy Hacket impersonating an angry carp, so I clapped my hands over my face. But I swear, the tears oozed right between my fingers anyway and fell onto the table with a veritable damp clatter you usually hear only in the movies, when the soundtrack is, like, mega-amplified.

Margaret immediately put her arm around me and said, "Hey, Roger, take it easy, you poor soul."

Susan said, "Wow. Are you okay?"

"No I am not okay!" I wailed, my lips all twisted while bawling.

Debby and Libby quit playing the piano.

Leroy Shanti Bogdanovich threw a spoon at me that missed. It knocked over a vase of paper flowers.

"Take it easy, take it easy," Margaret whispered in her modulated, friendly voice. "It's okay, Roger, really. Tears are good for you. Let it all out, you'll feel so much better."

"No it isn't okay," I blubbered into my palms again. "It stinks. I hate it. I wish I could commit suicide."

"What's the matter?" Margaret urged like a professional shrink full of equanimity. "Tell me about it." She stroked me softly. "Take it easy, baby—gee whiz."

"I kicked out my own kid," I admitted. I don't think I had ever felt so desolate in my life.

"You had to," Susan said. "He's a fuckin' Nazi."

"He's a Nazi?" I yelled at her. "What about that thing over there that sprang from *your* loins?" I pointed—

j'accuse!—at Leroy Shanti Bogdanovich. Who gave me a bland evil eye, then poured more cream into his tabletop lake.

"How can you let him get away with that shit?" I bellowed.

Susan was somewhat taken aback. But she's a quick study and recovered à toute vitesse. "You live in a glass house," she retorted calmly, "so quit throwing stones."

The twins nervously began playing "Chopsticks" again. I growled at Margaret, "Would you please tell those two fucking circus midgets to quit fraying my nerves?"

"Okay, that does it." Margaret's professional shrink act went south. She arose in a huff, dropped a buck tip onto the table, said, "Let's go kids," and booked.

Susan warbled, "Oh Roger, poor Roger, Zelda's hung you in the closet and I'm feeling so sad."

I tottered home and went to work.

But my heart wasn't in it.

The dog came and scratched at the door, so I let him in and he curled up at my feet and went to sleep.

Working on a Zane Adams TV script is like eating meat loaf, wax beans, and powdered potatoes and gravy in a diner called Mom's. It'll keep you alive, but it sure tastes like shit.

Zane Adams is a detective who, believe it or not, has Down's syndrome. Also, believe it or not, he's deaf. He's played by Mort Gibbs, who, believe it or not, is six feet three inches tall, blond and blue-eyed and very muscular. In the series, Mort/Zane is married to Maggie Dykstraw, whose name on the show, believe it or not, is Maggie Pumpernickel. Maggie P. interprets all of Zane's sign lingo and bastardized mumblings when he's not talking to deaf people. When he talks to other deaf people, there are subtitles. The show, believe it or not, is a tad difficult to write.

At the moment in time we're talking about here, the show also has catapulting (cellarward) Nielsen ratings.

I was working on an episode where Zane is attempting to track down the murderer of an Arab translator at the UN who double-crosses the PLO because he's actually in favor of peace with Israel.

He is knocked off, believe it or not, by a Brooklyn hit man, who also suffers from a mild case of Down's.

Because of this, Zane has sympathy for the killer, who, believe it or not, was totally abused as a child because of his handicap.

Zane is also enabled by his own infirmity, believe it or not, to run a psychological profile of the killer, which helps in locating the assassin.

I won't bore you with the rest of this maudlin plot, believe it or not.

Suffice it to say that after ten minutes at work on the show, I started thinking of Zelda.

And, deciding to take the edge off with a quickie, I loped on into the house.

Zelda's Selectric was chattering like a pack of magpies. She wore a flamingo-red T-shirt and denim short-shorts. I sneaked up behind her, slipped my hand in under her armpits, cupped her delectable mams, and nuzzled at the nape of her neck.

Her fingers continued flying over the keys.

I nibbled on her earlobe, unbuttoned the shorts, and slipped my fingers inside.

Tap, tappety tappety tap tap tap.

With my other hand, I sort of nudged her chin, then

curled my index finger up lasciviously over her bottom lip and into her mouth.

She bit the finger real hard.

"Yeow! Jesus *Christ*, Zelda!"

"Jesus Christ yourself," she bleated. "Can't you see I'm working?"

I hopped around on one foot, shaking my finger. "But you're always ready for love," I whined. "You always want a quickie."

She said, "I see, *your* work is all-important. But *my* work is irrelevant?"

The brain is a magnificent instrument, a truly bad-ass computer. In but a tenth of a micromillisecond, mine had added up my projected income ($128,452.60) versus Zelda's projected income ($000,000.00), and it sent to my caustic outrage glands a message, which, fortunately, in another tenth of a micromillisecond, was countermanded by that part of my frontal lobe or medulla oblongata where the Instinct for Survival resides. And I replied, in a tactfully jocular manner, "You interrupt *me* all the time. Yet I'm always amenable."

"That's because you are oversexed. And I always ask first, anyway. And you can always say no. I never take you for granted. But you always take me for granted, and I'm sick of it. I really wish you'd get out of here, now. Maybe I can regain my momentum."

Believe me, I hit the road, Jack.

I went back to Zane Adams.

I wrote a scene where Zane catches his wife, Maggie, ogling the UN ambassador from Tunisia, so he breaks her nose, knees her in the groin, chops her up into little pieces, and grinds her down the garbage disposal.

Then I backtracked, wielded my mouse (whom I call Timothy) like a flamethrower, rubbed it all out, and began again from scratch.

* * *

But I did not advance very far.

Zelda suddenly appeared and pounded on my tower door.

"Whattayou want?" I shouted.

She burst into the room in a rage. "You've got some gall barging in there and disrupting me and then just walking away without so much as a by-your-leave!" she blasted, red in the face and trembling.

"Oh fuck off, Zelda. Leave me alone. Get out of here."

"I will not leave you alone, you pig. You think you're God, and every slut you ever knew treated you like God, but *I* don't think you're God, Roger. I don't even think you're halfway normal. I think you're so used to bullying people and getting your way that you've become a fucking monster control freak!"

I stuck my fingers in both my ears, squeezed shut my eyes, and grimaced.

Zelda grabbed the dog by the scruff of the neck and tried to tug him outside with her. He yelped and braked with his front paws.

"Hey, leave him alone," I said. "He's got nothing to do with this."

"He's my dog," Zelda snarled. "I brought him into this marriage. He always patterned on me. Now you're trying to steal his love and his loyalty and I won't have it. I don't want him sleeping here anymore."

She continued wrestling the poor boob out the door.

"Hey, sic her, boy," I muttered lacklusterly. "Go ahead, big fella, bite her wrist. Gnaw on her ankles. Don't let go."

Guess what?

Nobody laughed.

Guess what else?

Zelda went totally ballistic, released the dog, jumped into

the Subaru, and hightailed it once more for Hell in a bloody handbasket.

"I hope you have a head-on collision!" were the words I flung after her down the potholed driveway.

But later that night, when she returned looking as bedraggled as a wet cat, her breath tainted by booze, Zelda was remarkably contrite.

"I blew it," she admitted, drawing water for tea. "I'm sorry. I hope you can forgive me."

"Sure, of course." I don't know why her apologies always triggered in me a desperate need for expiation in return. So I said, "Actually, *I'm* sorry."

"Why don't you just let me be sorry this time around, Roger, without feeling a need to step on my lines?"

"Oh, sorry," I said, then I blurted, "I mean I'm *not* sorry. I mean—"

Zelda's laughter pealed loudly, and I followed suit.

"You can tie me up and beat me with a birch stick," Zelda said. "I'm so ashamed. I feel so bad. I had no right to be hard on Woody. I feel like I'm some kind of monster, I really do."

"You are not a monster," I protested.

"I get confused," Zelda whispered hoarsely. "I forget your kids aren't my kids. I know the styles are different, but I don't understand how to incorporate them. It's like I froze, or something, over the past twenty years. And now I can't adapt. I get frightened when I'm angry. I'm afraid I'll destroy everything. You must want to escape this trap you fell into. I don't blame you. You must ask yourself a hundred times a day how it could have happened to you."

"No no, I don't. C'mon, please take it easy."

Zelda pointed at the box she'd dropped on the table.

"I bought him a present."

"Who—?"

"Woody. It's a new leather jacket. It has all the proper zippers and metal studs and pocket flaps—the salesman knew exactly what I meant. It cost four hundred dollars."

I whistled.

Zelda stayed up until two A.M. baking chocolate chip cookies and a couple dozen Congo squares.

She wrapped the package in colorful paper, added a ruby ribbon flower and an Ansel Adams card, of Half Dome at Yosemite. In the morning she carried it to Woody in person, on her bike. She apologized for being a harridan and embarrassed him royally in front of his grody pals by giving a hug and saying, "I love you."

Next day (we discovered later), Woody sold the jacket to a buddy for two hundred dollars. Apparently he liked his old shitheap better.

The following Tuesday I'm traipsing along Main Street in a daze when I hear *beep beep beep* behind me, do a fast swivel, and there's Christie behind the wheel of what's left of her VW Beetle.

"Hiya stranger," she piped cheerfully. "How they hanging?"

"You don't wanna know," I said miserably. "Marriage is not a bed of roses."

"Tell me about it."

Christie's first husband had been an animal who beat her just for the fun of it. Hubby number two played around, then dropped dead of a heart attack on the links at thirty-seven. Husband number three was an aerospace engineer whom she had actually walked out on when he voted for Ronald Reagan.

I said, "How you doing?"

She chortled, "Hey, the rent's paid for another thirty

days, and Cazzie didn't slit her wrists last night. Life is a bowl of cherries."

I envied her her freedom.

"But how about you?" she added. "You look a tad blue around the gills."

"Just a momentary setback," I scoffed. "Actually, life couldn't be better."

"I thought guys were supposed to bulk up under a regime of wedded bliss," she teased. "But you look positively anorexic."

"It's a volatile situation."

"Wanna go have a drink and tell me all about it?"

Yeah, I really did. Oh, I had a major yearning to spill the beans to a friend. That would have been so nice. Can you believe it?—a sympathetic *neutral* ear. One thing Christie wasn't was judgmental. She'd hear me out in peace, and with compassion. But suppose an eavesdropping spy like Weezie Bednarik saw us and reported back to Zelda. I was terrified of that. It seemed every time I so much as nodded good day to a woman, any woman, Zelda heard about it and managed to hound my ass.

Small town, small people, no privacy.

"Gee, I'd like to have a drink," I said to Christie, "but I can't."

"Why? What else are you doing that's so important?"

"Actually, nothing. But I just can't."

Christie clicked off her ignition, wrenched the stick shift into first, hopped out, crossed the street, and gave me a great big old hug. She smelled like fresh-baked woman, straight out of the oven. My body wanted to melt right into her body.

She whispered, "Take it easy on yourself, Roger. Go with the flow. I love you a lot, even if I can't have you or help you. You're a decent human being, and a lovely writer. We need you. Take better care of yourself."

As she returned to the VW, I almost shed a tear. I wanted

to holler, "Wait!" She slid behind the wheel and flipped the key to start her engine.

Fat chance.

I wound up pushing her in heavy traffic in order to jump-start the car.

By the time I reached home, Zelda was fuming.

"I made a date to see Douglas," she said.

"Excuse me?"

"You heard me. You're not deaf."

"Why did you do that, Zelda?"

"See if you can figure it out, Roger." She stamped into the bedroom and slammed the door. Then she opened the door and fired another salvo:

"You said you told that top-heavy slut permanently good-bye!"

I thought: *Christie is not a slut, and I'm tired of your paranoia and accusations, so go fuck yourself and shut up before I bash your fucking teeth down your throat.*

What I said instead was "Her car stalled in a traffic jam. I happened to be walking by and I pushed her car."

So sue me, cunt.

"You also kissed her in front of a thousand witnesses."

"I didn't *kiss* her, Zelda. She gave me a platonic hug in gratitude."

Zelda reslammed the door in my face.

Behind that door her fingers began flying over the Selectric keys, creating a sound like that of flamenco castanets in the hands of a truly inspired dancer.

I scurried out to my writing tower and wrote Zelda a turgid letter:

Dear Zelda,

I can't take it anymore. I can't stand the way you

find a conspiracy against you under every rock. I'm so tired of the way you mistrust me and hate this town and glom on to every piece of negative gossip about me that comes down the pike whether it has any foundation in fact or not. If you hated me so much, why did you marry me? Just because you hate all your ex-husbands and ex-boyfriends doesn't mean I should be that way too. I hate being rude to the people I have cared for. You make me not want to defend you because you get off on trashing people I care about. What gives you the right to call everybody I once loved that's a female a slut? I think people are supposed to *earn* respect, it isn't just automatically conferred because they get married. It breaks my heart the way you dislike my children. They're not bad kids, they're just normal human beings, and all children go through phases, particularly at their ages. I feel so defensive anymore. I'm afraid even to think about inviting Woody over to the house for a meal or something, for fear he'll fuck up in your eyes. I'm afraid even to go have a meal with him in town because you'd say we were plotting against you. I hate being afraid to relate to my own kid. Why is everything so damn *loaded* to you? I can't keep track of all my little faux pas in your eyes. Half the time I don't know if I'm coming or going. I'm 45 years old and suddenly I feel like I'm 90. I'm smoking a pack of cigarettes a day for Chrissakes. I drink a third of a bottle of vodka. I'm not happy, I'm miserable. I love making love with you because you are the most beautiful and the sexiest woman on Earth. I have an incredible passion for you, you know that. I love this obsession. It's the most wonderful thing that ever happened in my life. But this other stuff is killing me. How can we stop it? It seems to have a momentum all its own. Every morning I wake up on pins and needles, wondering if the mood is gonna be erotic, fun, funky, humorous, or whether the mood is gonna be tense, edgy, confrontational. I can't stand all the confrontation. What's the point? Can't we call an allee-allee-in-come-free? If we don't, Jesus, baby, I think I'm gonna flip out. I think I'm gonna—

And so forth, ad nauseum, for another four pages.

Zelda fired back an answer one hour after I had slipped my lengthy epistle to her under our bedroom door:

Dear Roger,

I don't hate you. I am trying to learn how to love you and make a marriage together. You spent your whole life avoiding confrontation, so now you're a basket case. You have no idea how to communicate. Everything you do is dishonest because you don't even *know* any better. You're a professional at avoiding the truth. You kid yourself you're this wonderful, good-natured, outgoing, generous person. You're so terrified of not being liked that you fawn like Uriah Heep every time somebody so much as frowns in your direction. If your ego isn't being constantly stroked by five women at once, you go into a panic of personality-worth withdrawal. You're the most passive-aggressive human being I've ever met. You're Mr. Goodguy Save Everybody with everyone else in the world except with the one who counts—me. The one you're committed to, by the way. The one you promised to love for the rest of your life. The one you invited to share your home. The one you uprooted from her sense of place by capturing me with this false facade of bravado and passion and protestations of undying fealty. Maybe I should have known you weren't able or willing to deliver. Maybe I should have realized that you're weak and you're afraid to go for true intimacy with me. Maybe . . . but I am not an easily frightened person, and I believe we're all gonna be old hags in twenty years so why the hell not try and forge something *real* while we've still got the brains and the bodies to enjoy it? I want something original and profound with you, and dammit, I aim to fight for it. I don't want to be like everybody else, fucking dumbos compromising up the ass on everything just hoping not to make waves! I also refuse to be classified as just another repetition of your old dysfunctional tapes with women, because I am a *special* person, and we should be special together!

By the way, if you hate smoking cigarettes so much, quit smoking.

If you hate drinking so much, quit drinking.

And furthermore—

Duhduh duduh duduh.

Two questions:

1.) What is a "personality-worth withdrawal"?

2.) How would you define "true intimacy"?

I knocked on the bedroom door.

Zelda said, "Go away. Nobody's home. Your wife committed suicide."

I said, "I hate that letter you wrote. It's stupid and vindictive. And childish."

" 'Vindictive,' " Zelda replied snidely. "I bet you went to college. A real entomologist."

"An entomologist studies bugs," I retorted triumphantly. "An etymologist deals with words."

"Well, why don't you *bug* off and leave me alone, then?" Zelda snapped.

"I need to talk with you a minute."

"Tough beans. I'm busy. Go away. Go write another one of your pussyfooting misogynistic epistles."

"I'm going to open this damn door," I threatened. "I'm pissed and I want to get a few things off my chest."

"What chest? That concave thing that covers up your ice-cold heart?"

I heard her rise and walk over to the door.

"Zelda—" I warned.

"I don't care if you're Ronald Reagan's ex-hemorrhoid," Zelda said. "Leave me alone, you pig. I hate you. You're lower than whale shit."

I turned the handle and pushed against the door. But Zelda was pushing from the other side.

I said, "Hey, let me in. This is important."

Zelda said, "Beat it, buster. I want my privacy."

"You hate privacy," I reminded her. "You think everything should be shared and in the open. Now back off and let me in."

I pushed harder. She pushed harder, too.

"From now on, I'm doing it all your way," Zelda said. "You have your space, I have mine. Never the twain shall meet."

"Hey Zelda! *Open this damn door!*"

"Hey Roger! *Fuck you!*"

I stepped back ten feet and rushed the door, I really did. Just like a G-man, I lowered my shoulder and hit it hard.

Just like Abbot and Costello, Zelda stepped away at the last moment. The door banged open, my legs smashed the edge of the bed going sixty, and I almost broke both tibias just below the kneecaps, then somersaulted with a scream— "Aaarrrgh!"—over the bed and, upside down, slammed up against her precious nineteenth-century Ceylonese trastero, then crumpled into a heap on the floor, thoroughly dazed, counting stars, tweety birds, and exclamation points.

Zelda grabbed a vase from off the sill in front of her desk, walked over, and turned it upside down.

About one quart of water and a dozen carnations landed on my head.

* * *

Even though Gretal had rented another post-office box, from time to time mail continued arriving chez yours truly. I let it pile up to about a dozen letters, none of them very important looking. But finally I decided I'd better give the stuff to Gretal.

Here's the problem, however: I did not wish to drive up to her house. Suppose the Weezie Bednarik vice squad saw me, and Adrian reported my iniquity to Zelda?

After much pondering, I decided the most straightforward plan of action would be to call Gretal and ask for her new box number so I could forward the mail. But on further reflection, that seemed awfully cold-blooded. And besides, we hadn't talked since that phone call when Gretal had claimed to feel betrayed.

In the end, I saw no way of making contact without coming off as a shitheel.

Then one day I ran into Mimi Jeantete in the liquor section at Smith's. I asked after Gretal.

"She's holding her own," Mimi said, giving me a polite second-degree frost, a smile without sunlight, eyes devoid of a friendly light.

"Is she still sick?" I asked.

Mimi couldn't help herself. "No, Roger, she's fit as a fiddle. The cancer went into total remission. It's a real miracle. She plays tennis and volleyball on the weekends, and is planning a trip to Europe for Christmas. She always wanted to see Amsterdam in the snow."

Mimi's cart held three bottles of Myers' rum, a quart of half-and-half, and a jar of maraschino cherries. Mimi is actually a wonderful sculptor. She fashions grotesque angel gargoyles that dangle from the ceiling in clever mobiles. They are painted electric garish colors. I bet Mimi will probably be famous in another year or two.

If she lasts that long.

I don't know why Mimi has a drinking problem. She also smokes. She's fat. and rather slovenly. Dawn to dusk she wears sunglasses.

"Me too," I said. "I bet Amsterdam really *is* beautiful in the snow."

About a week later, I crossed out my box number on Gretal's letters, wrote PLEASE FORWARD on each envelope, and dumped them into the local-mail slot at the P.O.

I'm surprised I hadn't thought of that sooner.

Gabrielle and Jennifer spent Thanksgiving with their father, the Immortal Scumbag. So it was only me and Zelda and Woody and Kim à table for that special occasion.

Zelda had signed up for an organic turkey at the health co-op. But a tragedy befell the delivery truck. Its freezer mechanism went out between Oregon and our heavenly valley, allowing about five thousand birds to rot as the semi traversed the Nevada desert.

Loath to go Butterball, Zelda roasted up a pan of Rock Cornish game hens she had marinated overnight in Grand Marnier.

Woody hadn't shaved in about ten days, his Mohawk was drooping. His clothes were of the sort you usually see on slapstick vaudeville entertainers or rodeo clowns. To be more specific, he wore a Jane's Addiction T-shirt, a green fluorescent bow tie, his skeleton earrings, and his rotten old black leather jacket.

Woody refused to remove his aluminum-studded finger gauntlets during the entire meal.

Kim's attire included a 10,000 Maniacs T-shirt, a pair of men's boxer undershorts with the fly sewed shut, black panty hose, and a pair of red high-top Converse All-Stars.

Comme d'habitude, Zelda looked gorgeous in a high-neck long-sleeved Russian blouse with lacy cuffs and a ruffly jabot. An ultramarine-blue sash encircled her waist. She had on a beige pleated skirt and embroidered Chinese slippers.

An emerald-green ribbon in her hair completed the outfit.

I wore my usual: scruffy brown corduroys, sneakers, and a $1.98 Yves St. Laurent shirt from Thriftown.

Scented candles burned brightly, cut flowers were redolent, our linen napkins were held in painted wooden rings from Guatemala.

Never marinate Rock Cornish game hens in a liqueur—they taste like shit. But of course we all devoured them, commenting lavishly about their succulence and aromatic flavor.

About halfway through the meal I suddenly saw my children through Zelda's eyes and became appalled at their table manners. They were scarfing down vittles like jackals at a rotten wildebeest carcass.

Finally I could take it no longer. I said, "Hey, you guys, quit eating with your elbows on the table."

Woody never flinches. He never does. Woody is one of those people who, when the big earthquake happens, will simply roll over and fluff up the pillow and go back to sleep.

Kim reacted like President Kennedy in the Zapruder film, taking that third bullet in the head. Her fork clattered theatrically off her plate and bounced onto the floor.

Naturally, she burst into tears.

Then she bolted up, staggered loudly off to the guest bedroom, and banged shut the door.

I rolled my eyes to heaven, apologized to Zelda, screwed my face into a here-we-go-again expression, and hastened off to my daughter.

* * *

I knocked on the door.

No answer.

I went in.

Kim lay on her belly on one of the beds, sobbing hysterically. I sat down beside her and placed my hand on her shoulder. She growled, "Go away."

"Listen," I said, trying to sugar my words with an understanding parental kindness, "it's stupid to run away from the table like that."

"Not half as stupid as telling me to take off my elbows, Daddy," she grumped. "We *always* eat like that. You too. We've always been pigs."

"Try not to call me Daddy," I said, fearful that Zelda might hear.

That did it. Kim dried her tears, but continued lying there as inert as a stone.

"I'm sorry," I said. "But you have to make an effort to grow up. We all do, me included."

"I'm only fifteen," she said. "I don't want to grow up yet. And anyway," she added, "you're always telling us that *you* keep waiting to grow up. If you can't become an adult at forty-five, why do I hafta do it at fifteen?"

Good question. Spoken like a true Zelda.

"I wish at least you'd pretend, just a little," I said. "Why is that so difficult?"

"You always take *her* side," Kim whined. "How come *I'm* always the bad guy? You've known me for fifteen years, you've only known her for one."

"One year, two months, eleven days, five hours, fourteen minutes, and twenty-seven seconds," I joked.

Instantly, however, I felt guilty for betraying Zelda by mocking our marriage.

"I hate eating with you guys," Kim said. "I'm always on pins and needles. I'm always on pins and needles just being in this *house*."

"Me too," I admitted. "I'm sorry."

"Divorce her," Kim said. "I hate her guts."

"I love her," I said. "We're trying to put a marriage together. It isn't easy for any of us, but if we all stick it out, the rewards should be tremendous."

"The marriage of the turd brains," Kim said with her usual sophisticated wit and wisdom.

But suddenly we both laughed.

When Kim and I returned to the kitchen, Zelda was gone. "Where?" I asked Woody, who was happily demolishing his fifth Rock Cornish game hen, which he held in his fingers like corn on the cob. His elbows were planted firmly on the table.

"I dunno," Woody said cheerfully. "She just left."

I looked outside. The Subaru was gone.

Oh to hell with it.

We finished up Thanksgiving dinner, the three of us together. We relaxed. We laughed a lot, told dumb jokes, and performed a few stupid human tricks, like making spoons stick on our noses.

That was a riot. We laughed so hard we cried.

Between the three of us, we ate a half-gallon of Neapolitan ice cream, drank coffee, then did the dishes. After Kim swept the kitchen floor, Woody mopped it. Kim emptied the trash. I put away the dishes and scrubbed the counters. I used Comet to clean the sink.

Shortly thereafter, a trio of punk-rock Beastie Boys—correction, one was a girl—arrived, and spirited away my children in what appeared to be a 1949 VW Beetle, sans engine hood and muffler with EAT THE RICH and other clever slogans spray-painted across the rusted metal.

As dusk fell, I watched the remnants of a boring football game on TV.

Then I tackled *Return of the Perseid Meteor Thugs*.

Zelda returned about midnight. She parked, marched inside, went to bed.

Kim never came home. She had opted to spend the night at Woody's hovel.

I typed until two. Then I left Sidney Bard in deep trouble when his silver thread was severed by a pack of featherweight space gangbangers called Zorbitaks from the planet Twerp, and hit the hay.

Zelda was deathly quiet.

I whispered, "Are you awake?"

She didn't answer.

And here's the thing: I wanted to hug her. Because of guilt? Yes. Of course. Too, I felt sorry for Zelda. When I thought about it, Kim and Woody and I had ganged up on her. Seen from an outside perspective, we must have been a weird ensemble.

Suddenly Zelda lurched against me and moaned, "Oh jeepers, Roger, I feel so damn queasy."

I held my wife, stroking her hair, and said, "Take it easy, baby, it's all right. It's okay."

"No, it's *not* okay." Her voice was tiny and miserable. "It's like every time something beautiful happens, an ugly counterpoint bashes it to smithereens. I don't know how to make that stop happening, but I hate it. I wanted us all to be happy. Is that such an impossible dream?"

"We're happy," I muttered, for want of a better reply. I was really scared she might begin sobbing, like that other time.

Zelda squeezed me in such tight desperation, I thought I could hear my ribs crackling.

Wounded lovemaking reminds me of apples on a rainy autumn day. The sex has no violence or hilarity, it's more like a melancholy jazz tune—"Stormy Weather," "September

Song," "Tenderly." You touch her as if she's a sainted virgin, with utmost consideration. She frames your face between her palms and kisses you like a butterfly settling upon a blossom. Falling tears are impelled by muted emotions both asexual and erotic. Your measured breathing is blue and misty. An exquisite gentility informs every gesture. Each heart is woozy and penitent.

I said, "Baby, maybe we should be more social, get out, see other people. Take a break from all this one-on-one intensity . . ."

"Roger, it's going to be all right. I have faith in the process. Underneath, where we can't see it too clearly, the bond *is* happening. I can feel it, I believe in you and in myself. One day, I promise, it'll be like daffodils in the spring. Please don't give up on us."

I heard a lonesome train whistle far away.

Also the sweet, eerie strains of a violin.

Picture this scenario.

I'm at Smith's, pushing a shopping cart. In my cart is a bottle of vodka, a bottle of Kahlua, a bottle of Jack Daniels, a carton of Kool Filter Kings, a six-pack of Miller Lite, a six-pack of caffeine-free Diet Coke, a three-pack of wooden kitchen matches, two Bic lighters, and a jug of Knudsen's Cranberry Nectar.

I'm not paying attention because I am also reading a copy of the *National Enquirer* while shopping. The feature cover story is about Siamese-twin girls who sued to enter the Gladvine, Pennsylvania, Little League, then won the batting title with a .586 average.

A lot of ideas for the pickles Sidney Bard finds himself caught in in outer space come from rags like this.

Bam!

I collide with another shopper.

Not just any old shopper, either, mind you. It's my old friend from the Redoubtable Framing Company, Sandra.

"Oh golly," I half chuckle, feeling—as usual!—embarrassed and flustered, "I'm sorry. Are you okay?"

Sandra is staring at me.

After an uncomfortable pause, I ask, "What's the matter?"

Sincerely devastated, she sputters, "Roger, what happened to your hair? Suddenly it's turning *gray*!"

Moe Bubbles is the one who told me Gretal was back in the hospital again. He was on a bicycle at the spa, reading *Esquire* as he pedaled. Zelda and I had just attended a Tuesday night aerobics class with Jane Raines.

Zelda had left to shower and dress when I stopped to say hi to Moe and he gave me the scoop on Gretal.

"Do you see her?" I asked.

"All the time," he said. "I drop by at least twice a week."

"How's she doing?"

"I told you, she's back in the hospital," he puffed.

"I know. But I mean how does she *look*?"

"Tired," Moe said. "Très fatiguée."

"Does she ever say anything about me?"

"Never."

"Well, I guess I don't blame her," I said.

Moe quit pedaling. Sweat streamed off his face, which had turned purple.

"How's it going with Susan?" I asked.

"Oh, God, please!" he groaned, gesturing toward the highest altitudes of lunacy. "Let's not diminish ourselves by massaging that subject."

"Well, how's old Leroy Bogdanovich?" I asked.

"Yesterday he managed to start my Toyota, and he drove it through the clothesline into her chicken coop."

I laughed, Moe laughed.

I said, "Hey, please, if you go to the hospital, tell Gretal I love her, and I'll pray to her archangels daily."

Then I ran off to the men's locker room, hoping that Zelda hadn't seen me with Moe and intuitively deduced the content of our exchange.

On December eighth, Don Perry's assistant, Melissa Hornblower, managed to offend Zelda by asking for yours truly without performing any amenitory ablutions.

"And who shall I say is calling?" Zelda asked sweetly.

"His agent," Melissa replied. Period.

"His agent is Donald Perry," Zelda said. "And, unless I'm mistaken, you're not Donald Perry."

After a pause on the other end, Melissa asked, "I'm sorry, is this the right number? The Roger I'm after is a writer."

"This is Roger the Writer's wife," Zelda said. "And I, too, am a human being. I have a name. It's Zelda. This is also my house. Roger and I share it."

Another pause.

Melissa eventually said, "Listen, Zelda, it's important I talk to Roger."

Zelda said, "Don't any of you people ever say 'please'?"

Melissa Hornblower hung up on my wife. Zelda recounted the story to me in a rage. She wanted sympathy, yet all I could muster was anger. I raced into the kitchen and dialed New York. I fell all over myself apologizing to Melissa.

"God, I'm sorry," I said. "It's my fault. Zelda and I just had a fight. It was terrible. She's real upset. We were married hardly a minute ago, as you know, and things are

179

tense. I'm sorry. She didn't mean to be impolite. But you caught us at a hairy moment—"

At this point Melissa interrupted. "Excuse me, Roger, but I don't have all day. Don wanted me to call and say that Ed Barsano over at NBC wants to make sure the Zane Adams script will be in his hands day after tomorrow. Don hasn't received it yet. Is it on the way?"

"Almost," I said. "Don't worry, you'll get it. I have a few minor adjustments to make, a bit of tinkering, nothing major."

"Don says after the *Catacombs* fiasco it'd be a good idea if you mailed this one on the button."

"I will, Melissa, I promise."

I figured if I worked all tonight and all tomorrow, I could finish the final forty pages, no sweat.

"Don wants to know how it's going."

"Tell him great. Capital G. Tell him I've elevated Zane Adams to art."

Melissa chuckled, "G'wan, Roger—I don't wanna give him a heart attack."

After I hung up, I explained the situation to Zelda. "I'm dead if I don't deliver," I said.

She answered sweetly, "Do you wanna make love?"

Writing is easy, a pundit once cracked. All you have to do is sit down at the typewriter in the morning and open a vein.

I camped in my office for thirty-six hours, opened a half-dozen veins, and actually put together the pages. I smoked about eight packs of cigarettes and drank a bottle of vodka. Zelda handled all callers with her usual aplomb.

When it was over, I sat in the kitchen drinking coffee. Federal Express turned left at the end of the driveway and headed for New York, two thousand miles away.

"You poor baby," Zelda commiserated. "I don't know how you do it."

"Talent," I joked. "Charisma. Stupidity."

"You are not a stupid man," she contradicted. "You're brilliant."

"No I'm not, sweetie. I'm a real dumb bunny."

"Why, because you married me?"

Oh shit. "Hey, Jesus, no. I'm a lout because I took that job. I hate writing like fast food."

"I haven't helped any, have I? Mostly I'm just an incredible hindrance, aren't I? I muck everything up."

"No you don't, baby. You're wonderful. You're full of life, chutzpah, sparkle. You're sexy, you're beautiful, you're my inspiration."

"I inspire you to write *that* shit?"

My jaw fell open. I stared at her. She stared back irately. Zelda added, "You never feel happy, do you Roger, until you've managed to humiliate me?"

"I wasn't trying to humiliate," I babbled. "I was trying to be supportive."

"It's a shame you have to 'try,' isn't it? Wouldn't it be nice if the support came naturally?"

I said, "Zelda, I am a very tired human being."

"You're always tired, Roger. It's your main excuse for everything."

"I just wrote for thirty-six hours straight. I've had two hours of sleep. My headache you could drive a locomotive through."

"So why do you suffer it?" she asked.

"We need the money."

"If you're doing it on account of me, *I* don't need the money. *I'm* not the one to blame."

"Nobody's blaming you, honey."

Zelda said, "Every time you open your mouth, I'm to blame."

I pointed my finger at her, shot her dead, and giggled.

181

Then I rolled out of the chair, landed on the kitchen floor, tucked up into a fetal position, and went to sleep.

When I awoke, Zelda was sitting in the living room surrounded by curious yet disinterested cats, wrapping a present.

"Who's that for?"

"Gretal," Zelda said. "I heard she's back in the hospital." Okay.

Without missing a beat, I asked, "What is it?"

"A float bowl. For roses. You fill it half full of water, then set a rose blossom inside. No stem. It's very Japanese, and beautiful. On your way to the hospital you can stop by the flower shop and buy a rose. I think she would enjoy it much more than those usual drab bouquets people give."

I didn't have the heart to admit I was persona non grata with Gretal. So I bought a rose and tracked down Moe Bubbles, who said sure, he'd take it over.

But we decided to unwrap the float bowl and not say it came from Zelda. I had mixed feelings about this, but it seemed like the proper thing to do—sort of.

Life: the original no-win situation.

The network dropped me from the Zane Adams rewrites, which cost a bundle.

However, in this business, for what you played you get paid.

Without thinking, I kissed the check and handed it over to Christie: ten big fat ones, minus a buck for Don's commission.

Thank you God, thank you NBC, thank you Writers' Guild West.

Christie whistled. "Holy cow, nine big fat ones!"

She diddy-bopped her fingers on the computer, inserted a deposit-receipt slip in the slot, and transformed that check into electronic money.

I could breathe for a couple of months.

Christie said, "What'd you earn all this for?"

"Selling my soul to the devil."

"I'd like to meet your devil."

"No you wouldn't."

"Wanna bet?"

That's when I finally remembered to ask, "How's Cazzie?"

Christie burst into tears. "She ran away from the girls' home. She stole their TV set and the VCR and some jewelry. If it's not recovered, I have to pay. They figure she must of had an accomplice."

I didn't want to hear it. Krupke . . . I got . . . troubles of my own. Still, I had to pretend sympathy, n'est-ce pas?

"Geez, I'm sorry, kid." I started to back up a little.

"You hate me, don't you?" Christie said. "I'm nothing but trouble. I'm like a joke to you, aren't I? I'm like that disaster-prone dope in *L'il Abner*. You and your beautiful wife and all your money. What a contrast. I must seem like such a pathetic boob."

I shook my head vigorously. "No, no, not at all. I think you're a very courageous human being. You have more guts than all of us combined."

She halfway smiled through her tears. "Well, you know something, Roger? I think *you* are a pathetic boob."

Then she pointed her finger, fired the gun, and chortled, "Gotcha!" I never knew anybody who could laugh and cry at the same time like Christie.

That afternoon I mailed her five hundred dollars. Christie sent the check back covered with lipstick prints and a message:

Thanks, sweetie, but I'm doing just fine.

"He sold it to one of his stupid friends for two hundred dollars!" Zelda exclaimed.

She was bug-eyed with outrage, hurt, and disbelief.

"How do you know?" I asked, my heart sinking.

"The whole damn *town* knows, Roger! I'm a fucking laughingstock! How could you let him do a thing like that?"

"I don't *let* him do anything, Zelda. I hardly ever even see him. He's on his own. I can't tell him what to do."

Zelda sat down at the kitchen table. Then she got up, grabbed a bottle of Kahlua, poured about eight ounces into a glass, and added a dash of half-and-half. She sat back down at the table and essayed a hefty swig. About half the liquid disappeared. She laughed, and her eyes began tearing.

I fetched a glass and poured the rest of the bottle into it. Chin chin.

Then I sat down at the table and stared at my drink.

Zelda took another strapping belt. I could hear the glugs as she swallowed.

"I don't understand you or your children at all," Zelda wailed.

"I know. I don't either." Boy, was I mortified.

"It was a gift. A peace offering. It was a *gesture*. I was trying to reach out."

"I know. It was a lovely gesture."

"He sold it for two hundred bucks. *I paid four hundred!*"

I couldn't help myself. I said, "You can't give a gift with any strings attached. That's not fair."

"Is that the only way you can see it?"

No, not at all. I could see it every which way but loose. I could see Woody as the devil, as a scumbag, as a victim, as a desperado. I could see Zelda as a woman scorned, as a manipulator, as an angel trying to love us heathens. I could see—

Zelda finished her Kahlua, staggered across the kitchen, grabbed a bottle of Wild Turkey 101, and poured another eight ounces into her glass.

She came back and plunked down a mite tipsily.

I managed to stop myself from blurting "I'm sorry."

"Do you hate me?" Zelda asked wearily.

I shook my head.

Picking her words carefully, my wife explained, "The reason I'm like I am, Roger, is I feel, deep in my bones, that there is *a correct way to be* in life. The world is so sloppy and cavalier. I care about what matters. It's *important* that things matter. People should respect and love each other, and take responsibility and be *honest.*"

"I agree one hundred percent."

"Then why don't you support me, baby?"

I gave up and gazed out the window. Magpies scrawked in the apple tree. Last night new snow had fallen onto the mountaintops.

"Roger—?"

I bit my bottom lip.

I made impotent fluttering gestures with my hands.

I went into my files and located our marriage vows. It seemed impossible that only a few months ago we had recited them to each other in a public ceremony of great rejoicing and celebration.

Let me count the ways we had enumerated the ways:

1.) We promise to respect each other's freedom and independence and differences.

2.) We promise to be open and loving in ways that each of us says they need.

3.) We promise to listen to each other, and to support each other, with care and compassion and an open heart.

4.) We promise to stay open to each other's needs, in work, in the universe, in sexuality.

5.) We promise to try hard not to be mean to each other.

6.) We promise to always keep a good supply of olive branches in our hearts.

7.) We promise not to be afraid of, or to suppress, each other's vitality, flamboyance, energy, or chutzpah.

8.) We promise to choose a joyous life.

9.) We promise to be open to the humor in life and to the healing powers of laughter.

10.) We promise to be thankful for this life, and for our time, and for our adventure together.

I reread the list about twenty times.

It made me sad.

While Zelda was at the spa, I taped the vows to our refrigerator. Next day I noticed the paper was gone, but I refrained from comment. The following afternoon Zelda glanced up from the book she was reading (Pär Lagerkvist's *The Dwarf*) and said, quite calmly, "I hate you, Roger."

"Oh? And why is that, Zelda?"

"You know why."

"No, actually, I don't know why. I commit so many transgressions in your eyes, I'd be hard put at any single moment in time to place my finger accurately on the exact one you're thinking about."

"I hate it when you're snide," Zelda said.

"I hate it when out of the blue you say you hate me," I answered.

"You never notice anything," she said. "You don't give a damn."

"Notice? What are you talking about?"

"When I change a picture on the wall, or rearrange the furniture, or clean all the books in the poetry bookcase, or make the bed with clean sheets, you never notice. You take everything for granted. You don't care about those things."

"I notice," I said. "I just don't acknowledge it every time. You're always changing everything. I would get dizzy if I tried to comment each time."

Zelda said, "I think it was a low blow to tape those vows on the fridge. You are a cruel human being. I bet you roast in Hell."

"I won't mind being in Hell," I replied pleasantly, "as long as you're up in heaven."

She stuck out her tongue at me. I returned the favor. We both laughed. But it wasn't very funny.

It was cynical.

And so a brand-new tone entered our peripatetic pas de deux.

That night, when I clicked off the lamp and left my office, I accidentally kicked apart a pastrami sandwich on my stoop, and toppled a mug of beer.

While at work, furiously typing away, I had never heard the elf Zelda as she laid down those offerings and silently stole away.

I sat on the stoop, aching with love, and patched together the sandwich. Then, slowly, I ate it, scratching the dog's ears while staring across the driveway at our house. A lamp on the kitchen table burned golden. Otherwise, all was dark and peaceful there.

Great feelings of love for Zelda welled up inside me, and I began to weep.

"I love you, Zelda," I whispered.

How much between one and ten? she asked.

I went overboard this time because the ache inside me really meant it. "A million," I said gently. "And maybe even more."

At Christmas we had a jolly time.

As a child, I had loved Christmas. I believed in Santa Claus until I was six. I put wish lists in the fireplace for brownies to pick up and deliver to the North Pole. I arranged glasses of milk for Santa on the mantel beside peanut butter and marshmallow cream sandwiches and chocolate chip cookies.

In later life I mellowed out. Bonnie hated Christmas. So I always got Woody and Kim. We practiced Noel anarchy, with little obeisance to all the time-honored traditions. Yet we always chopped down a tree; we *loved* tramping through the snowy forests. And I threw presents at the kids willy-nilly. Of course, countless friends came by to scarf junk food and get shitfaced on cheap wine or top-notch bourbon. I remember once we had sixteen cartons of eggnog in the refrigerator!

We never stood on ceremony. On Christmas day I usually threw a naked bird on the table, handed my kids and each guest a blowtorch, and told them to have at it.

This was not exactly Zelda's style.

She wanted a bit more order *and* panache.

For starters, we went out and chopped the holy tree—so far, so good.

Then we made wreaths for all the doors and for all the windows. This took heaps of time, but the results were pretty.

We hung sprigs of mistletoe in every doorway.

We made popcorn necklaces and colored-paper chains for the Christmas tree.

On Christmas Eve we had a formal party. A hundred people came. Beforehand, Gabrielle, Woody, Kim, Jennifer, and I lined the driveway with candles burning inside paper bags—luminarias. Every ten minutes somebody rushed into town for more tablecloths, more liquor, more candles, more nutmeg, more ribbon, more cards and wrapping paper, more hors d'oeuvres. We cooked up a huge pot of clam chowder. We baked sugar cookies until we were blue in the face.

We scrubbed the house until it was spotless. We vacuumed. We washed the windows. We put lemon oil on the furniture.

The preparations killed all of us, but the party was "a great success."

All the kids were perpetually broke, so naturally I had sent each of them a hundred bucks to buy presents for the others. I gave Zelda five hundred dollars to purchase goodies for me and for them. I spent another five bills on crap for her and for them.

Christmas shopping is sheer torture, I hate it. This year I particularly hated trying to figure out how to give everyone equivalent gifts so nobody would feel slighted.

Woody used his hundred to purchase penicillin (for a case of the clap), to pay the landlord for a hole punched through his kitchen wall, and to acquire food to keep from starving.

Kim used her hundred to lavish crud on Bonnie.

Jennifer and Gabrielle cleverly parlayed their respective century notes into thoughtful and timely presents for me, Zelda, Woody, Kim, and each other.

I hated them.

While seated in the twinkling living room on Christmas morning opening boxes, we pretended to be the most cheerful little group of assholes on the planet.

When it was over, I forked out another million so all the

John Nichols

youngsters could go skiing, while Zelda prepared the turkey (which had been soaking overnight in Grand Marnier).

"I thought you gave Woody and Kim money for presents," she said. I was sitting at the table, swilling eggnog.

I shrugged, too drunk to care. "Yeah, I guess I did."

Long pause, then: "I wonder whatever happened, then?"

I shrugged again. "Dunno. My kids've never been real great on the Christmas-exchange orgy."

Zelda said, "Maybe if you quite treating them like 'kids,' they wouldn't act like kids. They wouldn't just rip you off like this."

I nodded. "Maybe, I dunno." I wanted to say, *Fuck you, I don't care, it doesn't matter. Why does everything always have to* matter *so much?*

"They are really spoiled," Zelda said. "I wouldn't say it if it wasn't true. You know it's the truth. I don't believe how you let them get away with it."

I said, "I'm sorry."

She said, "That's all?"

I said, "What do you want me to do, buy a hair shirt and suck on stones?"

I hated Zelda. I hated myself. I felt guilty. Part of me knew she was right. Part of me knew she was dead wrong. Part of me knew it was all my fault. Part of me knew it was all *her* fault. Part of me was scared because of this *thing* fluttering deep down inside me, which I would later learn to identify as hatred.

"Maybe it wouldn't hurt if just once in your life you held them accountable," Zelda said. "I can't believe their lack of consideration."

I wanted to tell her that my children resented the whole scene. That Zelda's opinion of them right from the start had created a self-fulfilling prophecy. So many new rules. So many regulations. So many rewards and punishments. Her "good" girls always pitted against my "bad" children. Her obvious dislike of Kim and Woody's mother.

190

Ranana ranana ranana.
It made me so weary.
But I could not deal with yet one more battle royale.
So I poured another eggnog, loading it double.
Zelda stuck a weed in my mouth and lit it.
I said, "Thank you."

Let me describe for you our Christmas dinner that evening.

About six o'clock, Zelda announces, "The turkey's ready." So we all sit down. Woody and Gabrielle, Jennifer and Kim, me and Zelda. Perhaps I should add that Gabrielle is a beautiful young woman with a 4.0 academic average, who also teaches aerobics to pay her way through college. Jennifer could be beautiful, but she's rather plump and introspective, and rarely speaks, though she listens attentively, absorbing every word.

At the start of our feast, I'm chipper as a little old cricket in the pea patch, babbling away. But it seems as if a pall is hanging over the table. Zelda is in one of her remote, zoned-out phases. Gabrielle and Jennifer merely dig into their vittles, eyes lowered, and won't speak a word. Woody, a professional trencher-man, rarely talks while devouring helpless nourishment anyway. Put grown-ups at the table and he's twice as quiet. And Kim simply picks at her heaping plate, nibbling at a pea here, a thin slice of breast there.

It's like Christmas dinner in a café next door to a makeshift gymnasium morgue after a plane crash in Iowa, and we've all recently identified our relatives who were dragged in out of a nearby cornfield.

I finally came up for air. I said, "Excuse me, but what is going on here? This is Christmas. It is supposed to be a joyous occasion. What's the matter? Did I miss something? Who died?"

Nobody utters a word.

I said, "Zelda, what's the problem?"

My wife surveyed me the way a mongoose sums up a cobra and replied, "Nothing."

I made one of those flip helpless gestures and decided to be jovial. I said, "Kim, old girl, what the fuck is the matter with *you*, anyway?"

She fired a .357 magnum glare in my direction and said, "It's none of your damn business."

I tried Woody. "Hey, old sport, what's the matter? C'mon, spill the beans, cough."

Woody grinned moronically and actually coughed.

I thought that was funny. I giggled. Nobody else cracked even a diminutive smirk. Finally I said, "Well, gee whiz, this is a helluva Christmas dinner. I'm sorry we didn't invite Bela Lugosi and Vincent Price."

Zelda could hold back no longer. She said, "I can't believe the three of you would come to Christmas dinner looking like such shitcan bums. You are so contemptuous of the rest of us."

"Excuse me?" I checked Woody and Kim, and then I realized: *Oh.* Woody was resplendent in his usual sadomasochistic punked-out filth-oriented attire. Kim wore a sweatshirt and shorts; her feet were bare. Me, I had donned my usual raggedy Levi's shirt, dirty dungarees, and sneakers. Gabrielle and Jennifer, on the other hand, resembled yuppie mannequins bedecked in high-end Orvis college fashions. Zelda, comme d'habitude, was strikingly beautiful in a green peasant blouse, a red pleated skirt, and matching heels. A flower brightened her hair.

Yup, obviously, it was the Grunge Family versus the Vogue-Elle contingent, Gloria in Excelsis Deo.

Bursting into tears, Kim wrenched away from the table. Her champagne glass tipped over and her knife and fork clattered to the floor as she bolted off into the living room.

I said, "That's *it*? You guys don't like our *clothes*?" I

hadn't dressed up for a meal since the day Lincoln was shot.

Zelda said, "If you were sensitive to anybody else besides your own selves, you would know exactly the problem here."

"Well," I countered, "I don't know the problem, and this whole scene stinks. I've never had such a rotten meal in my life. What does fashion have to do with good eats, the birth of Christ, and familial camaraderie?"

Jennifer said, "I don't feel at home here."

I answered, "I got news for you, baby, *I* don't feel at home here."

Zelda said, "You've made no attempt to make Gabrielle and Jennifer feel comfortable."

"No attempt?" That accusation cut to the quick. I tried to keep it cool, however, in deference to the holy occasion. I said, "I talk to them, I rent videos for them, they have warm beds, I spent a fucking grand buying them presents, I give them liquor, food, love—what does it take to make them feel comfortable?"

Zelda said, "Woody and Kim ignore them."

Woody surprised me by speaking in his defense. He said, "I invited them to a party each of the last three nights but they refused to go."

Gabrielle said, "Your friends are punk-rock morons. They're hopeless adolescents. They all act about fifteen."

Kim hollered from in front of MTV in the other room, "What are we supposed to do with a couple of dweebs?"

To me, wounded, almost in tears, Woody explained, "They like Madonna and Stevie Wonder and Michael Bolton. They *hate* the Dead Kennedys and the Circle Jerks and the Nazi Butthole Surfers."

"Their friends are so immature," Gabrielle said. "They're boooo-ring."

Jennifer added, "This whole town is retarded."

I said, "What makes you guys so fucking superior?"

Zelda leaped to their defense. "Nobody's superior, Roger. They're just stating an obvious fact. And if you can't see it, you're blind."

Woody mumbled, "Can I be excused?"

Zelda and I said "No" and "Yes" respectively in exactly the same breath.

After the sullen lad and lassies had tripped merrily off to see a show, Zelda and I washed the dishes. At first we worked in silence. But in due course Zelda said, "Don't you need to call Bonnie and wish her a merry Christmas?"

Yes, of course, I wanted to do that. And as soon as the dishes were done, I had plans to pop into town for cigarettes and make the call on my card from a public booth at Smith's.

Zelda's tone of voice, pleasantly noncommittal, caught me off guard.

"Well, yeah, I guess so," I said, affecting nonchalance. "It's no big deal."

"You go ahead," Zelda said sweetly. "I'll finish up here."

"I can help you finish—" I began.

Zelda grasped my shoulders, gave me a firm little peck on the lips, smiled reassuringly, and murmured, "Go. Use the bedroom for privacy."

I went into the bedroom. I actually had the audacity to close the door.

I dialed Bonnie.

She lit into me even before the "Merry Christmas" was halfway out of my mouth. "How come you waited so long to call? Where are the kids? How come they didn't phone to wish me a merry Christmas? I'm all alone, Roger, and those bastards broke in again last night and stole my blender and the ghetto blaster and the TV, and a whole tray of tapes, and they must've been really hard up because they took a humidifier, also."

"I'm sorry I'm calling so late," I said. "Believe me, around here it isn't easy."

"Where's Woody? Where's Kim?" she asked. Bonnie was crying. "Don't they even give a damn?"

"You already had a Christmas with Kim," I reminded her. "She bought you arm loads of useless trinkets."

"This is Christmas *day*, Roger."

I hate Christmas, I really do. It's like a plot, cooked up by financial Nazis, to demolish collective peace of mind.

"I'm sorry," I said. "It was all so chaotic. I should have made them phone."

She blubbered, "If you have to *make* them, what's the point?"

"It's not their fault," I said. "It's a little tense for them right now, up here, trying to cope with the situation."

"You said they went to a movie with Gabrielle and Jennifer."

I nodded. I said, "Yes. It was a move to promote family togetherness."

"*I'm* their true family," Bonnie said. "What about togetherness with *me*?"

"I'm sorry," I said. Meet Joe Blow, the Apology Machine. "I don't know what else to say," I added. "I'm sorry."

"What's the movie that's so important they couldn't take the time to call?"

"Zelda," I said, "please calm down. We ran a little late here, so they—"

"Zelda?!?!?"

Oops. "I mean Bonnie. Sorry."

Bonnie said, "I hate what you're turning into, Roger. I hate what's happening to everybody. It's like one of those Stepfather movies, only it's a Stepmother."

That irritated me. She had no right to be trashing Zelda.

195

But (fortunately!) I held my tongue. I explained, "It's only a stage. The first year is the hardest, they say, then things have a tendency to smooth out."

"Like they did with us?"

Touché.

What sort of people is it who always come up with these self-defeating reasons why nothing ever works out? Is it people in Personality-Worth Withdrawal?

"We should be proud of us," I told Bonnie. "We have beautiful children. We're good friends. I like you. I like Woody and Kim. So what if we aren't perfect? Who's perfect?"

"You mean besides your new wife?"

"Zelda never said she was perfect," I fired back.

I have a weird thing about being a patriotic American. At home, I can't berate my country enough. But when I'm in France or Spain or Amsterdam, the minute some asshole European starts berating the United States, I become almost jingoistic: that's *my* country they're trashing.

Same deal when Bonnie started ripping Zelda.

"Actually, they're selfish little brats, aren't they?" Bonnie said.

"Excuse me?"

"Woody and Kim."

"Well, yeah, sorta, maybe, I suppose, sure. But what else is new with adolescents?"

"It's my fault," Bonnie groaned. "I wasn't at home enough when they were little. I was so concerned about my own little garden, I never gave them enough attention. I never even—"

"Bonnie," I interrupted, "they're okay. Don't worry about it." I was groggy from tension and eggnog, so I resorted to mindless literary quotation: "Everything is for the best in the best of all possible worlds, really."

"Are you mocking me, Roger? On Christmas?"

I couldn't help it, I hung up on her. I was drenched in sweat, smoking two cigarettes at once. I stood up, raised a window, shooed out the smoke with my hands, then opened the door.

Zelda was sitting five feet away, watching *A Christmas Carol* on TV.

I sat down and ran my fingers through my hair while staring blindly at Bob Fucking Cratchet and Tiny Fucking Tim.

"I couldn't help overhearing a little," Zelda said gently. "And if you want my advice—"

I saw fucking *stars*.

New Year's Eve was a real lulu.

But it started great.

Gabrielle, Jennifer, and Woody had departed early for a Scumbag Fritters concert. Kim was back in the capital assuaging Bonnie (and, coincidentally, tormenting her boyfriend, Larry the Lug). Zelda and I had declined a dozen invitations in favor of a quiet evening at home.

With the children, earlier, we had built an eight-foot-high straw devil wired onto a cross, which was stuck in a hole on the lawn. Come midnight we would burn it and shoot off guns, a yearly ritual in my family.

In the meantime, we quaffed champagne, watched TV, and indulged ourselves in a passionate marathon root.

At five to midnight, we scribbled our New Year's resolutions on pieces of paper and stuck them into the straw devil on the lawn. It was a bright, chilly night bereft of snow on the ground. All my resolutions had to do with loving, fighting for the marriage, being tolerant and compassionate and grown up and saintly.

Zelda did not reveal hers to me.

I gave her the .22 pistol loaded with blanks. I fitted two number 8 doveloads into the Stevens 12 gauge. At midnight we each struck a match and, in unison, torched the devil. As flames rushed up through its twisted body, we let 'er rip. I reloaded the pistol and the shotgun, we exchanged weapons, and blasted away again. The devil danced in bright agony. We dispatched another salvo, then lifted high champagne glasses and toasted the New Year.

We stood with our arms around each other watching gibbets of fire float twistingly to earth. Guns went off all across the valley. I never was happier in my life.

Zelda crowed, "Oh Roger, I love you so much. I'm so happy I could die."

Woody called at 2:17 A.M. The truck was overturned in a ditch. He and Gabrielle and Jennifer were okay but at the jail, awaiting deliverance. In his inebriated state, Woody could hardly talk. Yet he managed to mumble, "I'm sorry."

Like father, like son.

"Who was driving?" Zelda whispered over my shoulder.

"Woody," I said mournfully. "Who else?"

Zelda said, "If you bail him out, if you pay for the lawyers and all the fines, it'll just exacerbate the situation. He'll never grow up. He'll keep doing it all over again until you force him to be weaned."

I ignored her, tugging on my socks and sneakers, tying the laces, snagging my checkbook, heading for the door.

"He has to learn to take responsibility," Zelda harped, rolling over in bed.

I found a package of breath mints in her purse and popped a half dozen, then started the Subaru.

I drove slowly into town, taking my time. I wanted to hold Woody in my arms and caress him like a puppy and apologize and tell him I loved him no matter what.

I wanted him to embrace me and caress *me* back.
By the time I reached the jail, I was crying.

Bill Witherspoon said, "What's going on out there, Roger?"

I implied he would not believe me if I told him.

Bill said, "Aw, just for fun, go ahead and try me."

I said, "Well, I think it's called jockeying for position. We're establishing the parameters of our relationship."

"Tell me more."

Bill, as I understood it, had been happily married for thirty-six years to the same wife, Rosalyn Teeter. She was a big-shot literary agent in the Apple. One of her clients was Meridel Gardiner, the romance novelist. Another was Danny Gillespie, one of those young turks on the best-seller lists who wrote about cocaine, sado-porn, and Soho bars.

"We screw often and we talk and we fight a lot," I said. "We also drink, and I smoke multitudinous cigarettes. To stay healthy, we jog and exercise at the spa. If there's any time left over, I write."

Bill said, "Roger, you're a professional. You've been doing this how many years?"

"Twenty-six," I answered without hesitation.

He sighed. "I gather you don't know when you'll be finished?"

"I'm having a little trouble concentrating," I mumbled. "Sometimes there's squiggles dancing in front of my eyes. I don't sleep very much."

"Come to New York," Bill urged. "During the winter, Roz and I never use the house on the Island. You could stay out there and write. It has heat."

I stated the obvious. "I wouldn't without taking Zelda."

"Christ, man, this is your *career* we're talking about."

"I'm working on it," I promised. "I mean it. I'm almost done. I can see the light at the end of the tunnel."

Also:

The check is in the mail, my herpes is dormant, and I promise not to come in your mouth.

It snowed frequently in January.

The temperature dropped, and every day big flakes fell onto our pretty little valley.

I love snow, I love the cold. It's great working weather. I'm a writing fool in winter.

I also like to chop wood when it's snowing. I like to build roaring fires and drink bourbon at dusk in front of the snapping logs, and get a hard-on just looking at my sexy wife cuddled up on the couch reading the autobiography of Arthur Miller while wearing a baggy old beige sweater, a pink silk thong, and green satin slippers.

Usually we jogged around three thirty. It was wonderful to run in quiet snowstorms. When we pulled up at our driveway after a three-mile workout, Zelda's knitted cap and sweater would be covered in white flakes. Her cheeks would be flushed and rosy. We always kissed and said, "Thank you," then walked up the driveway holding hands.

The dog usually bounced out to meet us. Him, and a couple of the cats, also. They'd advance halfway down the driveway, prancing and meowing and whining. We stooped over and scratched and patted everybody on the way back up to the house.

We bathed after running, then dressed sexy. I built a fire. We made drinks and elaborate canapés. We read the newspapers, chatted, or turned on the five P.M. TV news.

I preferred Peter Jennings. Zelda was partial to Brokaw. Neither of us could stand Dan Rather.

The cats lay about, soaking up the piñon bennies. The dog twitched, dreaming about squirrels and rabbits.

All the world was muffled, warm, peaceful, sexy.

I brought a mattress in from the guest bedroom.

We put Satie and Kitaro on the cassette player, and began making love like two virgins in a fourteenth-century madrigal. We caressed each other as gently as a doe licks her newborn fawn. We luxuriated in an erotic wooziness so beautiful you'd think it had been painted by Monet during an early morning on the Seine. We—

Hey! It felt like maybe we were turning the corner.

You *could* see a light at the end of the tunnel.

"How's the old novel coming along?" I asked casually, praying I wouldn't blush.

"I don't know," Zelda said. "Sometimes I think it's good, sometimes it makes me vomit. Sometimes I hate the writing, sometimes I love it. I wish there was a way you could tell if it had anything on the ball or not."

"I would love to read what you've got so far if you want."

My wife smiled nervously. "Roger, if I was roasting down in Hell pincushioned by long-shafted arrows and rusty sabers, and the devil himself said, 'Zelda, you can get out of this hole by giving Roger a glimpse of your novel,' I'd probably let you read the damn book." She patted my cheek affectionately. "But until then, sweetie, I'm gonna keep it to myself. We'll both live longer that way."

The phone rang.

We ignored it, of course.

We lingered against each other, barely touching, on the brink of premature orgasm simply because the sensation of well-being was so unrelentlessly dreamy and powerful.

We nibbled on each other's lips like angels licking dew off the petals of huge red roses at Versailles.

Insistently, the phone continued ringing.

My penis lazily leaked seminal fluids against the soft pink skin of Zelda's thighs.

"God I love you," I murmured.

"God I love you back," she murmured back.

Firelight flickered against us, it caressed the purring cats and undulated across white walls. It reflected off the picture window. Heat from the flames twittered against our arms and our cheeks and our legs.

The dang phone just would not quit, and finally it killed the mood.

I said, "Shit." Zelda replied, "Ditto."

I lunged into the bedroom and grabbed the jangling apparatus.

"Jesus Christ who is *this*?" I blurted angrily.

A voice said, "Gretal's dead."

Oh.

I wasn't sure if I had heard correctly. I guess I muttered, "Huh?" or "What?" or "Come again?"

The same voice said, "About fifteen minutes ago she passed away."

I didn't like that euphemism "passed away." Never have. It irritates me. It seems unctuous, obsequious, hypocritical. After all, dead is dead, isn't it?

I sat on the edge of the bed, gaping down at my Mother of All Boners, listening to a ringing in my ears, a momentary deafness. My flesh clung to squeezings of erotic pleasure, reluctant to pull away completely.

I said, "Excuse me? Who is this?"

"It's Mimi," Mimi said. "Do you want to talk with Moe?"

"Mimi who?" I whimpered. Nothing made sense. I reached down, taking myself in hand, and stroked to keep it from wilting.

"Mimi your friend," she said. "Mimi Jeantete." Then she hiccoughed and said, "Here's Moe."

"Moe?"

"Hi Roger, it's Moe," said Moe.

"What do you mean she's dead?" Nobody had indicated Gretal was that sick.

"She died about fifteen minutes ago," Moe said. "It took everybody by surprise."

"But how . . ." I started to protest. "But I mean why . . . I mean, how come . . . I mean, *dead*? How could she die?" I blurted finally, as it began to sink in. I quit stroking and the hard-on faded. I heard Kitaro in the background, all mellow and New Age mellifluous. Logs in the fireplace popped and crackled.

Moe said, "We're all here at the hospital."

"What are you gonna do?" I asked meekly.

"Well, we already called Daisy," Moe said.

Daisy was Gretal's daughter. A sort of delicious kook, about twenty-five, who worked for a travel agent in New York.

"And—?"

"She'll fly out in the morning."

"What about—" I couldn't bring myself to say "the body." So I asked instead, "What about Gretal?"

Moe said, "She's dead." He sounded very wifty and un-comfortable.

"I know that, I mean what happens now with the body?"

"A guy from the funeral home is coming. Daisy wants to burn it. I guess there'll be a memorial for all her friends."

I felt abysmal. I had abandoned Gretal. I hadn't talked to her in a long time. I felt lost and uncomfortable and yearning and angry, and weird. And oddly humiliated, or guilty, or simply far out in left field. Writer though I pretend to be, I can't explain this emotion.

Call it all of the above, and none of the above.

"Should I drive in?" I asked awkwardly. "Is there anything I can do?"

Moe said, "I guess not. Everything is under control. Mimi and I just felt you should know. We'll call when Daisy arrives, I'm sure she'll want to say hi. We'll give you all the particulars on the service."

Moe sounded tired, unflamboyant, barely alive. Like a hurt little boy.

Many sentiments bubbled around inside me. The worst had to do with being estranged. From Gretal. From Moe. From Zelda lying on her back in the firelight, so provocatively serene—

I scratched a kitty that rubbed up against me.

Eventually I said, "I'm sorry, Moe. I'll catch you tomorrow, I guess . . ." Then I asked abruptly, "Were you there?"

"No. It happened too quickly. There was just a nurse. And I guess the doctor at the end. McLean was on call."

Javier McLean is a sweet man from the Dominican Republic. His wife Bridget had been a torch singer in Gretal's combo. They had a sixteen-year-old daughter with cerebral palsy, and an eleven-year-old son who during the previous summer had pitched four Little League no-hitters. Javier was my doctor, also. Shortly before Zelda and I became legal, he conducted my yearly checkup. My prostate was a trifle enlarged, and Javier prescribed antibiotics (which did the trick). I don't know why, but now, listening to Moe, I remembered my reaction when Javier diagnosed my prostate. To prove I was at ease with the concept of my own mortality, in a cavalier and debonair manner I had paraphrased a Marlon Brando line from *Last Tango in Paris*:

"I may have a prostate the size of an Idaho potato, Javier, but I'm still a good stick man."

To Moe I said, "I'm sorry." He answered, "Yeah, we all are. Apologies for wrecking your evening."

"It's okay," I said. "You didn't wreck it." Then I asked, "Are you okay?"

A ray of the old Moe broke through the clouds. "Truth to tell, this old corpus delicti is a wee bit deflated."

"Well, you better get some sleep," I said lamely. He allowed as how he would, and we hung up.

I sat quietly. I frowned portentiously, trying to think, concentrate, figure out how to act, what to feel. Many emotions roiled around inside.

After a long silence, Zelda finally called, "Roger, are you all right?"

From the bedroom I could see her tempting hips and attractive gams. One leg was lifted and bent. Firelight pulsed against her skin. Those sexy little slippers sure applied the icing on her cake.

"Come here, please," Zelda called. "I miss you."

I went in and sat in a chair. Zelda's arms reached up for me. So I lay down beside her. She touched my prick, saying, "Oh dear, what happened?" I shook my head, couldn't speak, held her tightly.

"Roger," she asked, "who was that?"

"Gretal died. A few minutes ago. That was Moe and Mimi."

Zelda stiffened and withdrew. She said, "Oh dear, I'm so sorry."

"I am too."

Zelda whispered, "It's not your fault. You aren't to blame."

"I know that." I didn't want to be with Zelda at this moment, but I buried my face against her neck.

She said, "Gretal was a beautiful person. She had so much courage."

I hated Zelda talking about Gretal in a sympathetic way. It was so phony after all her attacks. I resented her use of the past tense. Maybe Zelda was being sincere, but I was in

205

no mood to hear or accept that. Because of Zelda, I had been cheated of a terribly important friend in my life. I had rejected Gretal. And—

And I kept my mouth shut. I clung to my wife, loving her, needing her, hating her (or was it my own?) guts.

Zelda said, "I'm sorry, Roger. I know how much you once loved her, and how much you cared for her. I don't know what else to say."

Don't say anything, I begged. *Spare us both.*

Her phrases "once loved" and "cared for" really grated. Zelda using the past tense about Gretal was *wrong*.

I wanted to cry, but was ashamed. Yet in the end I could not keep my mouth shut.

"I feel like such a creep," I admitted. "I hardly spoke to her the past two months. I always helped care for her when she was sick. I should have been by her side. I can't believe I arbitrarily cut her out of my life. What a coward."

To me my own words sounded spurious, immature, self-serving. Somehow we ought to be more grown-up and dignified when a person dies. Yet there I was, apparently feeling sorry for myself because Gretal had kicked the bucket.

Despicable. If only I had the courage to wrench free of Zelda and be alone where nobody could witness my duplicity, or whatever it was.

"I hate myself," I whispered.

I guess Zelda assumed I was accusing her. She said, "Maybe you should have thought of this when Christie showed up in that pink jumpsuit, and immediately you took a walk from Gretal. She was on her deathbed back then, too, if I remember correctly."

I stiffened. Had I heard correctly? I said, "What?"

In a matter-of-fact voice, Zelda elaborated. "Roger, you deserted Gretal a long time ago for a younger piece of ass. She wasn't yours anymore. Not for a long while. You abdicated responsibility."

Then Zelda breathed heavily in my ear and murmured, "I love you, sweetie. I love you so much. I need you to be inside. Make love to me."

And here's an interesting fact: Zelda touched me, and I got hard, and I did.

But around three A.M. I went for a walk. It was still lightly yet insistently snowing. No tire tracks marred the layer of white, and I advanced unhindered down the middle of the road. I was bundled up in a knitted cap, a wool-lined parka, and fat moon boots. Not a single dog barked at me. Laden tree branches were bending toward earth and the houses appeared enchanted, with roofs of vanilla icing. It wasn't very cold.

The scene was incredibly peaceful.

A few times I halted and listened to the falling snow crickle as it landed.

I did not weep because somehow that felt like betrayal. I thought about Gretal, remembering times we had shared. For some reason I recalled our visit to the Meramec Caverns in Missouri. Gretal and Daisy and I had stopped there on one of our cross-country jaunts. Daisy must have been about nine.

In the caverns there's a room full of impressive stalagmites and stalactites. It could have been a Gothic cathedral invented by those crazy Spaniards Salvador Dali and Gaudí. The tour guide activated a light show for us during which the recorded voice of Kate Smith sang "God Bless America." Scornful me considered it mighty hokey, but Gretal and Daisy actually placed their hands over their hearts and sang right along with Kate.

* * *

About a mile down the road I turned around and traipsed back. The snow lightened and then ceased altogether. I tramped in the line of tracks I had made on my northward journey. I did not want to further disturb the snow on that deserted road.

I couldn't erase Gretal, dead, from my mind.

I remembered her in the hospital tub. Her misshapen body. Old age. Disease. Struggle. And her unbroken spirit.

I could hear her raspy voice calling good-bye. She always cried, "Ciao, bello. Arrivederci!"

Nobody could say it like raucous Gretal.

I remembered touring the Metropolitan Museum with her and Daisy. We all raved at the Degas ballerinas. We ate an extravagant lunch in the courtyard cafeteria and treated ourselves to a bottle of champagne. Daisy kept asking to see an ostrich in the Central Park Zoo.

The dog cavorted down the driveway to greet me. I ruffled his ears. He danced away in the snow, twisting this way and that, kicking up his heels. A cat scampered off in quick little splashes of white stuff.

The sky had cleared and a crescent moon cast more light than I would have predicted.

I said, "Ciao, bella. Arrivederci."

A note tacked to the kitchen door was decorated by an arrangement of paper flowers. Carefully I pried free both the note and the bouquet and went inside. I put on water for tea, and while the concoction was steeping, I added a splash of bourbon and honey to the cup.

My hands were cold, so I held them over the cup. Then I opened the note.

Dear Roger,

It must hurt you deeply to lose such a treasured

friend. I didn't mean to intrude. I apologize for what I said earlier. I wish I could disappear for a while and let you grieve in love and privacy. All you have told me about Gretal has touched me deeply. You were lucky to know such a wonderful human being, and she was lucky to have you for a lover and a friend. I haven't experienced much death, so I feel awkward, and I'm sorry. But I am here for you in any way that I can be of help. And I love you with all my heart.

Zelda

Daisy is a cute kid. She's real mature for her age. She had to be, as the child of maniac Gretal. Gretal, who would take her to hear Chick Corea or Gary Burton or Carla Bley, but who could never get Daisy to school on time, or to a doctor if her appendix burst. At an early age, Daisy had learned to ask for money, which Gretal disbursed with an utter lack of concern, and Daisy put those bucks aside for a rainy day.

Every time Gretal overturned their blue VW bus (Celeste), Daisy had the repair bread stashed in a tin box in the crawl space of their bungalow.

Daisy the adult was a scrawny, haunted thing, tall, angular, sort of vampy, with long glossy black hair and bruised-looking eyes. She had bouts of bulemia and always seemed concentration-camp thin. She hoped to be a dancer, but everyone said she was too awkward, too tall.

Never mind, Daisy was dancing her heart out in the Big Apple and selling tickets to Polynesia while awaiting a break.

In the late morning I drove over to Gretal's house. New snow coated a magic world, and bright sunshine made the atmosphere unbearably cheerful.

Daisy was already packing books in boxes. Jane Raines, the aerobics instructor, was helping. As were Mimi and my artist pal, Margaret. The twins, Libby and Debby, sat in a corner morosely enthralled by TV.

Daisy wore an old navy pea jacket, black stretch pants, a pair of those thick knitted warm-up socks dancers favor, color of mauve, and sneakers.

She hugged me hard and burst into tears.

I said, "Shit, I'm sorry."

"You and me both."

I asked her about the trip out. I asked why they were boxing the books.

"I'm gonna rent the place," Daisy said. "I know it sounds cold-blooded, but I gotta move fast. The bread'll save my ass. And I'll get fired if I'm not back in five days."

I offered to help. "I'll be your agent if you want. I'll find a good person to rent it."

Daisy regarded me sadly. "Thanks, Roger old buddy." She kissed my cheek. "But I don't think your new wife would take kindly to you being involved with Gretal, even after she's dead."

Mimi opened a book called *Picasso's Picassos* and commenced sobbing. On the island of Ischia, once, Gretal had met Picasso and schmoozed with him. To me, she had never confirmed or denied the rumor that she had also hauled his ashes.

I went to the memorial service feeling like a phony. A lot of people treated me as if I was among the most deeply and intimately aggrieved. Both Sandra and Megan gave me a gentle hug. But don't you know how uncomfortable it is when people confer a legitimacy that is not deserved? Though I do suppose I had been one of Gretal's last main squeezes. And, until a few months ago, we had certainly been close friends.

A surprise, Woody showed up. In an odd, subterranean

way, he'd always been pals with Daisy. I had once thought maybe they were messing around with each other. Woody wore a coat that might have been hand woven by bloodthirsty drunks in Afghanistan, and he never took it off. He inhaled about six beers in ten minutes and lurked on the edges of the crowd, speaking to nobody. Then he disappeared.

It had started snowing again, and I knew Woody lacked wheels. So I stepped outside to offer a ride. But already his line of tracks trailed off between all the cars into darkness.

I had an urge to follow, but instead merely stood there awhile, thinking about Woody, life, death, Gretal, families, weather.

My kid had big feet; they left huge prints in the snow.

Woody and Roger, dysfunctional yetis connected by blood.

Shy creatures, yetis, yet peaceful, or so we've been led to believe.

I guess when someone dies, you always realize—suddenly—just how much you cared. In this case Gretal's death was like a great hollow blow to my head and to my abdomen. I almost shrieked and then doubled over in pain.

I wanted to go somewhere neutral and sob my guts out, but I felt that wouldn't be fair to Zelda. So instead I crammed all that intense feeling about Gretal back down into its foggy lair, and I put on a routine face.

I bought a bunch of flowers for Zelda. Daisies, carnations, baby's breath, a couple of pink roses . . . a fey and varied bouquet. Zelda loves Chagall. Demure brides in white lace floating among flowers and sly-eyed goats and twisting fishes.

Also the moon and plenty of stars.

Zelda *ooh*ed and *ah*ed and placed the flowers in a vase. She set the vase on our bedroom windowsill. The late-afternoon sun was shining in, and the outside world was rich and puffy white.

We made love quietly among the cats sleeping on our bed without disturbing one of them.

Zelda stayed on her best behavior. When she kissed me, her lips seemed fabricated of chocolate foam. He body was slow, heavy, sad. I could do anything with it I pleased. She remained contrite, passive, wide open, pliable.

No denying it, sorrow is a very sexy emotion.

After a pair of pleasant orgasms, we lingered in each other's arms. Zelda drowsed, twitching a bit, making protesting fluttery noises. I contemplated the windowsill bouquet. Sunshine streamed through the petals, casting enormous colorful smudges against the white walls.

Zelda suddenly gasped and muttered sleepily, "Roger, I'm not ever going to hurt you again, I promise."

Truly heartfelt, I replied, "The same goes for me to you."

Next morning, when I awoke, Zelda had already been puttering for hours. While I remained only half awake, listening to magpies wrangling in nearby cottonwoods, I could also hear the *squish clack squish* of Zelda mopping.

At least once a week, sometimes twice, she coated the entire house with Mop & Glo.

I could also smell fresh-ground, fresh-roasted coffee percolating.

Into the kitchen staggered our satiated slugabed, scratching his stubble beard. Zelda's electric-blue bando top barely covered her nipples, let alone the rest of her tits.

Then came high-cut, lime-green panties.

And her high-heel fuck-me sandals.

Her hair had been tamed back into a ponytail tethered by a shiny lime-green ribbon.

Her lipstick glistened. Her eyes were mascaraed. She sported a residue of blush in her cheeks.

Yum.

I marched up behind my wife, tugged down the waistband of her panties, and slipped it in while she continued mopping. I followed her around the kitchen that way. The dog standing over by his empty dish gazed up raptly at us, wagging his tail hopefully. Two cats sat on the window ledge, drooling over a dozen juncos scarfing hen scratch on the bird feeder.

The phone rang. Zelda and I waddled over and Zelda answered it. She said, "It's for you."

Daisy said, "Yo, Roger, what's up?"

I had the presence of mind to say, "You don't want to know."

Since I was committed to a phone conversation, Zelda quit mopping and leaned over the kitchen table to make it easier for both of us.

Daisy said, "I need a favor. I can pay you back in about two months, I figure, but Gretal was broke. She had ninety bucks in the bank. When I flew out so sudden, I didn't have enough for car rental, the return ticket, food, the funeral home. Could you loan me five hundred dollars? I promise you'll get it back, I—"

"Hey, Daisy, say no more. Jesus, I'm sorry I didn't already offer. You'll have it by noon. No need to pay me back, ever. You know I don't loan money. If I got it, I give it. My small gesture to the unequal distribution of wealth on Earth."

"Oh, Roger, you're a sweetie. God broke the mold, you're one of a kind, I love you. I don't care how it went down in the end between you and Mom, but you'll always be tops in my book."

I came, good.

In fact, the orgasm was dee-*light*ful.

After I hung up the phone, I collapsed bent over Zelda, pressing her against the table. I gasped, I nibbled on her hair and tugged it back a little with my teeth. Grrrr. I said, "That was incrediburgable!"

A moment later I was splayed, in one of those rickety antique chairs, like some spavined drooling freak from the Karl Mangus-Richter Lobotomy Center, watching Zelda finish up the mopping, when she asked:

"How much are you going to give her?"

"She needs five hundred."

Zelda stopped mopping. She leaned against the refrigerator, eyeing me thoughtfully.

"Do you really think that's wise?"

I knee-jerked into my defensive mode. "Hey," I said, "we spend money on the house, we spend money on clothes, we eat like kings. It's important also to disburse bread on stuff that isn't self-indulgent."

Zelda said, "Everybody knows you're an easy touch. They all take advantage."

I said, "Aw, I don't think so. Mostly, I offer. People seldom ask. I like sharing extra cash. I should have offered it to Daisy the minute she arrived. But I didn't know Gretal was so broke."

"It's not my fault Gretal was broke," Zelda said.

"I know, baby, I'm sorry. That's not the way I meant it."

Zelda could have been near tears. "You give all our money away," she said. "You never consult with me. We'll be old hags in the gutter because you willy-nilly gave it all away."

"I *earn* it, sweetie," I said evenly. "I don't think I have to consult with you every time I want to help somebody out, do I?"

Zelda stood the mop in its corner, poured a cup of coffee, and sat down across from me. I thought, Oh good, she's clicked into a different, less confrontational mood.

Then she said, "It often seems to me that you've spent your whole life buying affection."

Zelda smiled at me serenely.

"Beg your pardon?"

"How many friends do you think you'd have if you hadn't laid gobs of money on everyone since time immemorial?"

"Excuse me?"

Lovingly, Zelda clasped my hand. She looked directly into my eyes. Her entire face was lit up by her typical irresistible sparkle. Yet her black pupils were flint hard and frigid and almost insanely belligerent.

That gave me a shock.

Zelda said, "Name one girlfriend whom you haven't supported, bailed out, financed, purchased vehicles for, or paid the rent or their doctor bills."

I was flabbergasted. "Zelda, it's not illegal to be generous."

She said, "Has it occurred to you that Daisy is taking over right where her mother left off?"

Incredulous, I said, "Hey, I pay for you. I buy you clothes, I feed you, this house is yours, too. I fix your car, I give you medical insurance, I pay your dental bills, I—"

Zelda removed her hand from mine, stated, "But I am your *wife*," then had a leisurely sip of coffee.

I said, "Are you implying that if I hadn't given any of my girlfriends money, none of them would have cared for me?"

"Why ask me?" she said. "Why don't you just ask yourself?"

I got up and ambled outside to take a leak over by the clothesline. It wasn't until I heard our neighbor, Bob Whitney, call out, "Mornin', Roger," that I realized I was stark naked and standing in a foot of snow.

My friend Alex has been known to harbor insights concerning the battle of the sexes. His own life has had its ups and downs. He and Betty are by no means the Perfect Couple, but they seem to have devised a way to scuffle without drawing fatal blood. I doubt they'll ever do anything so radical and silly as tie the knot. But they have logged almost a decade together, and that ain't hay.

I had to call Alex anyway about Gretal. I could hear him sucking on his pipe. After we had reminisced about Gretal, I recounted my personal story, the histrionic marriage. Alex listened politely until I was done.

Time passed. A lot of it.

Finally, I said, "Well—?"

He answered, "Hey, did you think it would be easy?"

"No. But who would've thought it would be like this? Dr. Jekyll and Mr. Hyde. We have a lot of fun, but I anticipated less stress. The sex is fabulous. But there's so many areas where I'm buffaloed."

"All animals have to establish a territory," Alex said.

"Thanks, but I am not an animal."

"Who sez?"

"C'mon, Alex, be serious. I am *hurting*, man."

"I am serious," Alex said. "Be patient. Once she feels secure, it'll be over."

"What is required to make her feel secure, my total emasculation?"

"Take it easy," Alex said, puffing away. "You're just pissed because you've finally met your match."

I said, "Love is not a contest. Nobody's supposed to win or lose."

"Spare me the Pollyanna, Roger."

"Alex, I can't sleep. I drink like a fish. I'm smoking a pack of cigarettes a day. I walk around on tenterhooks, always waiting for the next shoe to drop. I'm tired of being pilloried by the woman I love. Give me some helpful advice."

He said, "Bet on the Lakers to take it all come play-off time."

The thing about Alex is that he *is* intelligent, he *can* be compassionate, he has *wisdom*. It's simply a question of pushing the correct button.

I asked the inevitable question. "How have you and Betty lasted so long?"

"She threatened to kill me if I took a walk."

"Be serious, *please*."

"Betty gives me everything I demand, whenever I demand it," Alex joked. "She's my Stepford lady. When she strays from the straight and narrow, I beat the crap out of her until she comes crawling and sniveling to kiss my feet."

"You guys fight all the time," I said. "I've seen you be brutal to her. Why does she take it?"

"I'm hell in bed," he chuckled. "That's the secret. Hypnotize them with sex. Rub their big white tummies and coo like a dove."

"Stop joking. I need *help*."

"I don't know," Alex said in exasperation. "You're asking questions that are impossible to answer. For some reason it just works. Does that mean Betty won't take a powder tomorrow? How should I know? Is it preordained I won't jump out the window on Sunday? I can't predict that, either. It's all a total mystery, believe me."

"I'm very unhappy," I said. Then I told him about eighty-sixing Woody, about Christmas dinner, about the death of Gretal, and giving Daisy the five hundred dollars.

I related the Thanksgiving fiasco, and the incest cracks re me and Kim. I expounded at length on everything.

At the end of my litany, Alex said, "Go read Engels."

"Excuse me?"

"*The Origin of the Family, Private Property and the State.* Then read *The Kreutzer Sonata* by Tolstoy. Then blow your brains out."

He was hopeless, so I threw in the towel.

We chatted for another five minutes, then called it a day. Sometimes Alex is out to lunch and not even dynamite up his ass can trigger a humane reaction.

But I went to a shed and hunted through all my book boxes until I found the Engels. And I read it, stem to stern, even the densest parts.

I figured any book that advocates the abolition of monogamy can't be all bad.

But the insights it offered were that marriage is a capitalist plot, cooked up by a patriarchal world to insure patrilineal inheritance patterns, the dominance of men, and the utter economic exploitation and subjugation of women.

Had I been female, it would've made a lot more sense.

But nothing made much sense anymore.

For example:

Here it came, right up the bumpy driveway, believe it or not—Christie's VW Beetle.

From a window in my writing tower I can see all the way down the driveway about a hundred yards to the paved road. And I actually spied the Beetle *before* it turned into the driveway, and naturally the first thought that occurred to me was *Oh no!*

The dog started barking.

It was a warm sunny day in February. Despite snow on

the ground, the weather was downright balmy, almost springlike.

So balmy, in fact, that Zelda, in nothing but a pair of short-shorts, and smothered in sun blocker, was reclining on the edge of the portal soaking up the bennies.

I said aloud, "It can't be Christie."

Wrong again, Roger.

That little crapola junker German twitmobile jounced up the driveway perky as you please, and skidded to a halt behind Zelda's Subaru. And out stepped that diminutive tart in her fox-fur chubby and high heels, directly into the mud: *splosh!*

Zelda had darted inside for clothes.

Christie loves animals. The dog waddled over, splashing mud against her tight skirt and hose, but she just jiggled his ears and scratched his chest and called him "Big fella" until she had him writhing in ecstasy.

I opened the office door and, in shock, blurted, "What are *you* doing here?"

Christie reached into the passenger seat and removed a bouquet of daffodils and a sympathy card in a pink envelope. She tiptoed through the mud over to my office. Her face was flushed.

"I'm sorry if you catch hell for this," she said, "but it seemed important to deliver the message in person. I know Gretal was no fan of mine, but I also know that you cared for her a whole heckuva lot, and her passing on must be a heavy blow to you. So I wanted to hand you this in person, and tell you how sorry I am, and give you a big ol' hug of commiseration."

Christie presented the flowers and the card, and began the big ol' hug right about the time Zelda reappeared, wearing a black Sidney Bard movie sweatshirt and her fuck-me pumps. Her hand held the thirty-eight she kept in her lingerie drawer.

I said, "Christie, you better let go of me."

She let go of me.

And turned around.

Zelda advanced to the end of the cement walkway. Her hand gripping the pistol hung down by her side.

"Hey," I called. "What are you doing with that gun?"

Christie began tiptoeing back through the mud toward her vehicle.

Zelda cried out, *"Fuck you, Roger!"*

Then she raised the thirty-eight and, holding it in both fists, eyes squinched almost shut and her head tilted sideways, my wife shot a hole in the VW windshield.

The dog jumped about six feet and scrambled underneath my truck. Two cats, who'd been sunning on the portal, frantically scooted over the wood bin, a bench, and a rocker, and disappeared around the corner of the house.

The rocker tipped over off the portal, landing in a bunch of dry hollyhocks.

I dropped into a squat, horrified, both hands shielding my face.

Christie lost her balance and sat down—*plop!*—in the mud.

Zelda turned heel and clickety-clacked back into the house.

I jumped up and gave Christie a boost. I said, "You gotta get out of here," and hustled her, both of us hunched over like commandos afraid of enemy fire, to the Beetle.

"Shit, that bitch shot my windshield," Christie observed.

"I'll pay," I squeaked. "I'll buy you a new car, I promise. C'mon, Christie, hop in and skedaddle. Thank you for these." I gestured with the flowers. "You're sweet. I'll call you at the bank."

"Oh screw you, Roger, you chickenshit. If that bitch thinks she can simply shoot my car with impunity, she's got another thing coming!"

Christie kicked off her shoes and headed for the house.

"No!" I bawled. "Don't go in there, she's crazy!"

"I'll show you crazy," Christie said, plummeting through the open kitchen door into my happy home.

I arrived in the nick of time to bear witness. Zelda was backed up against the stove, looking scared. The gun was nowhere in sight. Christie had yanked open the refrigerator door.

"You coward!" Christie exclaimed. "You fuckin' sorry jerk! I oughtta kick your butt and bust your teeth in except I don't wanna get my hands covered with shit!"

Then Christie reached into the old Westinghouse and jerked out the top tray. Bottles of Evian and Crystal Geyser and Diet Coke and organic apple juice and fresh-squeezed carrot juice clattered to earth, spattering in many directions.

Point seven tenths of a second later the contents of tray number two joined the fray.

Followed by everything on the third tray and then both crispers and their contents: apples, broccoli, tomatoes, celery, lettuce, jicama.

While all that crap was bouncing around, Christie stomped through the carnage and lifted up Zelda's juicer, still dripping with carrot shreds, and hurled it through the kitchen window.

On her way out, Christie hollered, "Shoot your *own* goddamn car next time!"

Exeunt omnes, chased by bear.

Zelda and I stared at the mess.

Then, believe it or not, we laughed.

Around midnight I suddenly woke up and said, "Where's the gun?"

"Mmnph? Murphle?"

I jabbed her shoulder. "Where did you hide the gun?"

Zelda, asleep, can be difficult to awaken. She rolled away from me, muttering incoherently.

I continued molesting her shoulder. "Zelda, I need to know where you put that gun."

"Bag in m' lishery draw, dummy . . ."

I hopped out of bed, located the gun, ascertained that it was still loaded, and removed the five remaining cartridges. Then I went to my writing tower and emptied a bunch of knickknacks from a tin box. I wrapped the gun in several Baggies, which I tied tightly with rubber bands. After lodging the mummified weapon in the box, I locked the box and returned to my house, opened a trapdoor by the water heater in the Beverly Jog, and, using a flashlight beam by which to maneuver among all the venomous cobwebs in the crawl space under the house, I wriggled to a spot approximately dead center below the bathroom.

The dirt was loose and dry and dusty, so it did not take long to excavate a hole into which I nestled the box.

Then I covered it up.

And wriggled back through Black Widow Heaven, miraculously avoiding a fatal bite.

In the kitchen I poured myself a stiff bourbon, downed it in a single gulp, and drew a bath.

While lolling in the tub, I read *The Kreutzer Sonata*.

It made my hair stand on end.

Next morning Zelda was distant and aloof. She wouldn't talk on the exercycle. She wouldn't talk at breakfast. She wouldn't talk during her bath.

Finally I asked, "What's the matter?"

She pouted. "You know."

"No, I don't know."

"Well, if you don't know, you're a bigger asshole than I thought."

I said, "Using the word 'asshole' is not a good way to begin communication. It's like waving a red flag at a bull."

"I wish. At least bulls have balls," she quipped.

Theatrically, I threw up my arms, then buried my face in my hands. "That does it! I give up!"

"I hate how you give up so easy," Zelda said. "You're treating this whole episode so damn carelessly."

"I don't understand this marriage," I moaned. "When I think it's going to zig, it zags. When I adjust to the zag, it zigs."

"I hate it when I'm serious and you're just snide, Roger."

Quietly, in control, my voice modified, almost fatherly, I said, "You're unhappy, you're insane, you shoot out car windshields, I think I have a right to be concerned, I ask a simple question, you start giving me guff."

"Maybe if you were paying a little more attention, and weren't so fucking self-absorbed and concerned with being clever you'd have a couple more insights into this farce that you so jokingly referred to as a marriage," Zelda said.

I spread open two fingers and zeroed in on her with my right eye. "You're crazy," I said. "I don't want to play guessing games. Why can't you just lay it all out on a platter so for once I might understand?"

Zelda said, "I think we could use a mediator."

"Come again?"

"A counselor, a therapist, a referee."

"A *shrink*?"

"If that's what you want to call it."

I said, "Zelda, we haven't even been married half a year. Don't you think it's a bit early to call in the Green Berets?"

"Ha ha."

"I'm serious."

"What, I'm *not* serious? Why, because I'm a woman?"

"You know I didn't mean it like that."

"How did you mean it, Roger?"

I peered at her again. I couldn't figure any of this. I was lost. Please, somebody, tell me the right buttons to punch.

I said, "What do you mean, a shrink?"

"I was thinking it wouldn't hurt to see Madelyn Grinnell a few times. She'd take us on at a discount."

"How do you know?"

"Because I asked her."

Oh. How come I never tip ahead of time to the troop movements everyone else knows have been going on for weeks?

I said, "Define 'discount.' "

"Sixty dollars an hour."

I pretended to be casual and uninflamed. "Oh, and what is her normal rate, pray tell?"

"Seventy-five. But listen up, Roger, and get this straight. I will not have you mocking Madelyn."

I professed total ignorance. "Mocking? Where did you invent that idea? Since when have we become such experts on the slightest deviation, the most subtle nuance of voice tone, facial expression, and language?"

Zelda said, "No, sorry, I am not going to be dragged into this one. You always try and deflect me. You always change the subject."

Fair enough. I clammed up and waited.

After about fifteen seconds, Zelda said, "Well?"

"Well what?"

"Well, what about it?"

"What about *what*?"

"Seeing Madelyn."

I said, "This marriage is costing me a fortune. I spend fifty times what I used to spend on water, food, electricity, car care, medicines, health insurance, dentistry, eating at restaurants, college education, renting movies, buying newspapers and magazines, clothes, and other assorted items too numerous to mention, like cosmetics and dry cleaning and shoe repair. Christie is probably going to sue me for her windshield and all the trauma you inflicted. And you wanna pay the quack who told Weezie Bednarik to overcome her inhibitions by talking to the world through a perverted parrot hand puppet named Adrian sixty dollars an hour to referee our marriage? What the fuck do you think I am made out of—diamonds and gold and rubies—?"

Madelyn Grinnell is actually a rather attractive tall woman with green eyes and freckles. She wears sports jackets with padded shoulders, pastel pleated skirts, and sandals. She looks preppy. Also healthy and happy and well adjusted. She's probably an organic person who never touches alcohol, coffee, NutraSweet, sugar, or salt.

I tend to mistrust saints like that.

And the clincher? Madelyn also has a sunny disposition.

In our first session she shook my hand and said, "I'm pleased to meet you, Zelda has been telling me all about you."

A bell went off in my head: Conspiracy! I replied, "I bet she has." Which, as you can probably imagine, was the wrong thing to say.

"See?" Zelda said, instantly furious. "See what I have to deal with night and day?"

"Her?" I said. "She has to deal with *me*? See that temper? How am I supposed to be able to talk about anything candidly if that bazooka is ready to fire every time I open my big mouth?"

"Hold on, wait a minute, whoa," said our sixty dollars an hour.

Yes, I'll admit, already at that point the thought had creased my brain: *At least let's make this bitch earn her highway robbery!*

225

"Big mouth," Zelda couldn't refrain from commenting. "Exactly."

"Fuck you both," I said, bolting upright and walking out. Unfortunately, I forgot the door was closed. I walked right into it. It knocked me flat on my back.

Zelda sat in her chair despising me, but Madelyn leaped from her swivel armchair with a shriek of apprehension and fell to her knees beside my body. She actually cradled my head in her lap and asked, "Oh geez, are you all right?"

I was having trouble gathering my wits, largely because it felt as if my nose was imbedded in, and pointing backward half through, my brain, but I did hear Zelda's voice loud and clear when she said:

"Leave him be. He does this all the time. It's a ploy to grab attention."

That woke me up. I rolled over. I shook my finger at my wife. I said to Madelyn Grinnell, "You know what that person did for attention yesterday? She shot a bullet through the windshield of a woman who was bringing me flowers of sympathy because one of my best friends died."

"It was one of his sluts!" Zelda shrieked. "He probably boffs her in the bathroom of the Benedictine Café during her lunch hour from the bank. They pass notes back and forth whenever he cashes a check. What am I supposed to do, *sit still while my husband commits adultery?*"

Afterward, in the car toddling home, almost smugly Zelda asked, "Well, what do you think?"

My shirt was drenched in sweat. My armpits ached. I felt dizzy from exhaustion. I felt like maybe a hundred years older and counting. My shoulders were so locked in a forward slump of resignation that I suspect in silhouette I perfectly resembled a turkey buzzard.

And here was Zelda, chipper as a little old chickadee, asking me what I *thought*?

"I am not ever going back into that room," I allowed weakly. My voice was so hesitant and weary she had to decelerate in order to hear. "I don't care what happens. Wild horses couldn't drag me back. Divorce me tomorrow. You win. You can have everything. The house, the cars, the land, the pets, the children, everything. I don't ever want to go through anything even remotely related to that again."

"What are you talking about?" Zelda was giddy with elation. "We made incredible progress. We managed to communicate. We got things off our chests."

"Is that what it's called? I thought it was called Total War. The Ardennes, Dresden, Hamburger Hill, Khe Sanh . . ."

I started crying. I didn't even lift my hands to rub my eyes or hide my face. I simply sat there, slumped in the passenger seat with my hands lying limply in my lap, and great big tears rolled out of my eyes.

Zelda slammed on the brakes and pulled onto the shoulder of the busy street, and reached over and tenderly stroked my cheek. She said, "Oh baby, you poor baby, don't cry, we should be celebrating. It may not seem it to you now, but that was a real breakthrough. Oh dear Roger, you don't have to cry over this, you should be rejoicing."

Then I'm not sure quite how or why it happened, but Zelda fumbled at my fly and the next thing I know she was giving me head while multitudinous cars zipped past, back and forth, and saltwater continued to cascade off my chin and land in her hair.

For some reason, despite my weakened state, it was the best blowjob I ever had.

* * *

I remember that evening as a kind of epiphany, a real breakthrough in feeling. Yes, we jogged and ate hors d'oeuvres and read the newspapers, yet there was such a *glow* to the proceedings. We kept reaching out to touch each other briefly in loving reassurance. On occasion I surprised Zelda staring at me with the tenderest of expressions. She also caught me gazing raptly at her. Something had happened to my body—all the muscles were sort of deliciously flabby. I kept wanting to hunch, slump, and collapse, going as lax as jelly. The meeting with Madelyn Grinnell seemed to be triggering a belated catharsis. I have rarely felt more relieved and at peace. I had never been to a therapist before, and maybe the act was going to be exactly as triumphant as losing my virginity.

At one point I directed my calf eyes at Zelda and said, "Thank you. For *every*thing."

She thanked me back.

I took her hand.

When we got up to make more hay, our feet splashed through demure little puddles of schmaltz, but we couldn't have cared less.

The devil is a persistent adversary. I yearned for another peek at Zelda's novel.

"Roger, you are a cad, a slimy hypocrite, a skuzzball of major dimensions," I castigated even while reaching into that sacred file drawer and removing my wife's most recent chapter.

Yikes! Goosepimples pockmarked my shoulders!

Our narrator Samantha tells her hubby Nathan in no uncertain terms that she wants a divorce. They've only been married a year. Nathan freaks out and for emphasis sticks his hand into a burner on the gas stove. Samantha calls 911, but is so flustered she keeps dialing it wrong. Meanwhile,

Nathan barges around the house, banging his head into walls, mirrors, and assorted furniture. He loves her so much he'll kill himself if they separate. He can't live without her. She is his *every*thing. He drops to his knees and begs. He grovels, he crawls, he squirms. He is so obsequious Samantha wants to stick his nose in a moving electric fan blade, or beat him half senseless with a rubber chicken.

Instead, she decides to have an affair with Geoff, who has never quit carrying a torch. In her mind, Geoff is the guy she should have married. But on the day Samantha has an evening assignation with her skydiving former boyfriend, both his rip cords fail and he hits a cornfield like a ripe tomato shot from a water cannon against a brick wall (Zelda's metaphor, not mine!), and that is the end of that.

I didn't have the courage to read any farther.

On Wednesday I'm waiting in line at the post office to pick up a package when I hear that rasping parrot voice right behind my left shoulder.

I refused to turn around.

The voice said, "Hello, Roger."

I ignored it.

"Hello, Roger," it said again.

I ignored it some more.

The beak tapped my shoulder. "Hey, there, bud, I'm talking to you."

Staring straight ahead, I said, "Weezie, bag it, I'm not in the mood."

The parrot hand puppet said, "You're never in the mood to communicate with women, are you, Roger?"

I refused to answer on grounds that might tend to degrade or incriminate me.

"You're probably one of the most hostile and passive-aggressive slobs in this town," said Adrian. "I feel so sorry for Zelda. You misogynist. You are putting her through a nightmare that is unbelievable."

I rose to the bait.

"*I'm* putting *her* through a nightmare?" I hissed, still not turning around. "What are you talking about? I used to lead a happy life. Now, suddenly, I feel like a character in a Hieronymus Bosch painting."

"Maybe if you worked a little harder to release the inner child in yourself, you wouldn't be so uptight," the parrot said.

That did it. I cracked. I whirled around. I said, "I really hate that stupid hand puppet, Weezie. If you don't get it out of my face this instant, I am going to kill it. And kill you, too, into the bargain, if you don't watch out."

Weezie kept her eyes focused on Adrian, who squawked, "See what I mean, Roger? You're filled to the brim with hostility. You're, like, totally abusive. Zelda is at her wit's end. It's, like, she married a gargoyle that fell off the cathedral of Notre Dame. I bet you deliberately torment her. I bet you get your sexual kicks from making her suffer in bed. I bet you have a pornographic mind-set and you only care about her as a piece of meat. I bet—"

I committed a crime.

I snatched the puppet off her hand and bolted from the post office.

The shriek that followed me out the door was high-pitched, eerie, sensational.

Then Weezie screamed, *"Adrian!"*

But I had wings on my silver heels, I was flying. She would never be able to catch me in a million years.

I ran past four art galleries, the Sears mail-order place, a bait-and-tackle shop, the Army-Navy store, and Pizza Hut and McDonald's. I turned left at Kentucky Fried Chicken, jogged into the bank, and spotted Christie instantly. There was no line, so I scampered up, handed over Adrian, and said, "Do me a favor, hide this in your purse, take it home, shred it and burn it and dig a deep hole in the backyard and bury the ashes, okay?"

Christie is one of the world's most predictable Good Eggs. She accepted the hand puppet, saying, "Okay."

I left the bank and strolled toward the plaza, hands in my pockets, whistling Dixie. All the Christmas decorations were still up, twinkling, blinking, buzzing, and glittering.

As I was passing J.C. Penney's, I heard a cry in the wilderness:

"Roger, damn you, where's Adrian?"

I stopped and waited, still whistling Dixie.

The parrot's distraught alter ego caught up to me. Her hair was disheveled, her lipstick was smeared, her clothes were in disarray, one of her shoes appeared to be on backward.

Weezie gasped, catching her breath. Her eyes had swelled from hysterical crying.

"What did you do with him?" she sobbed. "Where's Adrian? I can't live without him. You're a beast! I'm calling the police!"

I chortled, "Go ahead, call the cops, I hope they give me the chair."

Madelyn Grinnell pursed her lips while making a tent of her fingers beneath her chin.

She said, "Why did you steal that hand puppet, Roger?"

"Because it was driving me crazy."

Madelyn said, "You *do* understand that Adrian is a channeler who is very important to Weezie's ability to communicate her true feelings?"

I said, "Adrian is a fucking crutch for a fucking bully."

"Bully? Would you care to elaborate?" Madelyn said.

Zelda slumped in her chair, arms folded, glowering

darkly. Rules were, she could not speak while I underwent interrogation.

I said, "She uses it as an excuse to bypass any normal human respect or sensitivity. She uses it to sabotage interaction. That parrot enables her to insult anybody at will and pretend it isn't herself doing it."

Madelyn said, "If a person had a broken leg, would you feel compelled to steal their crutches?"

I looked from the counselor to Zelda and back to the distinguished counselor again.

I said, "Excuse me?"

"He's deaf," Zelda said. "Whenever anything is really pertinent, Roger goes into his deaf mode. It's very convenient. It's totally passive-aggressive."

Madelyn said, "Zelda, I believe I can handle this. Now Roger—"

I said, "If the person with a broken leg was harassing me unmercifully by beating me over the head with their crutches, yeah, you bet, I would steal those fucking crutches."

Madelyn observed, "You say 'fucking' a lot, Roger. Would you care to explain why you feel it necessary to swear so much?"

"No," I said. "No, I would not."

"I see." Madelyn smiled her perky, freckled smile. She said, "Do you think your attitude toward Weezie has anything to do with the fact that she is a good friend of Zelda's?"

I said, "No."

"Care to elaborate?"

"Not hardly."

"Oh, all right," Madelyn said patiently. Then she glanced over at Zelda and asked, "What do *you* think about that?"

Zelda said, "I think he sucks shit up through his nostrils."

* * *

Do you recall those monarch cocoons I had brought inside in a fit of rapture last September, hoping to share the miracle of their butterfly metamorphosis with Zelda—?

Well, then you're doing a lot better than Zelda and me. Because in the k-fuffle of our chaos, neither my wife nor I remembered those helpless little critters.

Until one day, suddenly, I happened to glance at their jar half wedged behind a pot of lobelias up on the shelf of a hanging kitchen étagère, and I espied therein two beautiful insects that had emerged unbeknownst to us, filled their wings with air, and then, thanks to our inattention, expired.

We had never heard them fluttering to escape.

Zelda was gone when I made this discovery. I unscrewed the lid and tapped the butterflies into my palm. The poor creatures were dry and stiff and they crumbled easily into flakes.

I went outside and sprinkled this confetti into the irrigation ditch running beside our house.

And the water gurgled soporifically as I bowed my head in shame.

A miserable outcast peers through the front glass doors of the bank. Christie was at the third teller's window over from the potted rubber plant, underneath the silver mobile advertising the Full Service NOW Account.

I went in and waited in line for three minutes.

When it came my turn, I produced my checkbook and asked, "How much do you think it'll cost to replace that windshield?" Then I almost broke down. "Christie, you don't know how sorry I am. But you were crazy to come up that driveway."

"*I'm* crazy?" Christie giggled. "Roger, you poor baby. How can you be so deluded?"

I said, "Listen, I'm sorry, but I'm exhausted. I just want to give you the money. Here." I signed a blank check. "Fill in the proper numbers and deduct them from my account, okay?"

Christie said, "Okay. I need to accept it 'cause I'm broke. But what about the refrigerator? Did I break anything?"

"You were wonderful," I said glumly. "You're the best, kid. I mean it."

"So how come you didn't marry me?" Christie asked.

Good question.

I shrugged and gestured with my hands, properly rueful. Give 'em an inch, however, and they'll take a mile:

"Roger," Christie said, "do you think there's any chance we could ever sit down and talk about it? I mean, I'm not blaming you or anything, but I'd really like to know: why her and not me? Why her and not any of the others? Sometimes I lie awake in bed at night thinking about it. The whole thing was a real ego downer for me. You never said anything. We'd never talked at all. Just suddenly—*bang!* Sayonara. You were gone, and she was the Numero Uno. I mean, look at the two of you now. What did you see in her that you didn't see in me?"

A tear leaked out of her left eye.

The guy behind me said, "A-hem."

I jerked around, fists cocked, blurting, "Hold your fucking horses, buddy, okay?"

Moe Bubbles threw up his hands in a defensive posture. "Please, sire, no fisticuffs in an edifice of higher pecuniary manipulation. Have you no respect for the greenback, lad?"

* * *

That's when Zelda had her brilliant idea. "Let's throw a party for our six-month anniversary. We ought to celebrate. All love needs public confirmation rituals."

I should have mentioned that I would have rather worked, but I was too chicken.

So we invited Moe Bubbles and Weezie Bednarik and Ed and Emily Griffin and another couple, Madelyn Grinnell and her live-in lover, Charley Hirshburg.

Zelda cooked the veggie lasagna and baked that cherry pie. I concocted a big chef's salad and prepared all the usual hors d'oeuvres: kielbasy, smoked oysters, cheap caviar, and Bavarian vegetarian pâté, with Kavli crackers, low-salt Wheat Thins, and plenty of mustard and mayonnaise.

We offered a hard bar, plus several gallons of Almaden Mountain Chablis and Mountain Burgundy.

Zelda pretended not to notice that Moe had arrived with Susan Dice. Although of course that made Weezie the odd person out, so to speak. And Zelda is very aware of those social flaws, as you know all too well by now.

No matter. We ate, we laughed, we drank.

We sang songs, a two-hour medley of mostly Beatles, Stones, Dead, and Van Morrison tunes.

We scarfed some more and drank some more and smoked the doobie. Apparently, I made eyes at Susan Dice. And put my arm around her shoulders.

The conversation was hilarious. We balanced spoons on our noses. We laughed until it hurt while ridiculing modern relationships, dysfunctional families, and codependent people.

Weezie had a new hand puppet, Mark the Marmot. Obviously, nobody mentioned Adrian. Mark the Marmot had a very grating southern accent. I asked how come she had to channel through male puppets. Weezie ignored the question.

Madelyn Grinnell informed us that male-female was a yin-yang principle.

I said, "Oh," as if I understood a word that she was saying.

Madelyn's face was flushed and she repeatedly slapped Charley's shoulder, saying, "This big lug is the greatest gift that ever happened to me."

Then Moe produced that cocaine vial, and Zelda took it into the bathroom, and you all know the rest of the story: the mastiff belt, the boxing match, the shattered wineglass. If you want to refresh yourselves, please go back to page one.

Where our tale begins when all hell breaks loose.

On the morning after I woke up as if in a dream. Groggy. Credit the Prazepam. Which had knocked me out, but I'd slept for only two hours.

Zelda was still snoring, so when I slipped from the bed, I was very careful not to disturb her.

I creaked into the kitchen and fed all the cats and gave the dog his Alpo.

Naturally, I cut my foot on a little piece of wineglass my broom had missed last night.

It had been so chilly that frost feathers decorated the windows.

I clicked on the gas heater, selected the low setting, and went outside to pee. A lot of steam rose from the snow. Back inside, I dropped shaving stuff and a toothbrush into my Jansport knapsack. Then I tiptoed off to the truck, started it up, and drove away.

First I stopped by the Pig Pen. I knocked on what was left of the front door. Nobody answered, so I wedged through the splinters into the living room. Four or five bodies lay about, wrapped in old blankets and filthy sleeping bags. The place was freezing. It reeked of stale beer. Aluminum cans littered the floor like spent howitzer shells. A forlorn and emaciated yet still bright-eyed puppy sitting patiently in a corner wagged its tail, which went *thump thump thump* against the wall.

I wandered among the corpses until I found Woody. I squatted and jiggled his shoulder. He rose to the surface slowly.

I whispered, "Woody, are you okay?"

He gave me a quizzical look. "Sure, yeah . . . right?"

"I love you," I said. "I'm sorry."

Even as groggy as he was, Woody managed to look contrite. "Hey man, no problem," he mumbled, glancing away. His breath boiled in the air.

"I fucked everything up," I said. "I'm really sorry."

He started to look concerned. "No you didn't. It's okay."

"I'll make it up to you," I said. All I had was twenty bucks in my billfold, and I handed it over.

He frowned. "What's this for?"

"I dunno. Buy yourself a hot breakfast."

Then I leaned down to hug him. It was pretty awkward. He had one arm half freed and pressed it like a wounded seal flipper against my head. I breathed deeply a couple of times, then pulled away.

"I'll talk to you later," I said. "I love you a lot, Woody."

"I love you too, Dad."

At the 7-Eleven north of town is an enclosed phone booth. I pulled out my AT&T charge card and dialed Bonnie. Kim answered, angry at being awakened. She growled, "Who the hell is this?"

"It's me, your father."

"Oh, hi Daddy . . . I mean Dad. What are you doing up so early?"

"I just wanted to call," I said.

She waited.

"I just wanted to call and make sure you're all right," I said.

"Yeah, sure, I'm fine," she said. "Gosh, Dad, what time is it anyway?"

"Early," I said. "I got an early start. Can I speak to Bonnie?"

"She's still asleep," Kim said.

"Tell her I love her," I said. "Tell her I'm sorry. Tell yourself the same things."

"For what?" Kim asked. And then she gasped, "Oh my God, you didn't *kill* her, did you?"

"No no, nothing as rational as that," I quickly reassured my daughter. "But we did have a major blowout."

"*That's* unusual," Kim said, retreating a tad. Then she had the courtesy to ask, "What about?"

"I'm not really sure," I said. "I'm never really certain about these things. What they appear to be usually isn't what they are. Ask any shrink."

Maybe my voice was slurred or something, because Kim asked, "Are you drunk, Dad?"

I wished she would call me Daddy. I said, "No, baby, just tired, that's all. I better get off now."

Kim said, "You sure you're all right?"

"Fit as a Fido," I said, and essayed a chuckle.

I'm afraid it came out as more of a croak.

I was on a roll, so as soon as Smith's opened, I limped in and bought a single red rose. Then I drove east to the quiet cemetery behind a tiny Catholic chapel set against the foothills on the edge of town, and located Gretal's grave. Or anyway, the little bump of snow-covered earth where her ashes were buried.

It was the first time I'd been back.

I laid the rose down on the grave.

And yet again I said, "I'm sorry."

Some magpies, oddly silent for once, hopped around rattling the branches of a nearby spruce tree.

For a minute I could think of nothing else to say.

Then I sang a song we used to sing together. Who knows why, but it had been one of Gretal's favorite tunes.

> *You get a line, I'll get a pole, honey;*
> *You get a line, I'll get a pole, babe;*
> *You get a line, I'll get a pole*
> *And we'll go down and fish that hole—*
> *Honey, baby mine.*

After that verse, I guess I felt foolish, so I bagged it with the music and walked back to the truck and drove away.

Christie was on the telephone in her little apartment when I knocked. Her phone has one of those eight-hundred-foot-long curlicue stretch cords, so it required no great effort to keep talking as she walked through the living room from the kitchenette and unlocked the door.

She was wearing her old blue terry-cloth robe and mukluks with crossed tennis rackets on them that she'd knitted herself, and her hair was up in garish, rainbow-colored curlers. A residue of cold cream covered her face. She was smoking a cigarette.

I said, "Hi, kid, how are you doing?"

Christie motioned me to hush and listened intently into the telephone. She'd been crying.

The same hand that held the cigarette also clutched a Classic Coke can.

Breakfast among the hoi polloi.

She didn't say anything else, then hung up.

We assessed each other for a right long spell.

Then both of us gave miserable little guffaws, and we embraced.

"Don't talk," she said. "Just gimme a hug, asshole."

I gave her a hug.

Christie stepped back before it could become anything else.

"You look ... bad, Roger."

"*I* look bad?"

"That was the girls' home. They picked Cazzie up under a bridge last night. She was doing something with three homeless people. They refused to say exactly what. I guess she was drunk."

"Jesus," I said, "I'm sorry."

A male voice called from the bedroom. "Hey, babe, who's here?"

"Just a friend," Christie called back. "Roger. You know."

"Oh," said the voice, losing interest, already half muffled by a pillow. The bedsprings squeaked as the body squirmed into a more comfortable sleeping position. It sounded large and heavy.

"So," Christie said gently, "what brings a night owl like you out to my neck of the woods at this ungodly time of day?"

I shook my head. That male voice had taken away a bit of my steam. I was fearful of losing my cool. I had really hoped we could make love.

"Siddown." Christie grasped my hand, leading me to her small plastic dining table. "Take a load off, sweetie."

I felt awkward. "I don't want to interfere."

"You ain't interfering, Roger. I always got time for my friends. You're family."

"I just wanted to say I'm sorry," I said. "I came over to have that talk about why. It appears I'm a little late."

She touched my wrist with affection. "Thank you. But I

don't think right now is the best occasion for that talk. Promise me a rain check?"

"I promise," I said, standing up. "I really didn't mean to barge in. I guess I wanted you to know that I love you."

"I know that, Roger. I always have."

Christie remained seated. A sadness filled her eyes. Then she added, "You be careful, okay?"

I was halfway to the car when it hit me. I turned around, hustled back, opened the door, and stuck my head inside. She was still seated in the same place, same expression, exhaling smoke from the same cigarette.

"I'm real sorry about Cazzie," I said. "Is there any way that I can help—?"

Halfway to Megan's trailer, I pulled over to the side of the road. I frowned. I wasn't thinking very straight, was I? I tried to clear out some of the cobwebs by rubbing my eyes.

Then I hung a U-ey and drove to the Benedictine. The joint was steamy and noisy with an early breakfast crowd I hardly recognized. Margaret was there, however, gabbing with Mimi and Susan. The twins were still playing "Chopsticks" on the piano. Leroy Shanti Bogdanovich had built a large fort out of sugar packets. I wasn't feeling sociable, however, so I sat alone at the alcove table, drank three cups of coffee, ate a Hash Brown Heaven with *two* eggs, and read the paper.

Bad news, boys and girls.

Bad news all around.

About an hour later I went to the pay phone at the nearby Texaco station and dialed Argentina. After five minutes of confusion, miraculously María Teresa said, "Diga?" We talked in Spanish. I suggested we meet in Atlanta. She accepted—gleefully—all my demented proposals.

When I hung up, I can't tell you how elated I felt. In the

travel agency I told Nancy Gant I wanted a round-trip ticket to Atlanta, leaving tomorrow morning. She tap-tapped on her computer and about thirty seconds later the ticket emerged from a centralized printer.

I paid with a Visa card.

Then I trotted out and got in the truck, backed up to an unleaded pump at the Amoco station next door, and filled 'er up for the drive down south to the airport.

About a mile from town, however, I hit the brakes. I pulled onto the shoulder, cut the ignition, and contemplated the wide, white sagebrush plain. Two ravens flapped across the road from east to west. Otherwise, traffic was light.

I crashed from my momentary high.

"What the hell are you *doing*, Roger?"

I putted back into town, parked at the Holiday Inn, and called María Teresa. I said it had all been a big mistake. I couldn't do it. I didn't have the money.

I apologized profusely.

What happened is, I wound up in the local Motel 8 for three days. I drank a lot of beer and ate many bologna and cheese sandwiches. I watched a hundred TV shows. I did a whole passel of thinking. It felt luxurious to be out of touch, out of action, incommunicado, on my own all alone.

It seemed like forever since I had been *alone*.

I cataloged in my head everything I could remember about the marriage.

I tried to decide my next, appropriate moves.

I concluded that divorce was the only answer. I wanted out. I didn't have the energy. I wasn't strong enough. Maybe I lacked integrity. Or maturity. Perhaps I was shallow and lazy. If love needed so much work to make it work, I wanted another job.

Talk about guilt, I wallowed in it.

I felt sorry for Zelda.

It would kill her if I took a walk. Or would it *really* kill her if I took a walk? Would it kill *me*?

Just *do it*, I admonished myself. It doesn't matter if it's right or wrong, if you don't do it, you're a dead duck.

This is silly, but I would miss the dog.

Not to mention Zelda.

A whirlwind of thoughts traumatized my poor brain. I couldn't think straight. I couldn't bear to give up the house, but I would give it up just to be free. What would I say to Gabrielle and Jennifer? I wondered if, in a divorce action, Zelda would claim co-ownership of stuff I had written in the past six months. This is a community-property state.

No matter. If necessary, I would give her the whole ball of wax.

I just wanted to be *free*.

Then I started crying.

It began when I thought of Gretal. And I guess it was fueled by my awareness of loss, and human loneliness, and all our suffering.

I was actually looking into the bathroom mirror, studying my own perplexed features, when abruptly they twisted and wrinkled up like some sort of special effect in a werewolf movie, and the rain began to fall.

Oh how it fell.

I think prior to this occasion my record for weeping had been maybe ten minutes, max. Like in the car after that first session with Madelyn Grinnell. But now my sobs went on for hours. I couldn't stop. I tried several times. I clicked on the TV as a diversion, but instantly banged it off. I took a shower, but kept watering the soap with tears. I decided to put on a jacket, lunge outside, walk around—but I was afraid I'd keep on bawling.

So I sat on the edge of the bed and cried. God knows how many times I muttered, "I'm sorry." Then I curled up under blankets, knees drawn up, hands thrust into my crotch, and let the anguish continue flowing. I apologized a thousand times to Gretal and Zelda and Christie and Bonnie, to Woody and Gabrielle and Kim. Repeatedly I returned to Zelda, apologizing, apologizing, apologizing. I begged everyone to forgive me: Megan, María Teresa, Don Perry, even Susan Dice and Weezie Bednarik, and—if you can believe it—I also muttered trite entreaties to that fucking hand-puppet parrot, which had driven me so crazy.

•   I let myself be swamped by the dismay caused by my own shortcomings and betrayals, and by the sadness that stalks us all.

And not until long after dark did I eventually dry up and fall asleep.

On the morning of the third day I quit smoking forever. I held my last pack of cigarettes under the running faucet, peed in the pack for good measure, then dropped it out the window.

I knew I would never smoke again.

Last night I had written my game plan down in a notebook.

First things first. So, in the next few weeks, I would complete *Return of the Perseid Meteor Thugs*.

Moe Bubbles had an extra room; certainly I could stay there until I found a place to rent.

Actually, better yet, I would fly east, accept Bill Witherspoon's invitation, and complete my novel in his house out on the Island.

When I called Bill to make sure that was okay, he said, "Great. Oh Roger, hallelujah. At last you've come to your senses."

Zelda could have the house.

(Sob.)

And half the money.

(Sob.)

And all the furniture.

And every pet.

In return I'd get my health back, and my freedom, and my friends.

And my kids.

Would she fight? No way. My offer was more than generous. It was exhilaratingly stupid.

But the whole idea scared me. I was terrified of Zelda. Her wrath. Her tears. Her accusations. Her sophistical arguments. I remembered her vowing to die if we ever broke up. I recalled her saying she wouldn't mind if I had a prostate operation and was impotent, because love was much deeper than, and much more important than, banal genital sex.

Be honorable, I told myself, and commit suicide.

It's the only clean way out.

"Don't be a fool, Roger."

On the last night, everything decided, I slept like a baby for the first time in ages.

Come the dawn, after solving the cigarette problem, I shaved, showered long and luxuriously, and dressed in my clothes, which had become a trifle randy during their sojourn at Motel 8.

Then I paid and went home to break the news to Zelda.

Up the potholed driveway I jounced, splashing muddy water to either side of my filthy truck.

The first thing I noticed was Zelda's Subaru was gone.

The second thing I noticed was that the dog did not come grinning and panting and wriggling out to greet me.

The third thing I noticed was that no lazy cats lay about on the portal, even though it was an almost balmy sunny day.

The fourth thing I noticed was a white square of paper tacked to the front door.

When I descended from the truck, everything remained deathly quiet. No breeze. No smoke issued from any chimney. Not a single bird twittered on the empty feeders.

Gingerly I approached the front door. The note was addressed to:

ROGER

I pried loose the thumbtack and opened the paper.

You can have the stupid house.
I don't want it.
Zelda

What?

I turned the paper over and over, up, down, inside out, but there was no further message. What you see is what I got.

I tested the door handle; the door was unlocked. I opened it and entered the kitchen.

Everything had flown the coop. All the paper flowers and hanging baskets full of garlic and onions, and all the pictures of foxy women on the refrigerator. Also the tablecloth and the Mexican candelabras and the bowls of fruit and the vase of cut flowers.

The juicer and the blender were missing; the aloe-vera plants had disappeared. The dangling ferns were gone.

Likewise the air plants, the bonsai tree beside the toaster, and the windowsill paperwhites.

The floor had been freshly scrubbed with Mop & Glo. The place was as neat as a pin.

The living room was empty of all the furniture and flowers and her paintings and lithographs and couches. No rubber plant, of course. And no dry bouquets of grasses and eucalyptus, either. Too, her stereo cassette player was gone. Half the books, which had been hers, had been removed from the premises. No Two Grey Hills rug graced the floor.

I hardly dared peek into our bedroom, which was minus the trastero, the bureau, the étagères, the bed, the mirror over the headboard, the plants, the desk, and the IBM Selectric.

A single forlorn dust bunny lay in that space where once a bureau, trastero, and desk had resided.

Boy, howdy.

I stood in the middle of the living room. The floor had also been given the business with Mop & Glo.

A single note of optimism was that the TV set and VCR, which had been mine, sat quietly in a corner.

For several minutes I turned in circles, letting it all sink in.

Then I stumbled over to the major bookcase and perused the tomes. The gaps between books was unnerving. I tried to remember which volumes of hers had filled the now empty spaces. Back and forth I paced, toting up the losses. Sun streaming in through the picture window made the empty room bright and sarcastically cheerful and terribly *silent*.

After a while I plopped down and contemplated the emptiness.

In due course it finally registered: Zelda was gone. Out of my life. Leaving me *free*.

I did not understand. How could she just up and do it? All those times she had sworn to me that marriage was forever, and now *this*? The hypocrite. How could she be so calculating and cruel? Had she no regard at all for the love we had shared? You can't just up and empty out a house and call it quits. At least she owed me an explanation. At least she, at least she, at least she—

If humiliation could emerge from some metaphorical five-gallon shaving dish, you can bet right at that moment I felt lathered in it. My emotions raced around like a pack of frenzied green elves trying to finish all the toys before Christmas. I had hot flashes, cold flashes, then neutral flashes. I rubbed my eyes and locked my lips and frowned, and grew dehydrated.

Though I wasn't talking, my voice went hoarse.

No cats purred or squabbled. No dog thumped while scratching himself in the kitchen. No Kitaro music issued from behind closed doors in the bedroom. No comfortable tapping sounds issued from her typewriter.

Even the telephone was deathly silent.

I wondered: Where could Zelda have gone? What about all the furniture? Who had been her accomplices? Certainly not Moe Bubbles, he wouldn't betray me, would he? Maybe Weezie Bednarik and Jane Raines and Madelyn Grinnell. Or possibly Gabrielle and Jennifer came north in a rented U-Haul.

A sudden heavyweight punch of inexplicable loneliness sent me reeling. It was followed by sharp pangs of terror, such as a person might have after walking into their house and realizing that burglars had invaded it and ripped off an item of incredible value.

Five minutes later, something quite strange happened that I am at a loss to explain.

I started thinking about making love with Zelda. I remembered planking her up against the refrigerator. I recalled all those randy tumbles on the kitchen floor. I envisioned that wonderful hump while I was speaking to Daisy, and Zelda was bent over the kitchen table. And of course our wedding night, in the truck, out on the mesa.

Especially our wedding night.

Pretty soon I was stroking myself. Zelda gazed up at me all dreamy, her velvet brown eyes heavy lidded. Her tangled dark hair lay on the pillow. She wore a slinky black tear-away dress. Her nipples were prominently etched against the fabric. Her arrogant, lascivious tongue kept licking her glistening lips.

Oh, no, not *tears* again!

Zelda arched beneath me. She pressed her breasts together with her hands until they bulged up at me, obstreperous in their amplitude. I groaned, and by now my tears fell like rain. Zelda whispered, "Come on, big boy, you know what I like." And I did, didn't I? I knew what she had liked, and she knew what I had liked, and above all else the sex had been terrific.

In my mind I rolled her over, pushed up the tight dress, hooked down the panties, spread her buttocks. I watched her in the mirror as I entered her body. I was sobbing. She was the sexiest woman I would ever know. How could any man lose such a gem and not want to commit suicide?

Zelda reached back between her legs and tickled my balls. "Come on," she urged me, "faster, Roger, do it *faster*, and *harder*, and *better*."

And I did, oh yes I did, Onan the Barbarian, jerking away on my poor confused pud until the inevitable explosion occurred, and I gave one final sob of pleasure and pain and failure and ecstasy that echoed throughout my empty house as I cried in jubilant agony:

"Zelda! *Zelda!* ZELDA!"

* * *

At that instant the telephone rang.

Blessed synchronicity?

I grabbed the apparatus in a fever of erotic confusion and blurted, "Who's this?"

"Who the hell do you think?" said a familiar voice.

"Zelda!" I sobbed. "Where are you? What happened? How could you do this to me?"

Cool, calm, and collected, my wife said, "Roger, I hired a lawyer."

I said, "But ... but ... but what do you mean?"

"What do you think I mean when I say I hired a lawyer?"

"You can't hire a lawyer," I protested. "I love you. Divorce is unthinkable. You always said marriage is forever. We made a commitment. You cannot just walk away from that type of commitment."

This gave her pause.

And a rather long and portentous silence took place between us.

When Zelda eventually spoke again, her voice had changed. It sounded puzzled. She said, "Roger, what did you just say?"

I reiterated in detail. I amplified some of the points, elaborated others. I accused her of running away when she should have stayed to fight. I talked about responsibility, truth, honesty, *struggle*. I mentioned we'd all be old hags in twenty years, so it was insane to give up after only a few months. I told her I loved her, I needed her, she was the greatest adventure of my life, she was beautiful, she made me horny beyond belief, she was my inspiration, I could not live without her ... and so forth, ad infinitum.

Then I stopped.

After another long pause, Zelda said, "Roger, are you drunk?"

"I have never been more sober in my life."

She mulled that over and apparently decided to believe me.

Her next question was "Where have you been these past three days?"

I told her.

"Who were you shacked up with?" Zelda asked.

"Nobody."

"Do you honestly expect me to believe that?"

"I don't care if you believe it or not," I said, "it's the truth."

Zelda held her tongue.

In desperation I launched another flurry of entreaties and supplications. How could she give up so easily? How could she contradict her own line about marriage? How could she leave a man who adored her so profoundly? How could she desert the home we had made together? How could she give up the best sex either of us had ever experienced? How could she—

Zelda interrupted. "Bag it, Roger."

I bagged it.

Zelda said, "You left me. You shacked up with somebody. I know you talked to a lawyer about a divorce."

"I talked to nobody," I vowed. "I sat in a motel room for three days—*alone!*—trying to sort things out. I quit smoking."

Zelda said, "You're lying."

"May God strike me dead."

She mulled that over for a spell.

I stammered into another round of pleading and protestations of eternal love. I ended by asking, "Where are you? What happened to the furniture?"

"I'm at Weezie's. I put everything into storage. The cats are at the kennel."

"Who helped you?"

"Friends."

"Baby," I groaned, "please come back to me. Right now.

Right away. Today. I'm on my knees. I missed you. I can't
live without you. I'm sorry for everything I ever did that
was wrong, but I promise I'll do better. You can't give up
now, we've hardly even begun. Please, please, *please* give
me another chance."

Zelda hesitated until the air ached with suspense, and
then . . . can you guess what she replied?

She said, "Okay."

Moe Bubbles, Weezie Bednarik, Ed Griffin, and Madelyn
Grinnell's boyfriend, Charley, helped us load up all the furniture at the storage lockers and cart it back into the house.
We needed the better part of a Saturday to move, and then
Zelda and I alone spent Saturday night unpacking her
books from boxes and reinserting them among my volumes
on the shelves.

Around midnight, finally, Zelda's presence had been re-
established in toto, and we collapsed on antique walnut
chairs in the kitchen, clinked bourbon glasses together, and
wearily toasted each other:

"L'chaim."

The cats were back, snoozing on windowsills. The dog
lay at my feet, squeaking in his dreams. Zelda had changed
into something more comfortable—a black bustier, red panties, and the usual fuck-me pumps. My dick was so hard it
hurt. Love and relief oozed from every one of my pores.
Thank *God* I hadn't lost my Zelda!

"Darling," I whimpered ecstatically, "I can't stand it any
longer. Let's make love."

Zelda stood up and took my hand and led me into the
bedroom. It was all I could do not to have an orgasm the
instant our lips touched. I felt so woozy with erotic antic-
ipation that I thought I might pass out. When my fingertips

first brushed against her tits, I thought I would die and go
to heaven.

Then Zelda whispered softly into my ear, "Come clean,
Roger: Who *did* you screw in that motel?"

I must admit that even today, with so much time having
passed in which to analyze in hindsight, I am still not exactly certain what happened when Zelda spoke those words.

I'm sure it has something to do with the axon terminals
in my brain failing to release the proper neurotransmitters,
thereby fucking up (royally) the dendrites, gland cells, and
assorted homologous impulses resulting in a thoroughly
botched chain of synapses taking place in my brain over a
very short period of time measurable in mere fractions of a
nanosecond.

In short, I flipped a gasket and went berserk.

"Fuck you!" I hollered, leaping out of bed and over to
the multimillion-dollar chifforobe. I jerked open her lingerie
drawer and grabbed for the thirty-eight.

Which occupied a tin box buried in the crawl space, you
will remember.

So I pitched the lingerie drawer through the window.
Then, even before shards of glass had ceased tinkling upon
our lawn, I tipped over the entire chifforobe, yanked out all
the drawers, and flailed among Zelda's undergarments and
nightgowns and panty hose like Edward Scissorhands dancing flamenco with his fingers.

Zelda leaped out of bed, still wearing high heels, and
bounced into me like an NFL cornerback popping the tight
end on a buttonhook.

I slammed backward against the wall, flung her aside,
pulled a flimsy door right off her billion-dollar trastero, and
held up the door like a shield, fending off her next attack.

Hangers twanged as I pulled out her clothes. I flung them

around and about, kicking and stomping and ripping. I wrapped silken sleeves around my fists and shredded delicate material with my teeth, all the while growling, sputtering, and grunting like some primeval beast running amok in a sci-fi cinematic potboiler made in Japan.

With superhuman (and demented) strength, I deflected Zelda's next charge and proceeded to lay waste our domicile. Yes, she kept charging me, throwing punches, trying to grapple, kick, bite, pull hair, or deck me with a slat from her splintered trastero. But, as unstoppable a monster as ever destroyed a miniature city, I continued to raise havoc despite her furious advances.

The living room's plate-glass window succumbed with a delightful splintering roar as the TV sailed through it, followed by two air ferns, several pots of lobelia, an ornamental orange, and, of course, the fucking rubber tree! I picked up an armchair as heavy as myself and gave it the royal heave. Gasping, Zelda planted herself in front of a seventeenth-century china cabinet, but I would have none of *that*.

Reaching forward, I snagged her bustier and ripped it off her body—*screech*! Then I flung her aside, into a pile of random detritus, and reached for the Wedgewood china.

Zelda screamed, "I'm calling the police!"

I detoured, briefly, to yank out the phone lines. Then I returned to the plates and saucers.

Ah, what delight I experienced with each noisy clattering shatter of high-priced ceramics!

I could vaguely feel her tiny irritating fists tattooing my shoulders. So I turned, grabbed one wrist, and together we toppled among vases, knickknacks, and storm-tossed cushions. For a minute, as my wife bleated in shock and outrage and repeatedly slugged me, I tried and failed to (a) get it up, (b) enter her body, and (c) indulge in a bit of rape.

Then I jumped up and addressed the bookcases. Volumes

of great literature, their pages loudly fluttering, sailed back and forth, landing in tangled heaps upon the floor.

That made my dick stiff, so I pissed on the whole kit and caboodle. I drenched Joyce and Hemingway and Joyce Carol Oates, I peed on Jimmy Baldwin and Joan Didion and Charley Dickens, also Dylan Thomas and Sylvia Plath and André Fucking Malraux—

"Screw art! Down with literature! *Fuck it all!*"

I would never write a great book, would I?

Zelda had quit beating on me.

In fact, she was crouched over there in a corner, appalled, nearly catatonic.

I stormed the kitchen like Chuck Norris and Rambo hitting a thatched hut full of Asian communists.

Oh Christie, I thought while disemboweling the fridge, *if only you could see me now!*

You know how it is, while in the middle of a hurricane, how your eye somehow picks out the oddest little details—?

Even though Zelda, crouched in her corner, had been effectively naked except for a thin strip of diaphanous material wrunkled about her pretty waist, she was still wearing *both* high heels.

Plugs crackled sparks as I wrenched them rudely from their sockets.

I emptied the cupboards, floundering about in confettilike celebrations of raisin bran, trail mix, pumpkin seeds, and dried apricots.

I smashed all those antique walnut chairs to smithereens.

I broke every window by throwing a Crockpot, the juicer, a pressure cooker, half a chair, a Dutch oven, and an old-fashioned meat grinder through the glass.

Somewhere along the way Zelda reappeared and began hollering, *"Stop it, Roger, you fool!"*

I grabbed a leaping cat by the tail and threw *it* through an already broken window.

Zelda bit my ear and it hurt, so I grabbed the little lady, propelled her back to the living room, wrestled her down into the carnage, and this time I really laid on the timber.

My wife snarled and slapped at me and there seemed to be blood and mucus all over the place.

Then all of a sudden I realized we were making love. And—bingo!—the entire focus of my frustration, anger, love, and strangulating distress contracted—like the universe just before its Big Bang—into that tiny area of my genitals and Zelda's vagina. And I realized the whole point of this unnerving little episode was to fuck.

The transformation clobbered both of us simultaneously: I snapped, Zelda twigged.

She went crazy.

At ninety, my brakes burned out and started smoking.

Zelda let out a high-pitched squeal.

When I dropped my mouth onto her lips, powerful electric shocks jolted both our bodies.

"Ay, Zelda!"

"Oh Roger!"

How can I describe what now transpired? There aren't enough laudatory similies or transitive action verbs to do it justice. There aren't enough hyperbolic adjectives even to begin to elucidate the cataclysmic sexuality that now transposed (nay, virtually transmogrified!) our peppy interaction. There aren't enough succulent adverbs, dangling participles, or split and pornographic infinitives to paint the portrait of that bruising erotic k-fuffle.

Picture two crippled banshees high on PCP and psilocybin.

Imagine a rude cowgirl dervish riding a bull in Dante's infernal Las Vegas rodeo!

My cock was so hard I bet Bessemer himself would have scrambled for the patent!

Every now and then a cat whizzed by our heads in a furry blur, like a woodchuck shot from a cannon.

I don't know if rage was in the saddle, or if lust controlled the cockpit, or if adoration sat behind the wheel. I only know that every sensation I've ever felt on Earth now raised havoc within this chaos.

Somebody once told me that during the initial instant of an atomic explosion, every element on the planet is both created and destroyed. In Zelda and me, every *emotion* you can conjure now battered our frantic bodies.

Then I felt an orgasm coming from a hundred miles away, jamming like a diesel engine chugging across the western Kansas plains in a straight line at eighty miles an hour, and it seemed as if the jism unfurled for minutes and minutes up along a shaft seventy yards in length, until at last that halcyon squeeze and release and diaphanous prickling paroxysm of ravishing euphoria almost caused me and Zelda to black out as we came together—

I cried, *"Oh Christ, Zelda, I LOVE YOU!"*

She replied, *"Oh Jesus, Roger, I LOVE YOU TOO!"*

"HOW MUCH BETWEEN ONE AND TEN?" I bellowed.

"Six," Zelda answered.

The telephone rang.

How *could* it ring—?

I must have overlooked one in my hurry.

I found it in the bedroom, under the comforter and a mattress.

I answered, still dripping semen.

Don Perry said, "Roger, no more beating around the bush, we need to have those pages."

And what did the Master Writer of Sci-Fi Detective Parables reply—?

"Hey, worry no more, Don, you got 'em."

Epilogue

TWO YEARS LATER

Snow was falling softly upon the ground. I reached the end of chapter six in *By Jove, By Jupiter, By God,* my ninth Sidney Bard intergalactic thriller, and decided to call it a day. I punched the save button on the laptop, waited a minute, then removed the floppy disk.

The dog whimpered and fluttered his lips, having a dream.

I nudged him with my foot. "C'mon, big fella. Cocktail time."

He got up slowly, in stages, stretching and yawning. I scratched my stomach. Through the glass door I watched flakes drifting down in the dim light of dusk. They looked dreamy and nostalgic, like those childhood Christmas paperweights you turned upside down to make it snow. Peace on Earth, good will toward men.

I opened the door. The dog stood there a moment, looking out.

"Let's go," I said gently.

He advanced into the quiet storm, and I followed.

Zelda was in the kitchen, cooking things. Whatever it was smelled wonderful. Warmth from the oven and from the wood stove embraced me. Zelda's novel, *Samantha Troy*, had just been published to rave reviews.

My wife came over and gave me a sweet, lingering hug. Her body felt cozy and sexy against mine. I noticed that a big tall Coke and vodka in a frosted glass already waited on

the table. It stood beside a platter of scrumptious hors
d'oeuvres.

"Ay, it smells good in here," I exclaimed. "What's for
dinner?"

"Goulash. With Italian sausage. Over wild rice. And garlic bread."

"Yum." I fondled her playfully; she fondled me back.

"Any messages while I was working?" I asked.

"Bonnie called. She's going to meet me in the capital
when I go down on Wednesday. She knows exactly where
to find that East Indian raffia material I want for the new
bedroom curtains."

"That's nice," I said, patting her ass as I reached for the
vodka and Coke. "She seem okay?"

"Sounded great," Zelda chirped. "And Woody called,
too. Said he's doing fabulous. Made ninety-eight on a sta-
tistics exam last week. He's got a new girlfriend named
Lillian, and claims he positively *loves* being back in school.
He and Gabrielle are going rock climbing over the week-
end."

I took a deep, lingering drink of the cool narcotic and exhaled air expansively. "Aaah. . . ."

"Also, Madelyn and Charley said they'd love to come
for dinner on Friday. She beat Susan Dice in the club B
quarterfinals this afternoon. So we're going to meet tomorrow in the semis."

"You can nail her," I said. "I'm gonna bet Charley the
entire ten K we've sunk into therapy on the match. He'll
have to take the wager."

Zelda gave an appreciative tinkling chuckle and continued:

"Kim also rang, asking if she could come up this week-
end. I said sure. We're gonna go to *Godspell* together with
Cazzie. I called Christie, just to confirm. I also promised to
hike up Wheeler Peak with them both. You're invited, of

course, if you want, and think you can stand all the girl talk."

With a toothpick I skewered a smoked oyster and fed it to the nearest cat.

"I can't believe how everything has worked out," I murmured. "It's a miracle, isn't it?"

Zelda came over, a spatula in one hand. She leaned down, picked up my glass, took a sip, and set it back. Then she kissed my forehead with her delicious lips.

"You just have to have faith," she said demurely, tapping me on the noggin with her spatula. I watched her lovely buttocks sashay as she returned to the goulash.

"No other calls?" I asked.

"Just one," Zelda said nonchalantly, her back turned as she stirred our dinner. "Don Perry called to say that *Perseid Meteor Thugs* has been nominated for an Edgar."

With that, I couldn't help it, I gave the cat another oyster and started weeping, I felt so happy. . . .

Hey, dude! *You wanna buy a bridge?*

John Nichols

PUBLISHED BY BALLANTINE BOOKS.
AVAILABLE IN YOUR LOCAL BOOKSTORE.

Call toll free 1-800-733-3000 to order by phone and use your major credit card. Or use this coupon to order by mail.

__AN ELEGY FOR SEPTEMBER	345-37994-2	$5.99

The New Mexico Trilogy:

__THE MILAGRO BEANFIELD WAR (Vol. I)	345-34446-4	$5.95
__THE MAGIC JOURNEY (Vol. II)	345-31049-7	$5.99
__THE NIRVANA BLUES (Vol.III)	345-30465-9	$5.95

Name _____
Address_____
City_____ State_____Zip _____

Please send me the BALLANTINE BOOKS I have checked above.

I am enclosing	$_____
plus	
Postage & handling*	$_____
Sales tax (where applicable)	$_____
Total amount enclosed	$_____

*Add $2 for the first book and 50¢ for each additional book.

Send check or money order (no cash or CODs) to:
Ballantine Mail Sales, 400 Hahn Road, Westminster, MD 21157.

Prices and numbers subject to change without notice.
Valid in the U.S. only.
All orders subject to availability.   NICHOLS